# RETURN TO
# DOOMSTAR

## RICHARD MEYERS

D1487951

**POPULAR LIBRARY**

An Imprint of Warner Books, Inc.

A Warner Communications Company

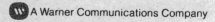

# MACBETH WITH REAL WITCHES!

The houselights came up. The actors looked down at a redeyed audience which was crawling on stage, led by a horribly grinning Merlin Master. His slithering manner and the expression on his face immediately spoke to Napoleon's heart, mind, and stomach. There was the timeless second when she just looked at the sea of bodies coursing toward her, but then her mouth was open and her feet were moving.

"Run!" she howled . . .

Harlan blocked the backstage door, watching in amazement as the sorcerers began to scale the sides of the theater, crawling along the balconies and lighting fixtures. Some had even reached the halfway point when a lightning bolt from the space bullet electrified the metal framework, sending sorcerers screaming off the metal bars.

The smoking bodies hit the stage and bounced. Before they settled, other sorcerers leaped on them, tearing at the corpses' heads. The still living witches and wizards dug into the dead people's heads, pulling out hunks of brain.

Then the Merlin Master untangled himself from the pile and began speaking.

"Patience," he said. "Patience, my loves. Quell your hunger. Calm yourselves until the desperation courses from your body." It had a promising start but a horrible finish. Merlin seemed to look right into Trigor's eyes.

"Then use the magic, my children," he said. "Use your magic to get your meal."

Also by Richard Meyers

**DOOMSTAR**

Published by
POPULAR LIBRARY

## DEDICATION

To Christopher Kelly Browne
We're having fun yet.

## ACKNOWLEDGMENTS

Paul Mills did the anti-BS poetry.
Christopher K. Browne did the foozles.
Christopher Browne did the Star Nosed Moles.
Chris Browne did the Governor.
Chris K. Browne did "savor."
Chris' T-Bird did some cat stuff.

"Would you look at the size of that footprint!"

# PROLOGUE: AMONG THE L.O.S.T.

# ONE

Roscoe Pound's back was turned when the thing appeared in the VU Port (tm).

"Uh, I think you'd better come take a look at this," said Zero.

Roscoe Pound sighed. He didn't have time for this. While it might appear at first glance that all Roscoe Pound had was time, all he might say in reply was that appearances could be deceiving. It might look as if he were sitting comfortably in front of a large, five-sided embankment, relaxing with a book in his lap, but this was not the case.

He was sitting, but not relaxing. Instead, he was going through hell and he didn't want to be disturbed. The sooner he got through it, the better. Walking over red-hot embers could only be termed enjoyable once one had already made the last step.

"What is it?" he asked Zero irritably, not even looking around.

"Uh," said Zero, unwilling to attempt describing the sight in twenty-five words or less. "You better take a look for yourself."

Pound sighed again (and not in a resigned way). It was the only thing he could do other than snarl at Zero for disturbing him or yelling on general principles. And he knew how she/it hated when he yelled. Upon thinking of her/it, he hazarded a glance up. As always, there was no expression (there couldn't be), but he could feel her disapproval and hurt.

"Zero," he said patiently, keeping his eye on the Book. "You have been a member in good standing of this crew for many, many years. And in that time we have come upon many interesting sights. But lo, in all those many years, there has not been one that I am certain you could not deal with on your own."

"You really mean that?" Zero asked.

"Of course."

Zero looked out the VU Port (tm) again, considering the compliment. "I still think you'd better see this," he decided.

"Zero!" Roscoe blurted, pivoting toward him. "I'm busy!"

"I know," Zero almost whined. "But . . ."

"All right, all right," she/it sniffed. "You had better go humor him."

Roscoe spun toward the embankment, his manner supplicating. "I'm sorry, my dear."

"That's all right." The voice was smoothly female.

"You don't mind?"

"This can wait."

No, it couldn't, but he wasn't about to argue with her/it. He supposed that any time out of hell was good. "All hell shall stir for this," as the Book would say. Of course, it only made returning to hell all the worse.

Pound struggled out of the cunningly comfortable seat,

waving his arms and kicking his legs to escape the sunken padding. He got to his feet and carefully laid the Book where he had sat. He smiled benignly at the embankment and then whirled to march right over and chew Zero's head off.

The white dots moved across the black squares as he strode across the expansive floor. The white dots were suns and planets. The black was space. The squares were plain ports set in the sides of the star-shaped ship which spun through the cosmos.

Looking through any of those things was an ultimately dizzying experience, since the ship had to turn to create gravity. She/it had their trajectory worked out so they could get where they were going without floating or being plastered against the walls.

Zero stood before the single VU Port (tm), which was the only window with a single view. A series of reflecting and refracting lenses outside the ship fed this one screen a consistent 180-degree image of whatever was "in front" of the ship.

As he approached, Pound looked at Zero with anger. It was hard to be angry with the placid, good-looking young man, but it was possible, especially when he interrupted what he knew were vitally important production meetings. It never occurred to Roscoe that Zero, of all people, knew full well what she/it was like, so if he interrupted the meeting, he had a trigor good reason for it.

"Well," Roscoe announced superciliously. "What is it?" (It was an unnecessary question and Pound knew it but he just didn't want to give Zero the satisfaction of simply looking. Things like that became important to the ego after twenty years in space.)

Zero would not be baited. He merely pointed at the screen. Roscoe finally looked. Outside was a hunk of slate-colored, rutted rock, human in shape though obviously much larger than a person—it looked like an unfinished sculpture.

There were suggestions of arms at the side, legs held together, and a lump of a head on top, but it could all have been a coincidence. Of all the billions of rocks in the galaxy, a man-shaped one was hardly unlikely. Certainly nothing to disturb a production meeting for. Riding on top of the rock, however, was a five-foot-tall cat.

The cat rode on the rock's back like a cowboy on a horse. There were even reins the cat held wrapped around the rock's "head." Roscoe knew it was a cat because its helmet was a large, clear dome, and its spacesuit was skintight (including the long part wrapped around its tail).

Its face was beautiful, even with the cat ears coming out of its furry skull. Its body was beautiful too, lushly female and human, even though the feet were almost paws. The fur itself was glistening orange with lustrous dark highlights, and the slitted eyes were golden green. She was making some arm motions which seemed to mean that she wanted the ship to pull over.

Roscoe looked into Zero's almost smug face. "How many times have I told you," Pound asked with mounting fury, "not to interrupt a production meeting!"

"But . . . ?" Zero said helplessly to Roscoe's back as Pound stalked back toward the embankment.

"So it's a cat riding a rock," Roscoe said, throwing up his arms without stopping. "So what?"

"But," Zero stammered, "isn't that unusual?"

"I repeat," Pound answered, stopping in front of his too-comfortable chair. "So what? So is the Walking Nebula. So is the . . ." Roscoe couldn't think of anything else. "I mean, if I stopped to look at everything that's the least bit out of the ordinary, we'd never get anything done."

"But," said Zero again.

"I saw it too," she/it interrupted, "and I didn't see any cause to even bring it up."

"There, you see?" Roscoe said, calming. He smiled benignly on his associate and appealed to his reason. "Zero, Zero, my dear fellow. I have work to do. You have work to do. And we have precious little time in which to do it. I would appreciate it if you would cease and desist from calling my attention to every hairy whore that you see riding through space on a rock!"

"Hey, everybody!" Spot cried as she swept into the room. "Did you see the cute cat outside?"

Roscoe raised his hands in exasperation and sank into his seat, thinking that he spent most of his time with his hands in the air. "Now, my dear," he said to the embankment, ignoring Spot's entrance, "where were we?"

But Spot had spent most of her short life preventing that very thing. When she entered a room, she prided herself on entering a room. "Well, did you?" she insisted, stamping her little foot.

"Act three, scene two," she /it said.

"Yes, we did," Roscoe sarcastically answered Spot. "Zero was kind enough to bring it to our attention."

"The Servant has just said, 'Madam, I will,' and exited," she/it continued.

"I think she's cute," Spot said.

"Beautiful is more like it," Zero said, garnering him a fiery-eyed look from the girl beside him.

"Page eight thirty-two," she/it told Roscoe as he flipped through the Book.

"Well, what are you going to do about it!" Spot demanded, stamping her foot again.

Roscoe stared at the two crew members. Zero's oval face, with its wavy brown hair, was bland as usual. And, as usual, he wore the white, short-sleeved body stocking which stopped at mid calf. His lithe form was clearly displayed. Spot's form was displayed in a different way.

She delighted in her wardrobe and always wore all she could. Today she had on a form fitting, floor-length, deep purple gown which showcased her creamy white chest and set off her shoulder-length red tresses. Of course, her hair changed color and style as often as her clothes. But she had the kind of fresh face that enhanced whatever fashion she chose.

Although Zero looked tall and Spot diminutive, they were both the same five-foot-seven-inch height. Roscoe stared at them for a second, then struggled to his feet to deliver his reply.

"Well, what am I going to do about what?" Although just over six feet tall himself, Pound seemed to bend over the others. It was his unique look, no doubt. While the others were prime examples of humanity, he looked every inch an eccentric.

His waist seemed to be wider than his shoulders, although they were both the same size. His shoulders were stooped and his back slightly bent from hours slaving over the Book. The top of his triangular head was hairless, but a long mane hung down on three sides of his skull, starting just two inches above his ears. He also wore his usual outfit, consisting of red, U-necked, long-sleeved shirt and blue pants hanging over his black all-terrain socboos.

"About the pussycat," Spot said. "I think she's adorable."

Trying to decipher Spot's logic was useless. She worked at being oblique. "What do you want me to do?" Roscoe asked.

"Let's take her on board," Spot suggested. "I think it would be wonderful to have a pet."

"That's not a pet," Roscoe said, his arm pointing at the VU screen. "That's a wild animal! Did you see the size of that thing?"

"She would be perfect for Ariel," Zero reminded him.

Pound stared at him in amazement, then suddenly thought about it. "Yes, she would," he considered, then quickly drove the insanity from his mind. "Yes, and so would a Devon from Inferno!" he yelled. She/it groaned behind him, causing him to lower his voice immediately. "I'm not taking that thing on board."

"Come on," Spot said, all artifice leaving her. "You can tell she's not untame by the way she acts and the cut of her suit. That's an intelligent creature."

Roscoe couldn't believe they were still arguing about this. It had to be some sort of travel fatigue, and OD lag, or maybe they were just getting tense with the tour coming to an end soon. "What is she doing out here, then?" Pound asked her. "She could be a thief or pirate."

"She does have a weapon," Zero told her. "I saw it. Two, in fact. A long one on her back and a more compact one on her thigh."

"Just for protection," Spot countered. "A girl can't be too careful."

"Not when she looks like that," Zero agreed. Spot elbowed him in the stomach.

"Let's just talk to her, then," Spot pleaded.

Roscoe looked to the embankment. "Well?"

"We'll never get anything done," she/it complained.

"We'll never hear the end of it," Pound told her/it mildly.

"Oh, very well."

Spot clapped her hands and giggled. Zero smirked at the girl's transparent mannerisms and walked back to the VU Port (tm).

Roscoe was now too keyed up to settle down into his padded chair. He waited by it as Spot and Zero wandered around the room and she/it attempted to establish contact.

"Communi-k (c) linkup complete," she/it finally said.

"What language are they using?" Roscoe asked her/it. "Anything we'd recognize?"

"It's an ancient mariner's vocabulary," she/it answered. "And English."

"All right. Let's hear it."

A deep voice filled the area. "This is a distress signal," it said. "We are in need of sanctuary. If you are able to assist us in any way, please leave your name, planet of origin, and destination after this signal is complete."

"That doesn't sound like it's coming from her," Spot said.

Roscoe frowned, more in anger than in sadness. "Link me up," he instructed her/it, then immediately continued, "We hear you. What assurances can you give as to your good intentions?"

The distress-signal voice answered with more animation than before. "What do you mean? Like promising not to blow you up or something?"

"That would be nice. And what kind of remuneration can we expect if we extend this consideration?"

"What do you want? Circash?"

The three humans looked at one another, a strange feeling of disquiet beginning to permeate the room. "Circash?" Roscoe eventually replied. "What would we do with circash?"

"What do you want, then?"

"How about services? Services rendered for services gained."

There was silence on the communi-k for some seconds, then, "Just a minute."

Roscoe looked at Zero, who was watching the cat out of the VU Port (tm). "She's talking," he said.

"Uh-oh," said Pound.

"Is that her voice?" Spot asked, her own voice tiny and vulnerable. "Who's she talking to? Herself?"

"No," Roscoe guessed. "Her ride."

"Fine," said the deep male voice. "Let us board."

"Us?" Pound echoed. "Who's us?"

"I am Harlan Trigor, space bullet of the planet Destiny," came the reply. "And she is a feline named Napoleon."

The three humans stiffened for a second, then Roscoe laughed.

"What's so funny?" the voice asked.

"You must think we've been flying the back holes for light-years," Pound replied derisively. "Come on, who are you really?"

He was met with stony silence, and then, "I've told you the truth."

"I'm not letting you on board, until I know who you really are," Pound maintained.

"You'll let us on or I will board myself!" the voice suddenly threatened. "No, I've had enough of this," the voice continued, obviously not to Roscoe. "Why should I . . . ?" The voice paused. "Why should we . . . ?" it blurted. "Fine. You do it, then."

"Hello," said a female voice. I'm Napoleon, and this is Harlan Trigor. I don't know what the problem is, but those are the only names we have."

The crew was stunned into silence. "It *can't* be them," Zero maintained finally." "Stranger things," Roscoe murmured. "Stranger things."

"We're being scanned," she/it announced.

Roscoe grimaced. "Can we outrace them? Take evasive action?"

"No," she/it, decided, never one for doubt. "On the basis of my input, he can make good his threat. They didn't need to ask us anything. They could have come on board anytime.

"Muse," Roscoe asked. "Are they—"

She/it didn't even let him finish. "They are who they say they are."

Zero started, looking out the VU in wonder. Spot looked faint. Roscoe just looked around the room, seeing nothing. "Well, I'll be trigored," he said. "It's them. It *has* to be."

# TWO

The feline released the nec-lip clasp on the spacesuit and pulled the globe off her head. Spot marveled at the luxurious golden-orange fur across her shapely, five-foot-tall feminine form. Zero appreciated her high cheek-bones, small nose, delicate whiskers, and lovely, upturned mouth. Roscoe noted the two black lines coming down from the inside corners of her eyes.

"You've cried," he marveled. "They said you never cried."

Napoleon looked at him sharply as Harlan maneuvered his suit behind her. They were in the ship's entry port, a nondescript section of the large spacecraft. They had been directed to the spot by Pound, who had automatically opened the sliding door. The space bullet had laid itself down for the feline to dismount, then stood itself up as the outer door closed. Air, and then the crew, rushed in.

"Who said?" Napoleon asked. Her tail lashing was the only sign of her sudden concern.

"It's an old Earthen story," Spot said brightly, either ignoring or not seeing the flash in the feline's eyes. "They said though you killed thousands of people, you would never cry because it would scar you for life. But you've cried. There're the scars to prove it." She pointed and Napoleon looked ready to bite off her finger.

"It's all right," Roscoe quickly interceded, stepping in front of the redheaded girl. "She's an SM."

"I am not!" Spot hotly replied. "I," she corrected loftily, "am an actress."

"Yeah, and I'm Zero," he said to Napoleon with a grin, extending his hand. "An FM actor." Napoleon took his proffered palm and shook it. Then she looked at the third person in the room, expecting some sort of explanation.

"And I'm Roscoe Pound," he introduced himself instead.

"An FM with two names?" Napoleon wondered.

Pound actually blushed. "Well, no, not really. I only feel like one after twenty years with these two," he joked. "Actually, my name is Roscodopolis-Pouneri."

A TM! Napoleon thought about going for her spitter, but then thought better of it. These three were unarmed and seemed totally unthreatening. Her paws stayed where they were, but her tail kept lashing.

"You can see why he shortened it," Spot told her. "Confidentially, we refused to call him anything but Roscoe."

Napoleon was nearly overwhelmed. She had not seen Earthens in years, and had never seen a TM (True Man) get along with an FM (Fake Man) and SM (Sex Machine) on an equal level before. And all three seemed to know more about her than she herself did.

"So," Spot continued in her conspiratorial tone. "What made you cry, huh? Was it Larry?"

Before Napoleon could react, probably by retreating around the space bullet's legs, Harlan made his presence known. "No, it was not Larry," he announced from inside the space bullet suit, which was still hovering some six inches off the floor. "They were . . ." The words trickled out.

"Tears of relief," she finished for him, still taken aback. They both remembered well the occasion. The aforementioned Larry had said good-bye to her on Harlan's home planet of Destiny. She had taken off into uncharted space, alone for the first time in her life. The combination of losing her best and only friend in the universe and plunging into the unknown darkness was nearly too much for her. But that hadn't made her cry.

She had seen and done too many tragic things to let such yawning despair defeat her. It was when Harlan had joined her that the tears finally came. He was almost as much of an outcast as she. It was knowing that she was not alone that did the trick. But as soon as she became aware of the tears, she purposely cut them off through a great effort of will. But it was too late to prevent the markings. Harlan, the complete soldier, never gave any hint that he noticed them.

"So you're Harlan Trigor," Roscoe said while Spot giggled. He lanced an angry look at her.

"Yes," he said gruffly. "Who the Destiny Mother are you?"

Pound could see more than names were in order. "Come with me," he invited. "You must be starving after . . . your long trip. Come on out," he said directly to the suit. "Have something to eat while we explain."

"I'll stay in here," Harlan said. "I don't trust you people."

"As you wish," said Roscoe. He led the entourage toward the door. Napoleon placed her hand on the spitter handle and followed. Harlan brought up the rear, floating in his suit like a flying sarcophagus.

Some things never changed. Although the prospect of a cooked meal was in the offing, all they actually got was the Greenfield Labs' foodstufs and vegemats. Still, it was nourishment and the feline accepted it gladly. They had been led down long, narrow off-white corridors to the low, narrow gray dining area. The food was taken from silver trays atop a plain brown table built into the wall.

They all sat on an all-in-one table-and-bench arrangement which could be folded up and attached to the wall as well. All except Harlan, who floated off to one side. He was ready to fry them at any given second should they say something he didn't like. And he wasn't wildly enamored of the things they were saying at the moment either.

"Sure, you're famous," Spot chattered. "Everybody knows the story of the NAO."

"The Noah's Ark Operation," Pound elaborated.

"I know what it is," Harlan interrupted irritably, even though he didn't know what it was. He didn't like the entire setup. He would have been just as happy to continue along as they had been doing, but Napoleon had felt too exposed riding on his back. And no amount of arguing that he could protect her could convince her otherwise. They had to get out of sight, as far as she was concerned.

Napoleon knew what the NAO was, even though this was the first time she had heard its proper name, and she was annoyed by its memory. It didn't help that Spot and Zero seemed to think of it as an entertaining fairy tale.

"Yeah," the FM said eagerly. "You and Larry killed everybody on the planet and then escaped to the stars, never to be seen again."

"We didn't kill everybody!" Napoleon snarled.

"Yes, you did," countered Spot brightly. "You unleashed such incredible devastation that the Earth started to crumble and all your FM brothers and SM sisters died and you even murdered your own feline family."

"That's patently untrue," Napoleon told the wide-eyed audience evenly, her tail like a metronome pacing an upbeat tune. It didn't help when Harlan started to laugh. "What?" she spat at him.

"It's funny," he defended himself. "They take everything that has happened A.N.D. [After Natural Disaster] and blame it on you."

Napoleon had to smirk, given these terms and the distance between her and the story's origins. "And you believe all that?" she asked Spot. "You believe that Larry and I murdered everybody on the planet?" The girl didn't say anything. Her expression didn't change at all. "How come you're here, then? Why aren't you dead?"

"Oh," Spot said primly, as if talking to a child. "That was years ago. Long before my made-day."

"Come now," Napoleon countered reasonably. "We've only been away from Earth, what, three years?"

"At this distance?" Roscoe asked. "With an OD [O'Neil Faster Than Light Drive]? Depending on how far you've gone, it could be hundreds of years in the future." The feline glanced back at the hovering space bullet, not expecting and not getting any reaction. "I mean, look at us," Roscoe continued. "We left Earth more than sixty years after the NAO and have been traveling in space for twenty more."

The aliens were stunned. Although they had been buzzing around for less than four years, they were lunching with folk who should have been eighty years older than they were. Although they knew it had to be true, it was still hard to tangibly face.

"Well, that's FLIT [Faster than Light] travel for you," Pound offered. "Who would have thought we'd be talking with two of the three most hated villains of A.N.D. history?"

Harlan was impressed. "Worse than Taplinger-Jones?" (He was the man who had started the WEA-War—the War to End All Wars.)

"You've replaced Taplinger-Jones," Zero informed them, nodding at Spot. "That's why she giggles every time your name is mentioned."

"Your names are our profanity," she said. "Like 'nap you' and 'I'll be larried.'"

"What a mouth," Zero gibed, then realized who he was with. "Sorry."

Harlan was continually amused. Napoleon wasn't. She scowled at her host. "For a TM, you seem to be taking a meeting with murderers in stride."

Roscoe shrugged and held his hands up. "The Earth you left probably doesn't even exist anymore. According to Muse, there've probably been revolutions, purges, several complete and total changes." Pound seemed almost wistful. "Your crimes, whatever they actually were, are probably shrouded in legend by now. If not totally forgotten."

For some odd reason, Napoleon felt something akin to disappointment. "But it's only been a few years," she quietly complained.

"Traveling at over light speed with an OD?" Roscoe asked. The feline nodded. "Forget it. Muse tells me that the farther you go and the faster you go, the quicker time flies."

"This Muse character seems to be a real information source," Harlan said cautiously.

Spot and Zero looked at each other, all smiles. "You could say she's a real conversation piece," said Pound. "Let me show you."

The quintet continued through the plain hallways until they reached a flat, dark yellow double door with a single small disk upon it. Roscoe carefully reached under his shirt and pulled a small metal T out. Harlan watched carefully while Napoleon's paw rested on her spitter handle. It reminded her of the universal translator Larry used to have.

Pound just smiled, sticking the bottom of the T into the disk. The two doors opened inward. Roscoe strode into the mammoth room first, looking perfectly at ease among its crowded, messy interior. It was almost like entering a gigantic warehouse, only the stored goods had a creative flair.

Everywhere lights dangled, wires coiled, steel structures rose to the ceiling, spiral staircases lined the walls, and huge, colorful drapes hung. Towering canvas sheets were tacked to wooden frames and were stacked upright as well as spread out on the floor. Implements of all kinds were strewn across tables (which popped up everywhere). Tools of every kind and description were bursting out of big metal lockers. Garbage, scrapings, wood chips, and hunks of metal littered the area. The cavernous interior completely defied comprehension.

Spot and Zero seemed to glow and swell in the room. They looked as if they were about to start dancing. Roscoe's smile widened until it threatened to chop his head in half. Napoleon and Harlan looked around and at each other in wonder. This was something they had never seen before. It looked as if chunks from different civilizations had been stolen and crowded together in this one room. The feline realized that this might be a pirate ship. That would explain the strange markings on its hull and the crew's lack of interest in the aliens' crimes.

But before either she or Harlan could decide, they came to huge doors which made up one entire wall. The portals stretched from floor to ceiling and were held shut by another tiny disk-lock. Roscoe turned to them at this juncture and took in their expressions with appreciation.

"This is Muse," he told them, his arms out and encompassing everything. "But that's not all. You haven't seen anything yet."

He touched the T to the lock, which clicked open. The two doors swept in without so much as a creak. Stretching out before them was a stage made from strips of highly burnished dark brown material. Curtains of deep red and black lounged on either side. To the sides were wall-sized equipment consoles, outfitted with wheels, buttons, dials, and charts, each section illuminated by a hooded ball.

Beyond that were the seats, plush red seating for the humanoid form. First, there was an inclined level, then a long balcony level taking up the rear half of the expansive room. On either side were three graduated tiers of boxes with four more seats in each. On both walls were four exit doors, split down their middles, with one side automatic and the other side manual. In the very back, even above the second level, was a tiny third level shielded by a wall of opaque glass.

Napoleon and Harlan were in awe. They had never seen a theater before. Both had been too busy surviving the theater of accident: reality.

"The seats can conform to at least twenty-three alien types," Roscoe proudly pronounced. "The exit signs automatically change to eighty-eight languages as the audience looks at them, and there are translators in the chairs. The lighting booth can't be seen into but can be clearly seen out of."

"Great," Napoleon breathed. "This is really wonderful. But what does all this mean?"

"It means, my feline friend, that this is the finest traveling theater in the entire trigored universe."

"O call back yesterday, bid time return," said an all-pervasive female voice coming from every corner of the theater. "It's the ONLY traveling theater in the entire universe."

"Who's that?" Napoleon mewed.

"Not who," said Pound, smiling beneficently to the air. "That's Muse. My Multi-Unit System for Entertainment. She/it is the producer of our ship, the *Shooting Star*. And we," he bowed, "we are 'The LOST.' Welcome to the Light Orbit Space Theater."

All three humans bowed elaborately. But all the feline could think about was the small compubot board she had secreted in her spacesuit.

Napoleon spun and stared slack jawed at Harlan. "A compubot?" she cried. "Oh, no! Not two of them!"

# THREE

Everyone was greatly confused until they all adjourned to the large, wide, tall bridge area to trade explanations. The bridge was as Roscoe had left it. The entrance was on the left wall, toward the back. The nearly hexagonal embankment stretched from one wall to the other; it was lined with monitors and meters which revealed the condition of the entire star-shaped ship.

The bridge was nestled in one point of the five-pointed star. The stage and backstage made up two more points. The last two were living quarters and a rehearsal hall. The center of the ship was all engine. Muse needed that for the practical and mechanical things she/it had to accomplish.

The only other things that interrupted the bridge's floor space were three small, solid T-shaped tables with a single, floor-installed seat on each side. Napoleon could see screens on the tables' surfaces, one which showed printed information, one which showed what was "behind" the ship, and one which showed a dark-haired man, a frizzy-haired man, and a bald man hitting each other.

"Oh, great!" Zero cried, running over to the third table's screen. "I love this one."

Roscoe paused as he approached his seat. He looked diffidently at the black-and-white images of slapstick comedy on the flat screen. Napoleon couldn't believe her eyes and Harlan his sensors. The men ripped saws over each other's scalps and banged each other in the faces with steel pipes and tools. It was worse violence than Napoleon had seen on Earthen VUs.

"We have to make do," Roscoe explained. "It's the only entertainment we have. Muse picks up ancient signals floating through space as we travel." He looked at the embankment, bending from the waist. "I wish you would be more selective. Can't you find any more episodes of 'Zatoichi'?" He turned back to the feline. "Now that's very exciting. There's this blind masseuse, you see . . ."

"I simply don't understand what you see in that," Spot pouted at the young man, bouncing her hip against his. "I don't think it's entertaining at all." She leaned down to give him a nice view of her chest.

Zero had already seen this particular adventure. "Why, you . . ." he said threateningly, then tried to get his hand inside her dress. She laughed and ran, with him on her heels.

"Come on, you two," Roscoe chastised, clapping his hands. "We have guests here." The others ignored him. Zero tackled the girl, much to her delight, and was slowly climbing up her body when Napoleon looked away and Harlan landed his spacesuit by the wall near the door.

"Nothing gynecological," Pound warned them as the space bullet head started to unscrew. The rocklike skull finally fell back like a parka hood and Harlan began to peel off the exoskeleton tubing which covered his actual head. He practically vaulted out of the nine-foot-tall space bullet suit, wearing only his black, long-sleeved body stocking.

Everyone but Napoleon did a double take at his wide, muscular body and strong, black-bearded face. His round head was also covered by coarse black hair. He suddenly felt a bit self-conscious under their stares.

Zero looked up from Spot's body (who was looking at the Destiny soldier upside down with her arms around the young FM) to Roscoe. "He'd be perfect." Roscoe nodded, his lips pursed.

"Perfect for what?" Harlan growled, standing in place.

"Perfect for the King of Scotland," Muse said. "Perfect for the King of Denmark. Perfect for Caliban, or Macduff, or Julius Caesar, for that matter. You name it."

"Name what?" Harlan nearly shouted.

"Harlan," said Napoleon quietly. "I think we'd better get out of here."

"But I just got unsuited," the space bullet couldn't keep himself from saying.

"No, please," Roscoe admonished, his hands out.

"We'll wait for another ship," the feline suggested, backing up.

"Please wait," Pound pleaded. "Let us explain." He looked angrily at Spot and Zero, who were still entwined around each other on the floor. "Get up," he barked, as if the whole thing was their fault.

"Let me," Muse suggested. Then the bridge was filled with the sound of stirring music. Napoleon backed behind Harlan, her spitter in her paw. Harlan looked around incredulously, wishing he were still in his suit. He felt incredibly exposed out here.

"Humanity went forth to inhabit the stars, only to find them inhabited already," quoth the Muse. "Naturally the Earth Central Government decided to instigate a Brotherhood of Planets, with Earth as the founding father. Unfortunately, as with the stars, someone or something had beaten them to that concept as well."

"A race whom I shall laughingly call of higher intelligence," Pound interrupted, "had already created a Federation of Worlds, which most of the civilized planets had already joined for their mutual trade benefit and defense. Quite naturally, not wanting to be left out, Earth put in their application."

"They were quite naturally turned down," Muse interrupted back. "No truly intelligent planet would have anything to do with the self-destructive, pompous, pretentious—"

"That's enough description," Pound directed. "Confidentially," he told the aliens as the others got up from the floor and brushed themselves off, "the fact that the Earthens had nearly destroyed themselves a couple of times over made entry into the Federation unthinkable." The music continued in the background.

"And they showed no tendency toward learning from their mistakes," said the militant Muse, the music accompanying her accordingly.

"Enough already," instructed Pound. "Continue."

"I have no appreciation of the Earth Central Government," she/it said defensively.

"That is readily apparent," Pound said. "Go on."

"After all," she/it said tenderly, "look what they did to you."

"Just go on," Roscoe almost pleaded.

"So life went on, but the ECG never got over the insult and humiliation of the Federation rejection. They passed it down from generation to generation and it grew and grew while the United World scientists created better and better artificials."

"Why haven't I heard all this before?" asked a bewildered Napoleon, the music muting. "I was on Earth for years."

Muse neatly sidestepped the question since there was no real answer. "Then you are aware that the TMs with the proper RH factor were a very bigoted lot. Any artificial or off-worlder was an automatic second citizen."

"Absolutely," said Harlan.

"Thank you," said Muse dryly. "When Earth had gained a certain amount of secondary stature, they again put forth an application to the Federation. Of course, they should have realized that such a misconceived move was prohibitive in itself. No planet should have the audacity to apply a second time. If the Federation found one worthy, they would be approached and invited to join. Earth was again—and finally—rebuffed."

"Ah, but we are a clever race," Pound interjected. The music suddenly snapped off.

"And impolite," said Muse. "Would you kindly stop interrupting?"

"Sorry, my sweet," Pound said quickly. "You're right. This is your story. Pray continue."

"I shall not deem to thank you," said the female voice as the music started up again. Harlan and Napoleon looked at each other in dismay. It had seemed inconceivable that there were two compubots in the universe like this. One they were listening to. The other had its existence programmed on the compubot board the feline had in her suit.

"But Earth was not to be ignored," Muse carried on. "They decided that if they couldn't join the Federation, they would beat them at their own game. So saying, they created a planetary organization of their own. The BOP: the Brotherhood of Planets."

"Of which we are but a humble part," Pound said with a big smile, which immediately disappeared when he realized what he had done. "Sorry." The music stopped again.

Her/its voice was cold. "Do you want to tell the story?"

"No, really, I'm sorry."

"You can if you want to, you know."

"No, that's quite all right. Really."

"You want to tell it, don't you?"

"No, I really want you to tell it. You tell it much better than I do. You're more objective. Isn't she?" he asked the aliens. Napoleon looked at him in disbelief, then grinned and shook her head. Forget it, she was telling him. You're not sucking us into this insanity. "Isn't she?" he asked the others.

"Oh, yes," Zero said with boredom.

"Absolutely," Spot added dully.

"There, you see?" he told her/it. "You simply must continue."

"Very well. I will continue." She paused. "If you're sure."

"What do you want me to do?" Pound suddenly shouted. "Rip out my heart and dance on it?"

"Where was I?" Muse said, ignoring the outburst.

"At BOP," Harlan told her, Napoleon looking at him in surprise. "When Earth found out that the higher intelligences had an organization of their own."

"Thank you," Muse curtly interrupted. "I remember. The Federation had already reached all the solar systems in the Milky Way area and was organized so tightly that the Brotherhood had nothing to offer the civilized planets. There was only one thing Earth could do."

"Enlist the other planets which the Federation had already rejected," Napoleon interrupted, daring the female compubot to take offense.

Silence reigned on the bridge of the Earth Ship *Shooting Star* while Pound and his crew stared wide-eyed and dry mouthed at the feline, whose tail was lashing back and forth around the space bullet's legs.

"So then every backward, nondescript world that had a society which knew the meaning of the word 'me' was put under the protection of the Brotherhood," Muse continued, seemingly undaunted. "And entitled to all the benefits thereof."

"Which is us," Roscoe said purposely.

"You have to have the last word, don't you!" Muse instantly cried.

"I'm sorry, my sweet," Roscoe said smoothly as Spot and Zero wandered away. "It's just that the whole thing is so close to my heart."

"How about my heart?" she/it complained. Napoleon could see what Pound was doing, much to her surprise. The feline had challenged the compubot, which had backed down. To save her/its ego program, he was letting the thing take out her/its hurt on him. The feline suddenly liked this human. He and she/it were nuts, but she liked them (which was saying something, considering the amount of hate in her heart).

"I'm really sorry, Muse, my dear, I truly am. I just wanted to supplement your telling of it. You had reached a segment that needed a dramatic bridge, so I took the liberty of supplying one. I didn't intend to upstage you. I wanted to enhance the story, that's all. Embellish it, not steal your spotlight."

"You said I could tell the story."

"And you did. You told it very well."

"How many times do I get to tell this story?" she/it complained. "This is the first time in years. When will I get to tell it again?"

"If not this story, then another one, my love."

"But you're always doing this! You never want me to perform."

"Now, that's just not true, Muse."

"It's always, 'Take care of the script, Muse,' or 'Take care of the costumes, Muse.' You never let me perform."

"What about the shows in our sixth and eleventh years?" Pound reminded her.

"Big deal," she/it sniffed. "The voice of Titania, and the voice of Hamlet's father."

"But Hamlet's father didn't have a voice originally, remember?" Pound countered. "I let you write that."

"It was so long ago I can barely recall it," Muse complained. "When can I perform again?"

Zero shook his head, wandering near the aliens. "More extortion," he whispered to Harlan.

"Soon," Roscoe answered blankly.

"That's what you always say. How soon?"

Roscoe's eyes were almost closed and his voice ice. "Very soon."

Muse immediately retreated but couldn't completely give up. "Which role?" she/it asked in a tiny voice.

"Excuse me," Napoleon called, getting her a look from Harlan this time. "Where do you fit in with all this?" Anything to end the argument.

Pound turned to the feline, then looked back at the embankment, motioning toward Napoleon. "There. Now you can tell the story without any more interruptions from me."

Her/its voice was plaintive. "I don't want to anymore."

"Muse" he said threateningly.

"I don't feel like it."

Harlan leaned down to whisper in the feline's ear. "I'm getting sick of compubots with erratic personalities."

"You're not the only one," Napoleon whispered back.

Roscoe Pound briskly turned from the embankment. "Very well," he said diffidently. "One of the benefits of joining the BOP . . ."

The music swelled again, drowning him out. "One of

the benefits of joining the Brotherhood," Muse broke in smoothly, "was partaking of its cultural services." Pound threw himself into his padded chair, almost lying down in its sunken interior. "We are the Light Orbit Space Theater, a division of the ECG-U.W. BOP Entertainment Subcommittee, or ENSUB. Our twenty-year play tour has taken us across the galaxy and back, on planets that solicit our services. The ECG has carefully calculated our speed and the time differential so we appear on our premiere dates."

"Wait a minute," Napoleon interrupted, one paw out. "I don't understand."

"What?" Pound asked from inside his chair.

"Anything," she replied.

"We are actors, who perform plays, on whatever planet has asked for us," Muse said slowly.

"The sad fact is, however," Pound elaborated, "that we got our itinerary in 594 A.N.D., and the Earth that exists on the same time plane now must be nearing 800 A.N.D. at least."

"The Earth we left might be three hundred years older than when we left it?" Harlan asked.

"Who knows?" Pound said, waving a hand. "You say you've been gone only a few years. We have been traveling almost twenty years. But we're talking to each other in the same ship at the same time. Neither of us is less real than the other. But the fact remains that you left Earth in the early five hundreds A.N.D., and we left in the late five hundreds. Why aren't you a century older than you are?"

"Don't bother," Muse suggested as the aliens struggled to understand. "There's insufficient data. There are laws of space travel we haven't yet begun to understand. But certain criteria are known to work, so those are the laws we go by."

"Twenty years?" Harlan marveled. "Alone?"

"I beg your pardon?" said Muse.

"Hardly alone," Pound countered. "In addition to my sweet Muse, there are my performers. Zero and Phyllis you've met—

"Don't call me that!" Spot cried angrily.

"Her real name is Phyllis," Zero said confidentially, "but everyone knows her as Spot."

"Why?" Harlan asked.

"Because she keeps missing it," Zero said.

"What?" Harlan replied, as confused as before. But Zero had already gone over to tease the pouting girl.

"Our hold is also filled with programmable robots," Pound revealed.

"What is all this?" Napoleon finally blurted. "What exactly do you do here and why?"

"What do you mean?" Pound answered. "What else would I do? I was a minor ECG Reg. And if you know Earth, you know it's one big decreasing spiral of ECG Regs. I was lower than low. This suicide assignment gave me a chance to get out of the shadow of the Doomstar .... Oh, pardon me. The deux ciel." He pronounced the quasi-French term for "second sky" or "second heaven" very carefully. "So now I'm twenty years older and probably happier than I ever could have been."

Roscoe looked pleasantly at the aliens' disbelieving faces. "Oh, come now," he reasoned. "Even with as small a population as we had, you can't believe that everyone was as bigoted and cruel as the TMs you killed. Larry-lovers had to keep quiet if they knew what was good for them"

"You," Napoleon stammered, "were a larry-lover?"

"I guess so," said Roscoe. "No one admitted it, even to themselves, but I hated what was happening to all the FMs and SMs."

"But you didn't do anything about it!" Harlan accused him.

Roscoe thought, his face sad. "No," he agreed.

The feline waved away the confrontation. She wasn't going to begrudge the strange man his apathy. It had taken Larry a lifetime to fight back as well. She wasn't exactly guiltless in that department either. "Everyone seems to be overlooking a primary bit of information," she announced. All eyes were on her. "What's a script? What's a premiere? What's a Hamlet? What's a Titania? What's a theater? What's a play?"

"I can answer that," said Spot. "A play is a dramatic performance of a written composition for one or more players of any planetology. 'The play's the thing,' as the Book would say. It's a dramatic exercise or entertainment for an audience. Do you want to know what an audience is?"

"I can tell you that," interjected Muse. "An audience is a thankless bunch of cretins incapable of appreciating a heartfelt presentation of any kind."

"Enough," Roscoe announced, struggling from his comfortable seat. When he had finally found his feet, he approached the perplexed aliens. "In order for you to understand, you'll have to know a little background. After all the wars before and after A.N.D., there really wasn't very much in the way of literature. There were plenty of military and scientific texts in the shelters, but little in the way of written entertainment.

"Thankfully, during the worst of the devastation, a certain high-ranking MM (Military Man) fell in love with a certain beautiful EM (Earth Mother), who was dying of radiation sickness. Rather than turning her over to the scientists for cloning or vaginal reclamation, he treated her with infinite care.

"But he had to separate her from healthy humans, so he placed her in a clear, radiationproof box. Even though it was only a matter of time before her death, he was desperate to please her and soothe her pain. When there was nothing else that would entertain her in the shelter, he even braved the outside world in a rad-suit.

"He returned to the shelter unharmed, carrying a bunch of written works under his arms. He brought the few books to her, but it was too late. The disease had progressed too far. She was unable to even read." There Roscoe paused, causing Napoleon to inquire, "What then?"

Pound smiled widely, having shown the feline the power of performance. He had both aliens on their toes. "The Military Man dropped the books, sealed off the room, took off the rad-suit, and made love to the woman. They died together."

"Such a beautiful story," Muse sighed. "I simply have to write a play about it."

"Zero and I will star," Spot offered.

Harlan was the one to break the spell. "I still don't understand. What does that have to do with a theater and a play?"

"Well," Roscoe answered pleasantly, "no one knew what to do with these books for years. But when the BOP was created, the ECG was desperate for something to offer other planets to get them to join. Finally the ENSUB discovered the volumes and hit upon the idea of performing them on newly joined planets."

"What were these books?" Napoleon inquired.

"*Her Lustful Passions, Rare Diseases of the Cow,* and *The Complete Works of William Shakespeare*," Pound told them.

"*Rare Diseases of the Cow*?" Napoleon echoed.

"It was very dramatic," Muse assured her.

"We finally settled on Shakespeare," Roscoe summarized, holding up the Book.

"I've always wanted to do something with *Her Lustful Passions*," Muse sighed. "I suppose I could always combine it with the cattle afflictions."

"We'll star," Spot called.

"Shakespeare wrote thirty-seven plays," Pound informed them. "Not counting his epic poems. The BOP ENSUB offered any one to the joining planets. We've been going from world to world the last twenty years performing them." He looked at the blank faces of the feline and the space bullet, unperturbed.

"And what have you two been doing all this time?"

Much to Roscoe's future regret, they told him.

# Flashback . . . Finally

# FOUR

They didn't tell Roscoe the whole truth, as much as Napoleon had wanted to. Although he deserved to know what he was getting into, discretion was the better part of valor. It was a much better idea for the LOST to harbor the aliens willingly than for Harlan to force them to offer the ship as a hideout. And if the feline had been Roscoe, and knew the entire story, she wouldn't have let them stay either.

She told them that they had been looking for her home planet of Mandarin, and that in itself was true. Once Harlan and she had left Destiny, the "mythical garden world, the piece of jade in the black velvet of space," as he had once described it to her, they plunged into the uncharted void aboard their new ship, *Felidae*.

Larry, the Experimental Fake Man, had designed it just for her, and the eager, able Destinian people whom she had saved from slavery built it to Larry's specifications. What resulted was a grand, eye-shaped ship,

tapered at both ends and thick in the middle. It bristled
with weapons and sensors that were as advanced as the
Destinians could make them (and the Destinians could
make them very well). The *Felidae* was essentially Napoleon's spaceship version of a space bullet suit.

They wandered the bottomless blackness until they
were nearly bored to death. When he wasn't tinkering
with his suit, Harlan wandered the roomy ship in his
black body stocking. Napoleon stayed on the intimate
bridge, wearing the rust-colored, sleeveless leotard
Harlan's sister, Hana, had made for her, the one with
the brown-and-green patch on the left breast which said
in the ancient mariner's language: "Seek long enough
and you will always find your Destiny."

Well, they sought long and found nothing. Both
decided to head back into known space to find Mandarin,
the equally mythical planet of Napoleon's origin. Or so
they thought. A predominant rumor which was given
some validity was that all aliens were descended from
Earthen creatures that had mutated among the stars.
Still, while Napoleon's ancestors may have come from
Earth, she had been stolen from Mandarin, along with
her eleven sisters.

They had all died on Earth, but she had managed to
escape, constantly awestruck by the planet's insidious
influence. She did not know her real name or her home
planet's real name. Earthen ego was so great that it
renamed anything it came into contact with. They had
named her Napoleon, after the name of the ship she had
come in on, and even told her that the god she worshiped
was called "Cheshire."

But the feline was strong-willed and athletic. Neither
she nor Harlan, a Destinian soldier who had been trained
as a warrior since birth, could handle inactivity for long.
They soon sought out inhabited planets where they might
find clues to Mandarin's location. It was all they had to

do, really. The whole idea of leaving Destiny was to discover Napoleon's purpose.

Harlan would shrug on his Destinian suit, a black, one-piece long-sleeved coverall with the built-in translator under the brown-green patch on his left breast, and they'd go planetside in one of the *Felidae's* "esc-globe eyes." These were the clear, OD-outfitted balls used to go from the orbiting ship to the planet's surface.

As they neared their first planetfall, Napoleon became increasingly paranoid. She was worried that her fame might have preceded her. But Harlan assured her that the reports of the eleven TM deaths they had caused were hardly of any interest to anything other than Earthens. And Earthens carried little weight out here compared to Destinians.

Sure enough, when the creatures they met on the galaxy's fringes weren't intrigued by their Destiny patches, they were intrigued by Napoleon's "look." Somehow she seemed attractive to every manner of humanoid. No one, however, could shed any light on Mandarin's location. Many felt that the Earthen name was misleading and they might have guessed better had they known its real name. But, no, they knew of no planet where felines were the norm.

"People don't get around much," Harlan decided as they sank in the esc-globe eye toward their latest planetfall.

"Interplanetary travelers are pretty rare," Napoleon agreed as she looked over the gray planet.

"Maybe things will improve as we move closer to the center of the galaxy," he hoped. They were dancing on the very edge, hopping from world to world.

Napoleon nodded noncommittally. Going deeper into the systems would mean coming closer to Earth, and even with the suit and the *Felidae*, she doubted she could hold off Earth's entire armament. Harlan knew that to be untrue. They could level Earth's defenses between the two of them, but the feline was still spooked. She didn't want to get close to the planet. She was not out for revenge. She was seeking a home.

The esc-globe sank below the thin cloud cover and emerged over Finally, the last Earthen-charted planet. In the days immediately after the creation of the O'Neil Drive, Earthen ships scoured the galaxy for planets interested in slave clone labor. Finally was the last planet they reached before they were unceremoniously forced back to their own world.

Ever since then, Finally was considered a last stop, a minor way station before either returning home or going farther to map the unmapped. Like all planets Earthens had recorded, it had humanoid inhabitants. In this case, light-blue-skinned people with a single nostril in their upturned noses. The sun was bright, but the cloud cover kept things cool. In addition, the atmosphere was light.

"It just gets so damn dull," the small spaceport globe parker said as he handed them their squeeze bottles of supplemental air. "For a while there everybody wanted to see what the last world on the edge of the galaxy looked like. But when they found out it was just another planet, that was the end of that. You two are the first aliens we've seen in I don't know how long. You want me to show you around?"

"No, thanks," Harlan told the overeager resident.

"Any ships from Mandarin ever come in?" Napoleon asked, putting the bottle's tube under her nose and squeezing.

"Mandarin?" There was a buzz from the translator, signifying an untranslated, regional word. "Not that I know of. Mandarin? Where's that?"

Harlan ignored the question. "You worked here long?"

"All my life," the parker said proudly. "It's been boring, I can tell you. So I'm studying agricultural design. Maybe I can move over to work in the tiered seed fields. Sure you don't need me to show you around? I can take you to all the good places."

"No, thanks," Harlan said. "Just keep an eye on the eye. What kind of ore do you take?"

"Don't worry about it." said the parker with disappointment. "You can keep the esc-globe on the surface and your ship in orbit for a revolution. But then you've got to make other arrangements."

"Fair enough," Harlan replied. Napoleon nodded, preoccupied. Both should have smelled something then.

They left the relatively small square and headed into what served as a town. There was a bank, a supply store, and a bistro. Harlan saw it was going to be useless almost immediately. This was a minor spaceport town, set some ways from whatever Finally cities there were. To get any information from citizens would require extensive traveling. Each of the last few planets they visited had let them land at a centrally located spaceport, usually situated just outside a major urban area.

Not Finally. Adjusting to the setback, the aliens wandered to the bistro, the last building set in the small town, which was surrounded by gigantic fields. Harlan and Napoleon looked across opposite fields into the gray-skied distance. The land was covered by reeds. Anything could be in or under those reeds and it was not a wise idea for them to find out what.

There was a door in the wall which Harlan could just push open. It was always a treat to see how different races on different planets handled the simplest things that Earthens took for granted. Like floors and walls and ceilings. But Finally was ECG Planet Directory approved, so there were no surprises. Larry had put the book, published by the famed Intercouncil of Brotherhood, on Napoleon's ship before she left Destiny.

The bistro was a single room with simple tables on one

central sector dotting the floor in front of a rear section consisting of several stoves and a food-filled cabinet. The smell inside was neither exactly good nor exactly awful. Even from here, Napoleon could see the Human System seal on much of the displayed items. But she and Harlan didn't need to eat. They had plenty of nourishment on board their ship. Instead, the two found a table. They needed to talk.

The four bored people inside perked up when the off-worlders entered. Even here, on the very edge of charted space, Destiny and its denizens were recognized. Destiny's legend and fame were sung and proclaimed on almost every human-harboring world. Of course, a five-foot cat accompanied by a man with muscles that looked like coiled bunches of hemp was pretty hard to ignore.

The other people inside the bistro looked to be long-term spaceport employees, so no one bothered the aliens until another man with one nostril walked in, took one look at the feline sitting next to the bearded man, gasped, yelled "Lil!" and fainted dead away.

Napoleon glanced at the man passed out on the floor and looked at the other four one-nostriled men in the bistro. They were as disinterested as she. She heard one mutter. The words came dimly out of her patch translator. "Lousy blackear."

The man on the floor's eyes fluttered and he raised his head to look weakly at Napoleon. "Lil," he called, then his eyes rolled up into their sockets. They heard the back of his head hit the floor.

Napoleon and Harlan examined him from their seats. Sure enough, his ears were black. Pitch black. The rest of his head was the same hairless light blue color as the others, but his human ears were a deep, shiny black. As they watched, his eyes opened again, locking on Napoleon.

"Lil, Lil," he mumbled, shivering as if deathly chilled. "Lil."

The feline threw a glance at her companion. He looked back. They both got up at the same time and went to the blackear. Harlan placed his hands under the quivering man's shoulders and lifted as Napoleon kneeled in front of him. She glanced around to see if the incident had any effect on the other patrons. Every eye was on her.

She smiled, waved, and then pointed at herself and said, "Lil." Meanwhile, the man had regained enough composure to look happily upon the feline and say the name strongly. "Lil."

"No," she corrected mildly. "Napoleon."

The man sat up as if a rod had been rammed through his spinal column, and his hands shot forward to grip her arm. Before his fingers could touch her fur, however, the feline's companion grabbed the base of the poor fellow's neck between his thumb and fingers and squeezed, paralyzing his arms in place.

"Harlan," reprimanded the cat, "please."

"Sorry," he apologized. "Force of habit."

"We haven't had a battle of any sort in two years."

"Old habits die hard," he said.

During the conversation, the man with one nostril had regained his breath. His hands sought the feline's arm again, but stopped just before touching, as if he suddenly realized something. With a troubled look to the glaring bearded man, he forcibly dropped them to his side.

"Lil, it is you," he said reverently.

"No, it isn't," said the feline.

"Maybe it is," Harlan interrupted.

"Do not make light of Lil," the blackear intoned to no one in particular. "You, out of all, should not treat him lightly."

"Her," Napoleon corrected. "He's raving," she said to Harlan.

"What are you talking about?" Harlan demanded, shaking the blackear. "Who is Lil? Why do you have black ears? And, for that matter, who are *you*?"

"Go to him," the man pleaded to Napoleon, as if no one had spoken but he. "He needs you." His hands rose to her face, the fingers vibrating like rung bells. Her visage, however, held only confused ignorance. "I know!" he suddenly boomed, clapping his hands sharply. Napoleon grimaced. "I know what's troubling you!"

The blackear scrambled to his feet. Harlan and Napoleon stood with him. "I will prepare your way!" he promised. "Do not worry. I will tell him of your coming!"

He spun to find Harlan blocking him. "Who?" the space bullet asked, but the blackear ignored him, stepping to one side. Harlan blocked him again. "Who is Lil? Who are you going to tell?" The blackear didn't seem aware of the words. He moved to the other side. Harlan was about to detain him further, but Napoleon called him off.

"Let him go," she said tiredly. "He's raving, I tell you."

Harlan stood in place and the blackear raced out. The frowning Destinian watched him go. "I don't know, Nap."

"Come on," the feline said, going over to the table. "Sit down." The atmosphere was making her nauseous. She needed to rest before they planned their next move.

Harlan looked over the others in the place. They were studiously ignoring the situation. Even with his vaunted Destiny-trained instincts, Trigor couldn't tell if they were really disinterested or faking it. But when he brought this up in hushed tones to the feline, she didn't want to talk about it.

For some reason, Napoleon didn't want to discuss the ramifications of the curious occurrence. Every time

Harlan tried convincing her that this was their first real lead, she would change the subject.

"He recognized you," Harlan said.

"He was delirious. He probably attacks every new person that way."

"He called you Lil."

"She was probably an old girl of his."

Harlan was stymied. He had never seen her this skittish. "What's the problem?" he asked.

She kept saying "nothing," and even after a lengthy discussion that bordered on argument several times, all she could think about was leaving the planet. Harlan finally left the bistro in disgust. The cat was turning irresponsibility into a fine art. She hated what had happened to her but didn't want to go back to Earth. She said she wanted to find Mandarin, but at the first clue she decided to turn tail and run. Harlan couldn't make heads or tails of it, so he simply marched back to the esc-globe.

"I don't feel well," Napoleon mewed, coming to his side, her tail wrapping around one of his legs. "Let's just get out of here."

"Fine," Harlan said. He wasn't going to start trotting out the relevant facts again. After all, this was her quest. If she wanted to ignore their first tangible lead, that was just dandy with him.

They rode the eye up and docked with the *Felidae* without a word. That silence seemed golden when they ultimately moved into the control area on the bridge. It was hard not to admire the shining new fittings, the wide, vaguely U-shaped front port, and the walls of bright machinery, highlighted by a red slot in the middle. There was even a large red arrow painted on the wall pointing to the thin, vertical slot.

"Took you long enough," said a disembodied male voice. Neither person took any notice of it.

Napoleon settled into her seat, the one with the

indented hole in the back for her tail, and started practical tests. Harlan moved toward the rear of the room where the nine feet of vaguely human-shaped, slate-colored rock was. The head was open, so a cup-shaped stone was hanging on the back. As the feline checked the warning systems, food stores, esc-globe eyes, and related circuitry, Harlan nimbly leaped up the monolithic slab and started lowering himself into it.

Soon he was shoulder deep in the piece of space debris, pulling the net of exoskeleton tubes across his head. As the gridded mask settled on his face, the dull hatching turned blue-green and pulsated like living veins. Harlan was back in his natural habitat. He was a soldier whose one purpose was to protect his home planet: a fable for strife-weary astronauts, a target for space pirates, and the home of a race of Earth-descended human beings.

A select few had been genetically developed into the double-jointed species which protected Destiny by fighting in the upper atmosphere, completely at one with their self-contained spacecraft and armament. Inside the suit, Harlan was at all-powerful, all-knowing peace. The only reason he ever left it was because it couldn't go everywhere and do everything. Once it landed, he needed zero gravity or a powerful launch to get it going again. It was not made for lower-atmosphere travel.

Harlan started humming a very familiar tune to himself. It was his space bullet song.

"There he goes again," the disembodied voice complained.

"Mess," Napoleon interrupted, "is the ship space-worthy?"

"Of course," replied Mess, the Multi-Unit Electric System for Space.

"Can we take off anytime?"

"Is there an echo in here?"

Napoleon knew that her caution had set off one of the

compubot's guilt traps. Now she had to explain the difference. "Spaceworthy refers to all the necessary checks. Taking off involves more than that."

"Such as?"

"Such as clearances."

"According to the cirquids filled by Palsy-Drake on the date of my conception and the niodes programmed by Larry on the date of my resurrection, spaceworthy means being capable of taking off."

"Don't bring them up again," Napoleon warned. The compubot took every opportunity to remind her that it was only taking orders from her out of the kindness of its connections. It owed its allegiance to its original inventor, the insane, drug-addicted Palsy-Drake (the only TM executed for crimes against RHs), and its original master, the oft-mentioned Larry. "Are we ready to go?"

"I'm hurt you should think otherwise," Mess said as Harlan disengaged himself from the suit and disconnected the exoskeleton.

"You don't have feelings," Harlan said as he climbed out.

"Yes, I do!" Mess flared. "And I proved it!" The compubot had overcome its original directive of self-preservation to save its master. As a result, it had been blasted apart, but Larry had pieced it together again for the *Felidae*.

"A calculated gamble on your part," Harlan theorized. "You knew you would never make it out of that wilderness. Your only hope was to return."

There was a long, cold silence from the console, during which Napoleon shot crinkler-sharp looks at the space bullet. Let her glare, he thought. He was still irritated at her. She was making the entire two-year search irrelevant by ignoring the blackear's actions.

"How dare you," Mess spat. "After all I've done for you. To be so callous. To be so thoughtless." The voice clipped off, then snapped on again. "That's it," it said briskly. "That's all. If I'm not appreciated, why not just disconnect me? Go ahead. Disconnect me. Right now."

To his credit, Larry had tried to amend Mess' previous paranoia. He had attempted to redirect the compubot's concern toward its new mistress. To his debit, all he succeeded in doing was making the paranoid personality guilt ridden. To be fair, playing with sealed cirquids was very difficult and chancy. Especially cirquids originally formulated by a madman. They were all lucky Mess' character was not more warped than it was.

"Would you two just stop it?" Napoleon howled, the nausea of the planet having left her completely. "Harlan, quit baiting it. Mess, you're not my mother. You're not anybody's mother. Damper down off the guilt trip." She silently cursed Larry. She cursed him for caring so much about her. Memories of his long, kind face began to assail her.

They had been a team on Earth. An Earth millions of light-years away now, but then it had been vital and dangerous. She was the last feline in the galaxy, sought out and lusted after by every vicelord and ECG official imaginable in a world where a naturally born female was at a premium. Larry was an artificial. Although the best of that kind, he was an artificial nevertheless, a TM-made commodity.

Subsequent to all the wars and all the natural disasters, the remaining military and government people (the only ones with enough time and shelter to avoid the devastation) created an Earth in their image. Clones were mass produced, but not ones specifically created as slaves. Although they wildly outnumbered the True Humans, the Fake Men and women were brainwashed and drugged into their awful roles.

Larry and Napoleon had escaped the crumbling Earth, only to fight to save Harlan's home planet. Now, after all the fighting, Larry was the only one to find happiness. He had remained on Destiny, partner to Harlan's sister, to become the ruling father of a new world. It was hard for the feline to comprehend that he was no longer by her side. Harlan was caring, considerate, and capable, but he wasn't Larry.

"Everything's set?" she continued briskly. "All right, then, let's go."

"Where to?" Mess innocently inquired as Harlan moved over to the co-pilot's seat.

"Anywhere," Napoleon replied, touching a tensor square on her console. Destiny technology had allowed Larry to install squares which only responded to Napoleon's or Harlan's touch. "Finally Central City Spaceport," Napoleon called. "We're ready to leave."

She waited for the double clicks which signified "message received" from the folks who had relegated her ship to a nearly deserted secondary spaceport. Instead, there was a longer pause than was usual and a voice speaking in English responded. "*Felidae*, you are cleared to the second moon."

Napoleon had already instigated takeoff procedures and had to forcibly stop herself from bolting. "What?" she spat, the very model of feminine manners.

"You are cleared to Finally Finished, the second moon, *Felidae*."

"What's the first moon called?" Harlan mumbled.

"Finally Over," said Mess.

"Mess"—she whirled on it—"I thought you said we could go."

"What are you looking at?" it said defensively. "This is news to me."

Napoleon jabbed the communications tensor again. "Finally Central, repeat."

"*Felidae*. We have duly received your shuttle request.

We have acknowledged it. We have cleared it. Please
proceed on the space lane we have opened for you."

Napoleon abruptly cut the connection. "I had nothing
to do with this!" Mess announced. Harlan put a hand on
the feline's arm. Her fur bristled, but she looked over to
see the communications tensor flashing. She pushed it.

"*Felidae*, please shuttle to the second moon or give up
your takeoff standing. You are holding up our patterns."

The feline's lips curled back over her teeth in a soundless spit. That took gall, especially after originally sending them to the deserted spaceport half a world away.
She looked at Harlan in consternation, then started tap-
ping the tensor. "Please stand by, Finally Central," she
said. "You are not coming through clearly." She switched
off the communications link.

"Lil," Harlan said.

"What?" Napoleon answered before realizing he
wasn't saying her name. Then it dawned on her. "The
little blue booger said he was going to prepare my way."

"That he was going to tell 'him' you were coming,"
Harlan mused.

The tensor had nearly strobed out by the time Napoleon tapped it again. Before the spaceport officials could
bluster, Napoleon said in her smoothest tones, "Sorry for
the delay, Finally Central. The problems have been alle-
viated and we're taking off now. Thank you for your time
and consideration." She cut the lines and lateraled the
takeoff complexities to Mess.

As the ship started moving toward its rendezvous with
the second moon, Napoleon stared at her control board
through gleaming, narrow eyes. Her brows arched down
toward the bridge of her nose and her lips were curled in
a smirk. It was thirty seconds before Harlan interrupted
her sneering reverie.

"What are you thinking, Nap? I know that evil,
insulted look on your face."

The gold-green eyes turned on the man, her lightly furred brows arching in righteous anger. "Nothing controls my life, Harlan."

"Napoleon," the soldier sighed, his broad shoulders hunching forward. "Please. I've told you before. Everything is not a plot to control you. Sometimes things happen because of a consideration, or a practicality, or, probably in this case, a mistake. It is not all part of a conspiracy to possess you."

"Nothing controls my life," the feline calmly repeated.

"And I'll be telling you again," the space bullet sighed, leaning back in his chair. "What are you going to do?"

Napoleon looked out the front window, her paws wide on the console lip. She smiled nastily at the approaching hazy, milky-white orb. "I'll visit their lousy second moon, all right," she said. "I'll even look into this Lil thing. But I'll do it on my terms. My way."

Harlan didn't like the sound of that. Not at all.

"Are you two finished?" Mess inquired. "Where do I land?"

# FIVE

They landed several miles from where Finally Central had directed them, and walked toward the location. The atmosphere on Finally Finished was thicker than on the home planet, and the satellite was closer to the system's sun. The proximity and atmosphere combined to make the weather a bit warmer. But the only chance they weren't taking was by coming to the spot from the rear wearing their skintight spacesuits and clear bubble helmets.

Harlan had wanted to fly her down on his space bullet, but the feline had refused adamantly. Once she got on this "nothing will control me" kick, she got independent to the point of idiocy. She refused to let Harlan accompany her if he put on the space bullet suit. Her very presence was superfluous next to that suit, as far as she was concerned. If he didn't care for her so much, her emotional impracticality would have driven him nuts.

So the pair walked side by side with the clear domes on

their heads, their spitters on thigh "magsters" (magnetic holsters) and the beamers on their backs. Everything was just dandy until the ground began to ripple.

"What is this?" she asked. "An earthquake?"

"No sign of that," came Mess' voice over the communication links. "Better get back to the esc-globe." It didn't like the situation either.

"No," Napoleon said. They stilled as the earth seemed to bubble several yards ahead of them.

"What happened?" Mess asked.

"The ground moved," Napoleon answered irritably. "Check it."

"I have checked," it called down. "And double-checked. There's no seismic activity in your area at all. Go back to the esc-globe."

"I said no. I said we'd walk, and I meant it. I just need to know what this stuff is."

"Trouble," said Mess.

"You're telling me?" the feline retorted.

"No, I mean more than that. Nothing is registering up here."

Napoleon didn't look at Harlan because she didn't want to see his face say, "I told you so." If she had looked, she would have seen Harlan's eyes intent on the moving dirt, with the barrel of his beamer making a third eye. Instead, she saw the ground rise up to smite her.

Her paw went for the handle of her spitter just as a wide orange beam smashed into the headstone-sized hunk of earth. It seemed to sink back into the planet. Napoleon didn't relax. Her spitter was up and in her paw. Her opposed thumb pressed the button at the rear of the barrel and the hilt extended to her shoulder.

She was ready when the second mound appeared like a wave directly in front of her. The weapon was as good as its name. As soon as Napoleon pulled the trigger, light green beams perforated the dirt. It seemed to wave slightly in place, then rained back to the ground as a dust cloud.

The two stood side by side, looking across a placid, reedless, field. Before it had moved, the land seemed to be a featureless plain. They had been moving toward an outcropping of rock some ways in the distance. That was where they had been directed by Finally Central. Suddenly the whole deal took on an ominousness it hadn't had before.

The two watched, all their senses coming into play. But only Napoleon grinned. After two years, she was seeing action again. She wanted to do something, and something else wanted to stop her. It made her feel like she was actually achieving something, not just floating around in space trying to avoid Earthens.

Harlan, in the meantime, did not smile. He may have felt some sort of strange exhilaration, but he was too good a soldier to show it. A battle of any kind was no time for levity. That came only after the battle was won.

The ground was pulled out from under their feet. Harlan fell onto his back heavily, but Napoleon always landed on her feet, even if she had to do a back flip. She landed on her rear paws after somersaulting through the air, and spitted the mound that came at her. The dirt tried to sweep over Harlan like a blanket, but he beamed it, then stood up in the hole he had created.

Napoleon kept spitting at the mound, but it kept coming. Harlan swung his weapon toward the charging ground, but it was too close to the feline. The soldier spun the ring at the butt of the beamer to its narrowest aperture, but it was too late. Napoleon turned as the earth hit her shoulder.

It was like a dirt wave. It acted the way water would. It knocked her back but broke and cascaded around her. Another wave started to rise behind it. Harlan made quick work of that with his beamer. He was not going to wait for her any longer. "Back to the eye," he ordered, not caring what mood the feline was in.

Napoleon looked to her soiled suit and the strange dirt dusted around her feet. "Right," she said. Then she was swallowed up by Finally Finished.

Two mounds came at her from either side. She howled in surprise, spitting the one behind her and tearing at the beamer on her back. Harlan immediately blasted a hole in the mound that was coming at her. She dove through it as the two mounds crashed together like cymbals. They exploded, sending hunks of brown earth everywhere.

Harlan could see Napoleon on the ground through the muddy fog. As the dirty mist began to settle, he saw dark fingers reach from the planet's surface and clutch at her legs. Fingers grabbed the hilt of her spitter and pulled. Fingers clutched at her beamer butt and pulled. The feline was being laid out across the ground.

She snarled and twisted, stabbing at the magster's release. Suddenly the beamer snapped off her back and she could sit up. She had to let go of the spitter. Both weapons sank into the earth and disappeared. Napoleon slammed her clenched paws on the roots of dirt that were wrapping around her legs. They broke as if they had never been tangible in the first place.

Harlan didn't dare shoot. Even though he was an expert, there was no way he could accomplish anything without hitting the cat. She just managed to stand when the ground all around her started to boil.

"Jump!" he shouted. She tried, but the curving mandibles trapped her right ankle. Napoleon was pulled back down. She collapsed onto her knees. The Mantases erupted from under the ground.

Harlan leaped forward, his trigger finger tightening and relaxing spasmodically as the beamer barrel was aimed at each target. He mowed the accursed insectoids down under the swashes of bright, deadly light. These creatures had almost subjugated his planet. The feline had helped him to defeat them, so he was not about to let them have her.

The first shot took out the large black Mantas behind Napoleon, the next a gray one coming out of the ground back first beside the feline. The beamer swung around to blast a Mantas head which appeared beside him as he ran. The creatures had tried to encircle him too, but he would not stand for it. He kept moving toward his friend, shooting the Mantases as they appeared.

But he could not shoot what he could not see. Just as he neared Napoleon, she fell into the ground as if a trapdoor had opened beneath her. He heard her howling screech and saw the ground start covering her. She looked like she was sinking in quicksand, only there was nothing laborious about her descent. She was swallowed up and there was nothing Harlan could do about it with his weapons.

The space bullet shot another giant insect as it reared its ugly blue head, then rammed his arm into the ground where Napoleon had just lay. His fingers clutched loose gravel. There was nothing down there. He felt the blow to his side and immediately rolled with the shock. Another gray Mantas skittered after him, trying to tear his suit, his clothes, and his skin with its razor-sharp mandibles.

Harlan fired the beamer into the Mantas' torso, leaving only the creature's head, arms, and legs. They fell onto each other like rolling pins. Insect arms rose from the ground all around him. He shaved them off where they emerged with a swing of the high-intensity beamer, its rays all the more powerful at this close range.

He cursed himself for a fool, then threw himself into the air. He did a midair somersault and landed heavily on his back. When the insect arms rose this time, he only put up an irresolute fight, his finger off the beamer trigger. He gladly let the arms pull him down through the dirt.

He watched the ground cover his helmet and heard it clatter against the clear plastic.

He emerged into an underground cavern just big enough for the six-foot insectoids to traverse if they bent double. He fell into their swinging arms and then kicked his assailants away. He eradicated the ones nearby with the beamer as he lay on the tunnel floor. He kicked out with his feet, not daring to fire the weapon unless he had a sure shot. He didn't dare cave the caverns in, blocking his path.

Harlan cleared the way and then crawled quickly along the tunnel, his Destiny-sharpened eyes searching the network of Mantas-made caves for his friend (his ears were more precise than his eyes). He heard her leonine roars before he finally saw her. He ran, crouched over, toward the sounds. He shot the Mantases who appeared to block his path and kept going until he saw the three who held Napoleon in their tight pincers.

Harlan shot the ground just above their heads. The tunnel ceiling collapsed on them. Then he opened a hole in the roof surface overhead to climb out himself. He ran to where the two arms and six mandibles were waving in Finally Finished's dirt. He grabbed Napoleon's hand and pulled her from the makeshift grave. He knew he didn't have to worry about her suffocating. Her air supply came from inside her suit. The Mantases weren't so lucky.

"Harlan," she started, but he cut off whatever she planned to say by handing her his spitter.

"Harlan, hell!" Mess blurted. "How about me? You've been screeching in my ear for five minutes. What is going on down there?"

"Get ready to go!" Napoleon shouted. "This place is crawling with boogers!"

"Great," Mess grated electronically. "You should have listened to Trigor!"

"Damper down!" Trigor shouted.

The pair headed for the esc-globe. They were within twenty feet when it began to sink in the dirt. Napoleon skidded to a halt and peppered the ground around the eye's base with green spitter tubes. It was not enough. The ground on one side of the esc-globe collapsed and the eye fell onto its side.

"We can still take off," Napoleon announced. "Get in." Harlan stopped her as a blue Mantas appeared from behind the clear ball. They couldn't shoot it without damaging the vehicle, but in a trice the whole thing was academic. The Mantas had a weapon slipped over its first two mandibles. A bolt of white lightning emerged from the weapon's two tips and cracked the esc-globe like an eggshell.

Napoleon riddled the damaged eye with spitter beams, but the Mantas disappeared into the ground again. The feline was then sent tumbling by a scratching kick on her shoulder. A winged, gray Mantas had flown overhead. Harlan kneeled and beamed it out of the sky. It fell heavily on its stomach, then sank into the ground, killed and buried in one easy step.

Then the air was filled with gray Mantases, and the soil was rich with growing blue and black Mantas arms. The flying insectoids battered at the man and feline. The arms clutched and tore at their legs. Harlan and Napoleon got the same idea at the same time. They hopped into the esc-globe from different sides and fought from there.

"You go up and I'll go down," the feline growled, already planting the spitter bolts into the earth. Harlan bathed the sky in yellow-orange beams. Napoleon swirled her tail around until its tip was in front of her face. Keeping one paw on the weapon, she tore out a spit-pak from the ammo ring on her tail. It only took a second to reload, but it wasn't enough. The two were rapidly being overwhelmed by sheer numbers.

The sky had become a buzzing, swirling gray, and the ground had become a Mantas field of clutching arms. The insectoids all shared a common mind, a common goal, and a common desire. It made no difference how many died fighting toward their purpose. They were not aware of their own deaths. The one mind, fighting for the one Rule, lived on.

A winged gray swooped down from Napoleon's side and grabbed the barrel of the beamer. It lay on the esc-globe ceiling and held the gun in its viselike pincers. Two more gray Mantases landed and charged Harlan. He kicked them back with two expert blows, but others were beginning to swarm.

Napoleon shot through the roof into the Mantas body, but it held on. Insect ooze began to pour down the roof and through its many holes. A black Mantas came out of the ground grabbing for the feline. She hastily redirected her aim, but the thing was upon her when she shot it. It blocked any other shots at any other Mantases coming from behind it.

They were losing. The Mantases were overwhelming them, and there was nothing they could do about it. Trigor took solace in the fact that at least they were trying to capture Napoleon and not kill her. For what purpose, however, he couldn't imagine. Otherwise he couldn't help wishing she had let him wear his space bullet suit. He would have made quick work of them then. Or would he? The last time he had faced the Mantases, they had possessed anti-space bullet weaponry. Maybe they had been wise to face them one on one after all. But it was useless to think that now. He was a soldier, and a soldier dealt with what he had, however he could. And a soldier went down fighting, protecting his . . . what? Harlan had no god, no country. He only had this friend.

Harlan let go of the beamer and gave the Mantases

crowded in the eye's doorway a devastating kick. He grabbed the spitter out of Napoleon's paws and shot a hole in the crowd. He pushed out of the esc-globe and ran around to the front. He fired away at the Mantases clawing at Napoleon on the other side.

"Take off!" he ordered. "Try the OD!"

Napoleon's paws reached for the controls and suddenly froze. She looked directly at Harlan and curtly shook her head.

"You can help me better from the *Felidae*!" he shouted, still firing, still kicking the Mantas arms which reached for his legs. He danced in place as only a Destinian could, his aim perfection.

"That's right!" Mess yelled in her helmet. "Get up here now!"

Napoleon looked to her right and hit the first Mantas as hard as she could. Its head jerked back on its body stalk, then the insect crumbled to the ground, tripping the ones behind it. The feline angrily slammed the controls into life, but the eye went nowhere. They had waited too long. The esc-globe was too damaged.

Mantas arms gripped Napoleon by the legs. The spitter trigger clicked on an empty ammo spit-pak. Harlan sank into the dirt up to his thighs. He felt the submerged Mantases tearing at his legs. The feline screeched as the insectoids bore her out of the esc-globe and away, holding her high above them.

Then the blackears fell upon the attackers. They had approached so quietly that even Harlan didn't hear them. The blue-skinned, one-nostriled men battered the Mantases who remained. They carried crystalline blue clubs which had edges as sharp as knives. They bruised and tore into the insectoids at the same time. The spitter and beamer only killed the creatures. These clubs caused them pain.

The Mantases began to scatter in panic, each feeling

the torture of the others. They ran from the blue crystal clubs, trying to take Napoleon with them, but the blackears would not allow it. They grabbed the feline from the Mantases, tearing the insectoid arms in two if they didn't release her.

Mantas ooze was splashing everywhere, patching the ground with pools of sticky mud. The blackears hustled Napoleon toward Harlan. He pulled himself out of the dirt and went to meet them. As he approached, he absently noted that while their mouths were open, no sound emerged. The only thing he heard was the rustle of the retreating Mantases and the movement of the blackears' running legs.

"Harlan," he heard Napoleon say with relief—and something else—and then they were by him. They just ran around the bewildered soldier as he was about to take the feline in his arms. He spun to watch them half pull and half carry the cat toward a cave entrance in the distant network of pointed, jutting boulders.

"What now?" Mess whined.

"I'm being kidnapped!" Napoleon yelled. "Again!"

"If they send up a ship, I'll blow it out of the sky," the compubot promised. "Trigor, do something!"

Harlan wordlessly gave chase, but he was constantly slowed by falling into the tunnels the Mantases had dug. The blackears seemed to know where the weak ground was and avoided it. Harlan tried to follow their zigzagging patterns, but they were too far ahead by then. Every time he seemed to get the hang of their movements, he dropped into another tunnel. But each time he leaped up and kept running.

He was ten feet from the cave entrance they were about to enter. "Guide me, Nap," he said just as a blackear exploded from the ground in front of him. The man with one nostril swung a blue crystal club at his head. Harlan ducked but it was too late. The heavy weapon smashed into his helmet, cracking it and driving him to the ground.

"Hey," he dimly heard Napoleon say. "That isn't— Look, I'll do it! Just undo . . . That's right. Taplinger-Jones!" Then her words were drowned out by the constant banging. Then even the banging grew distant and Harlan realized he was losing consciousness.

"No!" He shouted the word to mentally snap him back to full awareness. The space bullet had actually forced himself awake. The banging was not his imagination. The blackear was still over him, slamming the club again and again into Harlan's helmet. The dome was no longer clear. It was covered by spiderweb cracking.

"Hey, stop that!" Mess shouted. "Just stop. You hear me? I said stop!"

Though he was essentially blind, Harlan swept his arm around, chopping the blackear at the ankles. The man's feet flew up, his head fell down, and he crashed onto the ground. That in itself was enough to knock him out.

"I'm warning you," said Mess. "You better stop!"

"Damper down!" Trigor gripped the nec-lip clasp and pulled the helmet off. Mess wailed in consternation. Harlan ignored it.

The blackear was lying facedown and unmoving. Behind him came a veritable army of reattacking Mantases. They flew and ran in formation, charging the cave entrance.

Harlan ran inside, then stopped dead in his tracks. Outside, the cave looked like any other cave, a dull rock concoction. Inside was a different matter. The cave was made up of the same material as the blue crystal clubs. The walls were smooth, glowing gems. Crystalline stalactites hung from the roof and stalagmites jutted from the floor. Everything was bathed in blue luminescence.

Including the group that drew Napoleon deeper and deeper into the shining, reflective, almost transparent cave. Her helmet had also been taken off. She was no longer struggling. Although they still held her arms, she was carefully walking with them.

"Hey," Harlan called. His voice was taken by the slick walls and empty halls and echoed dozens of times over, making even that one word totally incomprehensible. The violence of the sudden, sharp echo was magnified many times until it pounded against Harlan's eardrums, throwing him painfully against the smooth wall.

He tried to clap his hands over his tortured ears, but two arms blocked him. The blackear had recovered and was right behind him. Before Harlan could protect himself, the blackear had covered Trigor's ears for him. Suddenly the pain was gone. His hearing was gone. All sound was gone. Harlan looked, blinking, into the blue, reflective wall. Now he was a blackear.

The one-nostriled men were not born with black ears. The blackness was a form-fitting covering which adhered so exactly that it seemed to be skin. It was so tight that it eliminated all sound. Harlan stared at himself until he saw the distorted reflection of the Mantases coming into the cave.

He spun around, pushing the blackear aside. The Mantases ran right for them. Harlan was about to meet them when the blackear grabbed his arm. Trigor looked at the innocuous blue-skinned human, who opened his mouth wide. The Mantases staggered back, the ones in front falling.

Harlan stared in amazement as the fallen insectoids started quivering, then actually contorting on the cave floor. He looked up to see one or two more gamely trying to complete the attack. Harlan looked to the blackear, who smiled and motioned toward the staggering Mantases. Harlan turned back and shouted as loud as he could.

He heard nothing, but the closest Mantas' head

exploded. Harlan jerked back in surprise and to avoid the hunks of insectoid cranium which splattered on the blue crystal walls. The other Mantases were thrown back as if by a blow. Harlan supposed it was a blow of sorts. Sound moved in a wave. This blue crystal cave made it a tidal wave.

When the stricken Mantases died, the others tried attacking again. Harlan waited expectantly for them. In his suit the Destinian's every muscle was a weapon. Every movement triggered a device. The space bullet had grown, knowing every single part of his body was important. Except his voice. His voice had only been for information. Until now. The shining blue stones magnified his sounds until they became deadly.

Like a child in a playground, Trigor killed the Mantases with his voice.

# SIX

The blackears pulled Napoleon deeper into the network of caves. Although her ears were protected from the deadly sounds, her eyes were hard-pressed to take in the crystalline beauty of the surroundings. She never knew there were this many blues. Every tint, every gem shape, every size swirled around her wide eyes as they walked.

They would be in a narrow, low hall, then suddenly step out into a towering vista of sparkling jewels. The blue-skinned Finally Finishers seemed to blend in with their environment. Unlike the first blackear they had met, these one-nostriled folk had hair. Most of it was on their heads and all of it was long enough to cover their ears.

Napoleon imagined it afforded them more protection from the killer echoes, and allowed them to move among nonblackears without discovery. The path had been carefully cut from the blue stone so it wouldn't be perfectly smooth but also wouldn't have sharp edges which could

cut into her boots. After many twists and turns, they
reached a large amphitheater.

It was a semicircular room with blue gem tiers cut
from the wall with a blue gem stage at the bottom. When
the entourage entered, the seats were filled with blackears. As soon as they saw Napoleon, they all raised their
hands and waved their fingers frantically, their faces
alight with wondrous joy.

The feline smiled, then laughed at the goofy sight.
They all looked like maddened chorus lines, gyrating
their hands like dancers having a fit. She was about to
clap her paws when the blackear next to her nimbly
placed her hand between Napoleon's closing palms. The
cat turned to the woman in confusion. She looked into
two of the biggest blue eyes she had ever seen.

They were like two gems stuck in the middle of two
spotlights. The rest of the face was young and attractive,
although not as striking, thankfully, as the eyes. The
girl's visage was haloed by dark blue, almost purple, hair
down to her shoulders. Napoleon realized that this girl
was probably the first step in an evolutionary cycle that
would make the blackears virtual chameleons inside
these caves. The girl's wide, thin, still lightly red lips
smiled.

She reached up and placed a single long, thin finger
against the black covering over Napoleon's ear. "You're
in the Temple of Quiet Ice," the feline heard. It was a
distant, ethereal voice which seemed to come from inside
her head, traveling from the wrong direction to get to her
eardrum. "Where every sound can be torture or death.
You mustn't make any sharp sounds, Chon."

Napoleon opened her mouth to reply, then thought
better of it, especially when the blackear girl placed a
finger to her own lips and directed the feline to face the
crowd. They were still waving like crazy. Napoleon
smiled beneficently on them and wiggled her own paw.

That seemed to drive them to greater heights of silent paroxysms.

She felt a gentle hand on her arm, leading her across the stage and out a side opening. There was a long, twisting cave hall before them, lined on either side by blackears. Napoleon knew what this was. She had seen one of these on an old Earthen VU program on the P Channel, "The Adventures of Vlad." This was a royal receiving line.

She put out her paw to shake their hands as the bluenette guided her forward, but all the blackears did was lightly touch her ears as she went by. The words were like whispers on the wind as she passed, like final echoes without the yelling part.

"Welcome." "Welcome." "Welcome, Chon." "Blessings, Chon." "Bless you." "Chon." "Richness." "Success." "Pleasure." It was weird, but very nice.

Napoleon smiled happily at the bluenette, which her blackear guide reacted to with a flush of pride. A feline smile was impressive enough, but her guide acted as if she had been touched by infinity. Napoleon was wildly flattered at first, but then concern began to creep in. Okay, she was great, now what did these people want from her? And who the Cheshire was Chon? What the Taplinger-Jones happened to Lil?

As soon as they were out of the long hall and into a relatively plain room, Napoleon stopped short and put a finger on the bluenette's ear. "Who are you?" she asked.

The bluenette grimaced and moved Napoleon's paw so her finger was directly over the ear channel. Then she lightly placed her own hand on the feline's neck. "Again," she asked demurely.

"Who are you?"

The bluenette smiled. "I go by no name. We don't call to each other here."

"Who is Chon, then?"

"You," the bluenette said even before Napoleon got the whole sentence out. Well, you ask a silly question . . . It was fairly obvious to "Chon" by now that these people didn't waste words. They answered directly, in as few letters as possible.

Napoleon didn't think "Why am I Chon?" was a particularly good tack, so she tried, "What do you want?"

"To guide you," the blackear girl said immediately. "I was chosen. I'm the honored one."

Curiousity killed the cat, but Napoleon couldn't turn back now. With a mental shrug, she said, "Guide away." The bluenette looked as if she were having a heart attack. Her already large eyes opened wider and most of the blue left her face. She was about to cry when Napoleon realized the problem. "No, no," she hastily said, pressing her finger tighter. "Just an expression. Please guide me."

The blackear relaxed, and the color returned to her cheeks. The rescue from shame made her more touchable. "Hungry?"

Napoleon nodded. It would give her some time to ponder. The bluenette let go of her throat and motioned for the feline to come along. She was led by her guide and two silent blackears through a good dozen caverns to a blue stone room with a blue stone table, blue stone chairs, and Harlan Trigor.

He looked calmly over at her, then raised his hands and madly shook his fingers. She leaped across the blue stone floor and hugged him for all she was worth, burying her head in his chest. "Are you all right?" she asked. "I forgot all about you!"

When he didn't answer, she looked up at his perplexed, almost comfortable face. She was suddenly glad he hadn't heard the last part of her greeting. "How are you?" she silently mouthed with exaggeration. He smiled and nodded, then motioned her to sit. She responded with

enthusiasm. She had escaped the Mantases, she was with
her space bullet, and all was right with the second moon.

She found the bluenette's finger against her ear. "We
found, guided, and saved you," the girl said. "You meet
with Lil soon."

To both their surprise, the blackears then left Napoleon and Harlan alone. After she watched them leave and
gave it a few seconds to sink in, the feline was instantly
up. She slid across the table and practically fell into
Trigor's lap. She rubbed her shoulder against his. He
patiently patted her back with controlled thanks.

She started talking, then closed her mouth. She took
his hand in one paw and placed his fingers against her
throat, then she put her finger against his ear. He sat and
she kneeled before him. Harlan looked particularly
uncomfortable in this arrangement.

"What happened?" she asked. He heard her as a tiny
little voice way back in his head.

She heard, "I killed ... Mantases ... voice ...
here ... me ... do this."

"Slow," she instructed. "Use few words." She got up
on one knee and put a hand on his throat, then reposi-
tioned his finger on her ear. Was it her imagination or
was he getting red? Must be a trick of the blue light.

"They drove off Mantases," he said, Tonto-style.
"Brought me here. Taught me this." She gathered he
meant how to communicate with the hands.

She looked into his eyes. Suddenly their gazes locked.
They were about to identify what they saw there when
the bluenette appeared again with her two helpmates.
They were carrying bowls of something that wasn't
foodstufs.

Napoleon broke the communication embrace and sat
on the chair beside Harlan as if she were a teenager
caught in her first tryst. As soon as she sat, she wondered
why she felt that way, then shook the feeling off. Hey,

this was a man she had been with for two years, a co-pilot and friend. What did she have to feel embarrassed about? What did he?

The pulpy globes in the bowls were vegetable and fruit in matter. Harlan snapped them open, smelling the interiors carefully. Napoleon held one up and touched the end of her tongue to it. The bluenette placed a finger on her ear, then kindly but curtly assured her that the nutriment was safe for feline interiors. One of the others put its finger on Harlan's ear and was no doubt telling him the same.

Napoleon looked over at Trigor's blank face, then linked up with her guide. "What happens now?"

"Wait." But Napoleon wouldn't leave it at that.

"For what?" She saw Harlan watching her lips carefully.

"For the commandment." For a girl who had been so helpful before, her new responses were clipped and hesitant.

"Whose?"

"Lil." The bluenette said it quickly, then actually jerked out of Napoleon's grasp. Harlan immediately linked with his own conversation partner.

"Who is Lil?" The blackear pointed at Napoleon. But the feline was watching carefully too. She rose immediately and took over.

"I'm Chon. Who's Lil?"

The blackear looked helplessly, desperately, at the bluenette. She bit her lip, looked around for a way out, then quickly linked with "Chon."

"The Last in Line," Napoleon heard, and then let the blackears scurry from the chamber.

An abbreviation. She should have known. Cheshire knew that the Earth she had left was rife with abbreviations. She had not been Lil. She had been L.I.L. And now something else was. The feline mouthed a silent "Oh" to

Harlan and furrowed her brow. He signaled her to lean in.

"I heard," he said innocuously, having adjusted to the new feeling form of communication. It helped that she wasn't kneeling before him this time. "Who are you now?"

"Chon," she told him. What could that mean? Cat High on Noses? Creature Hired Over Night?

"Religion," Harlan figured. "Lil is god. Blackear said, 'He needs you.'"

"Uh-oh," Napoleon said. Neither had to discuss the rest. The feline started to get excited. The space bullet started to get worried. Whatever waited for them inside the caves, the Mantases waited without. Harlan wondered who had actually cleared their way from Finally to Finally Finished. The blackears? The Mantases? Or both?

A great wind coursed through the room, ruffling Napoleon's fur. The bluenette seemed to sweep in on the gust of air, her flowing light blue gown fluttering around her. That was a change. Before they all had been wearing blue suits and boots to protect them from the crystal's cutting edges.

She frantically waved at the two to separate, then moved to the entrance again. She turned to face the wind. The feline and soldier heard the distant voice. It was deep and coarse, as if from the passing of time. It rolled toward them, moving from cavern to cavern. Even at its low volume, it was a commanding voice, one which should be respected and followed. It stirred something wonderful, something scary deep inside the female feline.

The voice finally reached the dining room. It was only one word, but it filled all their minds.

"Come," it said.

There was no denying the command. Napoleon and Harlan were led from the room by the bluenette. As they

walked through more spectacular caverns, the one-nostriled people they passed averted their eyes from the cat.
Mostly, they snuck glances at Harlan. He recognized
such expressions as envy, and, if he was not greatly
mistaken, near reverence.

Napoleon was disturbed that their attentions were
gnawing at her anticipation. She wanted to see the Last
in Line with near desperation, but she wanted them to
stop looking at Trigor just the same. She was beginning
to actively dislike the situation when the bluenette
stopped before a huge, mirror-smooth, oval wall. She
turned and stepped between the two companions, putting
a finger on both their ears. They laid their hands on
opposite sides of her neck.

"Chon must go alone," she whispered. "His face is for
her eyes."

Harlan heard one word echo again and again in his
mind. Alone. He suddenly reached for Napoleon's ear,
but the bluenette knocked his hand away with surprising
agility and strength. Before the feline could react, the girl
touched Trigor.

"She is His now." Her soft words spoke vehemently.

Harlan considered. He'd have to take on all the blackears bare-handed, or stand aside. He had no doubt he
could do it, but he wasn't sure whether Napoleon would
back him. She wanted to see the Last in Line. She didn't
know what "Chon" was. But he did. It wasn't an abbreviation. It was a contraction. Why they couldn't have
called her "Chone" to make it easy was beyond him.

Napoleon looked at him with concern. The bluenette
stepped between them and blocked her view. The feline
put a paw on the side of the girl's head and pushed her
away. She saw Harlan thinking, then meeting her gaze,
then nodding. She nodded back.

Oh well, she thought. When on Finally Finished, do as
the Finally Finishers do. The bluenette took Harlan's

arm and hastily led him away. As they rounded the corner, he looked back. Napoleon was looking at his reflection in the smooth wall, her face empty. He wanted to signal his support, but another blue wall blotted the view.

Napoleon waited. Suddenly the wall before her turned transparent. She found herself looking into a gorgeously appointed room. In the center of the bullet-shaped enclosure was a copper-colored chair, highlighted by bright shafts of blue light that created a golden halo. Beyond that was an impressive array of old-fashioned dials, switches, knobs and levers.

The feline was off to see the wizard. The chair was nothing less than a throne and the archaic scientific devices obviously came from a junked spacecraft. All of it danced on the déjà vu centers in Napoleon's brain.

Behind the copper throne was a large, blue, hollowed-out stone, its center piled high with opulently designed pads and pillows. Lying atop that was a massive figure, but the only part Napoleon could see was long, thick legs encased in rich yellow cloth. An arm draped in the same material appeared from behind the high, blue stone headrest and beckoned to her.

"Come." It was the same voice. It had a slight but nonviolent echo. It was much stronger than before.

Napoleon leaned forward, raising her arms to place her paws on the transparent wall. She discovered there was no wall. It was all done with blue mirrors. But she was a feline. She did not stumble or fall. Her balance was perfect. She lowered her arms and stepped into the room.

After several steps, she could not keep herself from looking over her shoulder. The wall was back. She was tempted to see if it was still false, but her mounting anticipation of the meeting took precedence. She turned back into the room proper. It was draped in dark browns and deep purples and ruby reds and rich gold. Anything but blue. It was garish but strangely suitable.

But it wasn't the sights that thrilled her. It was the smell. There was a palatable stink in the room. It was a musty, wet odor that others would find distasteful, but Napoleon recognized it and felt a near impassioned hysteria.

"Come," said the voice a third time, amused, eager, and impatient at the same time.

Napoleon suddenly stood her ground. She would not skitter to him like a crazy kitten. No one and nothing would make her do that. "You are the Last in Line?" she asked, unable to keep the thrill from the words.

"Not anymore," said the voice, not without humor. "Come here." It was a request and an invitation this time, not an order.

Napoleon walked over to his bedside. She took his paw. In the center of the huge, circular stone was the Last in Line, his old, battered, furrowed face smiling. Around the pale, but still magnificent visage was a mane of coarse, curly, straw-colored hair. Across the rough cheeks were long, steellike whiskers. The eyes were large, watery, and red on an ocean of beige. The nose was huge, black, two nostriled, and dry.

It was the face of His Majesty, the last of Mandarin's men.

"Hi, beautiful," said the lion.

## SEVEN

When the bluenette and Harlan returned to what would be Napoleon's chamber, it was filled with smiling one-nostriled people. As they entered, all eyes turned toward the girl's flushed visage. Harlan expected a whole lot of finger shaking going on, but they all placed their finger-tips on the smooth walls instead.

"They've met," she shouted. Then everybody shook hands. After that, they all went to their knees. They closed their eyes, their lips moved, and their fingers shook in front of their torsos. Harlan grabbed the bluenette's elbow as she sank and stood her up. Looking at the gathered prayers, he took the girl out of the room and into the hall.

He walked until he reached a wide, hollowed-out sta-lagmite, grown so high that it attached directly into a stalactite. He pulled her inside, then put his hands on her ears and throat. She slowly returned the favor, making it seem as if she were preparing for her first kiss. As demure as she seemed, she got in the first words.

"You should be glad," she chastised.

"Explain," he instructed.

"Chon and Lil are one."

"Continue."

"It was all a sign," she said, in an explosion of verbosity. "Chon's heaven-sent."

Trigor was beginning to get disgusted. He had heard religious dogma before, from the insectoid race which had threatened Destiny and almost got them here. They were also answering "heaven's" call. For them it was the Universal Rule—one order, their order, brought to this galaxy and beyond. If the Mantases' religion could be dangerously warped, so could this one.

"Details," Harlan demanded.

The girl looked at him in surprise, then nodded knowingly. "You're testing me." Harlan did not reply and allowed no expression on his face. "You're born from demon womb and know all," she continued soberly. "I'm sentinel of your work."

Harlan didn't like being lost, but the only way he could get out was to keep going. "Continue."

"The attire's prepared," she assured him. "Mandarin will rise. Live again."

The blue light at the end of the crystal tunnel. But the girl was still talking in religious code words. Harlan had to have a crystal-clear picture before he could proceed. "Speak the unspeakable," he demanded.

The girl was shocked. She looked away, then returned her gaze with resolve. Her expression said that if he, the partner of Chon, demanded it, then it must be so. "Lil and Chon make new one. Lil'll die. New one and Chon make more. We tend. We worship."

That was clear enough. Harlan stared at the bluenette's embarrassed face for a long, deathly minute, trying to understand the implications and his own feelings. Then he tried to figure out what he was going to do about either. They stood in their strange embrace, the girl not daring to let go, until Harlan spoke.

"What if new one's girl?"

"Lil says no."

"What if Lil's wrong?"

"Can't be."

"Oh."

Harlan couldn't bring himself to punch the girl, so he simply leaped out of the room. Trusting his instincts, he began to retrace his steps back to the opaque blue wall where he had left Napoleon. He heard nothing, but he felt her death behind him. He whirled to see a blue Mantas leaping at him, its sharp pincers up.

He clapped his hands violently, and then pushed the joined hands forward. By the time they reached the Mantas head, they were fists. Even as he sought to smash the insectoid down with sound, he knew that the Mantases could not have gotten this deep in the caves without protecting their antennae. These boogers didn't have ears, but could feel sound vibrations about the same as eardrums. They must have found a way to deafen themselves.

He smashed the Mantas back, revealing the bluenette lying in the stalagmite. There was a Mantas blade in her chest. The insectoid's knives were horrible. They were a series of thin cones that slipped over the Mantas mandibles. When they struck, one cone stayed in the gaping wound.

Beyond the girl, the cavern was crawling with Mantases. Harlan ran as he saw the nearest creature violently move his arm in a throwing motion. The Mantas knife cones came off a mandible in a bunch. As they flew through the air, they spread in a razor-sharp line. Trigor got around the corner as the blades struck harmlessly behind him.

He raced back to the chamber and slammed both palms on the walls. He screamed the Mantases' name as loudly as he could, then grabbed the nearest chair. The blue stone was heavy, but with an incredible show of strength and will, Harlan smashed it into the door frame. It broke into five pieces and the hall wall cracked all the way down the line.

The mixture of sounds alerted all the blackears, who got off their knees and scurried to protect the Lil and the Chon. Harlan took the longest piece of debris and ran back toward the hollow stalagmite. It had to be more than noise which killed people in the caves. That booger's head had exploded before. The noise had to make a tangible force.

The Mantases started throwing their knife cones as soon as he appeared. He deflected and blocked them with his blue crystal sword. He screamed as he came, swinging at the antennae. The Mantases crowded back in the narrow hall, retreating to the open cavern. Harlan held them off until some blackears appeared, their clubs in their hands.

Trigor moved through them and ran for the place he had left Napoleon as the Mantases sought to kill or puncture the men's ear coverings. Harlan's legs churned faster. With the number of boogers he saw in the cave, it was only a matter of time before they broke through.

His expert sense of direction did not fail him. He found the wall. He desperately searched for some kind of entrance as he concentrated his senses on his feet. He couldn't look over his shoulder every few seconds. He had to feel the vibrations of the boogers' attack through the gem floor. He examined the entire smooth surface before hitting it in frustration. His fist bounced off.

He stared up at the wall's expanse with watering eyes

as he yelled the feline's name. He couldn't reach the top of the tall obstruction. The desire for his space bullet suit was greater than ever before. He felt more feeble and helpless than he ever had. It was like losing his immune system. He was easy pickings for the first germ that came along.

He felt the buzz through the soles of his shoes. He turned and pressed his back to the wall. Coming around the corner were the Mantases. Through his eyes, the approaching rabble looked like ravenous beasts. Their little round eyes glowed, stuff dripped out of their tiny mouths, and their limbs jerked in every direction at inhuman speeds.

"Come on," Harlan said, motioning at the nearest Mantas. "You. Come here. You first." He knew they couldn't hear him (he couldn't even hear himself), but it had to have the effect he wanted. It did. The one he motioned to surged ahead of the others.

Just as the black monster reached him, Harlan leaped in the air, his feet, as one, lashing out. They slammed into the Mantas chest and hurled the insectoid back. It fell into four behind it, which knocked over several more. They all scattered, tripping at least a dozen more. Suddenly the gang was piled up in the cavern entrance, falling over each other.

But Harlan was hurled back too. He flew backward into a sea of blue. He sank sideways in the coolness until it turned clear. It was like floating sideways to the surface of an ocean. But instead of just his head breaking the surface, his entire body popped out of the sea. He tumbled, heels over head, across a pillow-strewn floor.

"Is he all right?" asked a deep voice.

"Almost certainly," said Napoleon's voice.

Harlan was lying on the floor of the throne room. He could only see the giant wall from the other side, but in it was the distorted reflection of what the feline had seen when it turned transparent. That was only the first shock. The second shock came when he realized he could hear. The soldier vaulted to his feet, trying to peer through the wall, then spinning to face the throne.

The CHosen ONe was lying in bed with the Last in Line. Harlan saw her spacesuit and Destinian uniform lying on the covers as he approached. The lion's yellow clothes were also strewn aside. In the one tiny part of his brain that wasn't concerned with the boogers' attack, Harlan silently thanked whoever was responsible for the bed covers over their furry, naked forms.

"Where are the blackears? There are Mantases out there!" he almost yelled, stunned by his hearing ability. He couldn't bother with asking what magic let him into the room.

"The Timuns are in their special shelters," the lion said weakly, pronouncing it "Tie-muns." "They went there on my directive. Now we will take care of the Mantases." He directed Harlan's eyes to the wall in front of him. It seemed to turn transparent and the soldier could see the boogers crawling around the stalagmite where the bluenette lay dead.

A growl came from deep in back of the lion's throat. His paws flew across the dials and switches on the antique machinery. Then he reached for a bulb-topped switch on the copper-colored console. Harlan saw the cavern start to shake. He saw the outstanding stalactites break off and plunge down. He saw them shatter on the floor, spreading glass-sharp shrapnel in every direction.

The Mantases began to panic and scatter, but then the cavern walls shattered and exploded inward. All the boogers were caught in the deadly crossfire. The blue gems went through them like bullets, when they didn't slice them like flying guillotines. The lion quickly cut off the visual portion of the program. Such complete and sudden slaughter was even too much for the veteran soldier to take in one glance.

Harlan was indeed shaken when he turned to the bed. Napoleon had her head buried in the lion's massive chest. Trigor immediately cut off all emotions. To go from that to this would be impossible if he allowed himself to feel anything. He thanked whomever again for keeping the bedclothes up near the feline's shoulders. Just seeing her outline beneath the covers was troubling enough.

"I apologize for all the confusion," the lion said to Harlan, a comforting arm around Napoleon. "Although I am the Timuns' god, I cannot always control their beliefs. Ultimately, however, it is best that they follow their doctrines exactly."

"I imagine so," Harlan understated, afterimages of the Mantas massacre in his mind.

The lion chuckled. "Believe me, it isn't as easy as it appears. I owe my life to these people, but I have to be careful. If I contradict the Last in—I mean, my own laws, they can get very testy."

"Aarol is from Mandarin," Napoleon said excitedly. "He crashed here, and when he awoke, the Timuns had made him their god."

"Really?" Harlan said flatly, surprising everyone, including himself. "So because you say you're from Mandarin and are worshiped by a bunch of deaf guys, you think you can bury us in a mountain and force her to copulate? Who do you think you are?" He stopped because he saw Napoleon's face. The lion was unaffected, but her expression was sardonic, understanding, and slightly annoyed. Just what he didn't need.

"Don't hyperventilate, Harlan," she said, taking the bed cover to her throat and sitting up. "Come over here." Harlan looked around, sighed, and then sat down miserably. "Forgive my friend," she said to Aarol. "He is my devoted protector and a bit of a romantic."

"I am not a romantic," he said, looking at the console. The feline looked at his back, choosing her words carefully.

"Aarol has been . . . urging the Timuns to seek out others like him for his entire life. When they saw me, they went a little . . . crazy." She carefully avoided mentioning that no one was forcing her to do anything.

"Aarol." Harlan spoke the name. He looked over at the lion. "That's it? Any other name?"

"I've forgotten," he rumbled. "I'm getting pretty old, you know." The lion took the initiative. "You must understand, these people worship me. I'm not sure why and I'm not completely happy about it, but I'm not all that displeased either. I thought I was the last of my kind, after all. The Timuns have kept me alive and safe, and I'm grateful—even if they are religious fanatics."

"Alive and safe," Harlan echoed. "From what?"

The feline and lion looked at one another. "We're not sure," Napoleon ultimately said.

"I came here as a cub," Aarol explained. "What I know of my past comes from fading memories and what Timuns, now long dead, told me. I . . ." He looked again at Napoleon. "We are from Mandarin. We were a proud people . . ."

Of course, Harlan thought.

"But not strong enough. Or perhaps not wise enough. We did not prepare defensive weapons against possible technologically superior invaders. We seemed to think that our personal strength would always save us. We were plundered for our food, our mineral resources, and our . . ."

"Women," Harlan said, an undercurrent of frustrated anger in his voice.

"Our felines seemed to be universally attractive," Aarol continued. "We were invaded by fleets of slavers with drugs. Our planet was lush and tropical. Although we could hide and kill, the attackers were well equipped with tracking devices. They were ultimately successful."

"I don't understand," Harlan interrupted to relieve some of his anguish. "Then why aren't there felines in every corner of the galaxy? Why not their descendants, at any rate?"

"The feline cannot reproduce with any race but its own," Aarol declared. "No amount of laboratory tampering could change that."

"That was why my sisters died," Napoleon said.

"And a feline will die if forced to . . . ?" Harlan guessed.

Aarol nodded. "The slavers had stolen only the felines. And when they returned, no male would allow himself to be captured. Even when the cub or lion was drugged, it would soon die in captivity, as I am dying."

Harlan looked into the lion's eyes. The two males shared something there. More than one thing, actually. Trigor's inner pain left him. "What happened to Mandarin?"

"I cannot be sure," Aarol admitted. "But I remember the Mantases."

"They came to our planet," Napoleon said. "But even the few who remained were too strong-willed, too defiant for the boogers. They destroyed the survivors. Then, to insure the complete destruction of our race, they destroyed the planet."

The loss was palpable in the room. It made Trigor's minor heartache seem microscopic in comparison. He didn't even ask them how the Mantases destroyed the world. He just took it for granted that they had the power.

Napoleon's hair was standing on end, her eyes aflame with hatred. The Last in Line leaned against the luminous blue headboard and closed his eyes. Napoleon leaned on him, her paws on his massive, matted chest.

"Where was it?" Harlan asked about the planet instead. "What part of space?"

"I don't know," Aarol sighed.

Harlan didn't want to, but he had to ask. He felt like a third wheel on the bed. "What are you going to do?"

"I don't know," the lion said again. "That is up to Napoleon." Harlan wasn't expecting that. He had been expecting an awkward suggestion that he leave the room.

"Aarol has given me two choices," she said without moving. "I can stay to continue our race or I can seek out the home planet of the Mantases for revenge."

Harlan was physically taken aback by the declaration. He saw no choice in the choice but could tell from the way the feline had spoken that each had equal weight with her. He didn't dare try to sway her, so he used a little shocked misdirection.

"But no one knows where the Mantas home planet is. Destiny scoured the known solar systems for it."

"But we are on the edge of unknown space," the lion decreed. "Each person's knowledge of this place is unique and individual. Thankfully, my eyes and ears have many extensions." Namely the Timuns. "The planet is called Nest. Once a generation it gives spawn to a renewed race of Mantases."

"Boogers do not reproduce," Napoleon elaborated. "They go through waves of hatching. Nest consists of a genetic city capable of making millions of Mantases. We don't know the exact process, but every millennium or so, the city releases its offspring."

It made cunning sense. No matter how many millions die in purges like the one on Destiny, millions more will soon replace them, all slaving to force The Rule on the rest of the universe.

"I cannot tell which is more important to me," Napoleon finished. "That civilization's destruction or the continuance of my own sad race."

"Why not do both?" Harlan couldn't help himself. "Have the child, then, if you desire, go in search of Nest."

"Precious time is so short and I could not leave the litter," Napoleon said blankly. "And I would not risk taking them with me."

"Bend a little!" Harlan blurted. He knew better as soon as he said it. She just cuddled closer to the lion man who smiled sorrowfully down at her. Trigor saw more than paternal concern on Aarol's face. There was an apology there too. He was begging forgiveness for being so stupid as to let his civilization die.

Both cats looked up as Harlan rose quickly. "You can do both," he assured her.

"What are you saying, man?" Aarol exhorted.

Harlan looked at the aged, regal face and the uncomprehending look of hope on Napoleon's. He knew he was doing the right thing—the only thing.

"I know you are forthright in your wishes," the soldier said. "I know what is right. Both deeds should be done, but the feline can only do one or the other. This is a solvable problem." Harlan didn't wait for questions. He had to roll over any objections with his wisdom. "Of the two deeds, there is only one that only she can do. No one else could accomplish it. Of the two deeds, there is only one that does not require her. A deed that could be attempted and accomplished by anyone."

Napoleon's natural independence took control of her addled brain. "Are you saying I'm only fit for motherhood?"

"Of course not," Harlan laughed. "But if not you, who else? And do you honestly think the Last in Line could wait until you found and destroyed Nest?"

"I don't think I could wait until morning," the aged embattled lion wisecracked with more exhaustion than lust. Napoleon looked to him, then at Harlan. Finally she smiled in resignation.

Harlan was warmed by her smile. "I understand the need for the Mantases' destruction. They threaten the entire universe. They are an organically evil race, wishing to eliminate individuality. It is not just the Mandarins', but every human race's responsibility to defeat them." The soldier had to stop. He needed to summon all his willpower to finish his declaration.

"I shall find and destroy Nest. My reward will be the rebirth of your magnificent kind."

## EIGHT

"She's going to do WHAT?"

"I told you, Mess, she's going to stay on Finally Finished and resurrect her species while we—"

"She's going to . . . WHAT?"

"Regenerate. Replicate. Repopulate."

"Don't throw alliterations at me!" the compubot fairly shrieked. "You reprobate! That's repulsive, you repugnant recreant. I repudiate you, you rancid renegade. Relegate her there? You were remiss!"

"Mess . . ."

"Be repentant!"

"Mess . . ."

"I am recalcitrant."

"Mess!"

"You wish to rejoinder? Throw alliterations at me, will you? Cad! How could you do this to me?"

"To you? How do you think I feel? I had no choice. She would have hated herself forever if she left. She had to stay." Harlan suddenly heard himself pleading his case. "What am I defending myself to you for? Get ready for takeoff."

"I don't follow your orders." Mess huffed.

"What?" Trigor exploded.

The compubot was undaunted. "You're not my master. It's ingrained right here on my niodes. The *Felidae* is the feline's ship."

"I'm the co-pilot!" Harlan shouted.

"Then you co-fly it. Which half is yours?"

"I know enough to disconnect you, Mess," he threatened.

"Go ahead!" the machine dared. "Throw the wrench in! Throw the wrench in!"

"Get the ship ready," they heard.

Harlan whirled to see Napoleon, wearing regal yellow robes. She stood in the doorway to the bridge. One paw was clenched at her side and her eyes were devoid of emotion.

Harlan nearly jumped across the room to embrace her, but then steeled himself. He thought it must have taken enormous self-control for her to see him off like this. She must have followed in another Timun shuttle craft. He decided to make their parting as easy as possible.

"Thank you," he said.

In answer, Napoleon raised her arm and opened her paw. Blue light filled the bridge area, blinding Harlan for a split second and turning the feline's robe green.

"He gave me this," she said in a monotone. Harlan could now see it was a stone, a brilliant, flawless, beautiful gem. He looked from it to Napoleon's desolate eyes. He could now see the tears scarring her face.

"He gave me this," she repeated. "Before he died."

# NINE

Blissful confusion was one thing; brain cramp was another. Even before boarding the Earth Ship *Shooting Star*, Harlan Trigor had suffered from brain cramp. He had been perplexed by, and suspicious of, the ease with which they were allowed on, and then with the comradery with which they were treated. Roscoe took them into his confidence, Zero took them on a ship tour, and, finally, Spot showed them to their quarters.

Trigor handled it all with dull consideration. Pound had been theatrical, the FM had been coolly distant, and the actress had chatted away with abandon, filling the air with ominous mentions of things called Ariel and Caliban.

"It'll be a great pleasure to have something human to play off of," Spot said as she showed them the small, square rooms with the bed mats along the wall. "Well, not human, maybe, but real flesh and blood. Well, you know what I mean."

Harlan had no idea, and if Napoleon had, she didn't say so. Spot kept talking as she made a quick three-sixty of the tiny area, waving her arms like a display model. "It's been such a bore to work with the actobots," she rattled on, motioning to the wall-attached sink and the reflec-table. The mirror-table combination also had a swing-out stool attached. "Anyway, the bath is down the hall with an excremat and clen-z-closet. Do you know how to use those?"

Harlan just kept staring vaguely ahead. Napoleon nodded for both of them. It wouldn't take many brains to figure out the necessities. Spot nodded back and smiled. "Brilliant," she chirped. "Do whatever you'd like, but don't fool with anything. We're getting close to Covenfall and Roscoe is finishing his recon prelims."

Spot's smile weakened when neither hitchhiker questioned any of her purposefully vague revelations. She steeled herself, however, to exit on an up note. "Well, relax, enjoy yourselves, and I'll see you soon. Muse'll call when the next meal is ready. 'Bye, now." With that, Spot swung her dark red curls and rich brocaded hem out of the narrow doorway.

Harlan continued to consider the invisible air currents on the edge of his nose. He was not good at it. He was a soldier. His mind had been refracted into elaborate channels of strategy. Emotions came into play only in terms of how they weakened the enemy. As a soldier, he had to trust the dedication, loyalty, and inner strength of his comrades. He didn't have time to consider the emotional stability of his fellows. So accepting what had happened in Finally airspace was hard enough. Dealing with it was brain cramping.

The *Felidae* had sped from the second moon in silence after Aarol's death. The feline had been left without her race and had been robbed of her chance to resurrect it.

She was in despair, and Harlan knew no way to comfort her. Her fur was stiff and her tail lashed like a scythe. The atmosphere on the bridge was dank with desolation.

"Well, at least I don't have to listen to that space bullet song," Mess considered. Harlan didn't reply. "Well, at least now you can go find a nice planet somewhere to settle down." Napoleon didn't raise her head from her console. "Wow," the compubot exhorted. "You can't say anything anymore. What can I do to get a rise out of you two?"

"Damper down," Harlan instructed it uncomfortably, glancing at the feline's bowed head with concern. "Don't you have any feelings?" He had fallen right into the machine's trap.

"You're the one who keeps saying I don't," it sniffed. "And while I might have some empathy around here somewhere, I certainly don't have any sympathy."

"I said damper," Harlan repeated threateningly.

"Why?" Mess shot back.

Harlan's head went back. "Your mistress has suffered a great loss," he said with quiet anger.

"Loss?" Mess scoffed. "Good-bye and good riddance. Now you finally have a chance to live your own lives, rather than chasing after someone else's."

Trigor was taken aback by the compubot's directness. The machine's tone was almost bitter. There was more of Larry's voice than Palsy-Drake's there. Harlan felt a duty to explain. "We cannot allow the Mantases to go unpunished."

"There are millions of them," Mess pointed out needlessly, "and only two of you."

"It is better to fight," Harlan said fiercely.

"It is better to live," Mess replied. "Especially when to fight is suicide. Living, surviving, is the best revenge. It is the only revenge. To die in a hopeless attack only makes a mockery of the warrior."

Harlan was stunned by the compubot's sudden, vehement lucidity. "It is not hopeless!" he shouted. "We have this ship. We have my suit."

"Your suit?" it laughed, making the noise of a can being opened by hand. "I heard about the last time you used your suit. Flat on your face in the Mile Long Castle."

"You pompous ... plated ... piece of ... !" Harlan sputtered. "I'll show you!"

"That's enough," Napoleon said, raising her head with a sigh. Trigor looked over at the seemingly calm feline, suddenly ashamed of his childish argument. He stood between the *Felidae* control board and Mess' console, looking back and forth: at Napoleon with shame-tinged concern, and at Mess with reproachful anger. "Especially when Mess is right," Napoleon concluded, her eyes still facing forward.

"What?" Trigor blurted, forgetting about his embarrassment. "I could tear that compubot apart with my bare hands, let alone with my ... !"

"No, no, dear," Napoleon soothed wearily, but with surprising tenderness. "Not about your suit." She turned her pilot's seat to face him, one foot on the ground, the other bent under her rear. "About flying around, searching for something I'll never find." Harlan blinked at her, speechless. "I left all there could possibly be on Earth, Destiny, and Finally Finished." The words hung in the air like tombstones.

"Wow," said Mess. "Miss Self-pity." Harlan glared at it, but Napoleon just laughed. The last time Mess had said that was to Harlan, when Larry and the feline had first picked his drifting space bullet suit up in the hold of the Earth Ship *Black Hole*.

"My, my," Harlan heard Napoleon say. "Just like old times." He only turned, abruptly, eyes wide, when he felt Napoleon's arms encircling his neck. His arms rose to take her hands away, but he stopped when his eyes locked into hers. "Really, Mr. Trigor," she said. "It's about time you and I had a serious talk about what we're going to do about ourselves."

"What? We? You? Us?" Harlan stammered, cursing his stupidity. Her display of outright affection had taken him much farther aback than the computer's challenges. It seemed as if everyone and everything else knew something he didn't. And his stiff mind wasn't dropping any clues.

"It's been more than three years we've been together," she said. "Two alone."

"What am I?" Mess interjected. "Vegematter?" Napoleon ignored it.

"Earth as I knew it is gone. If we keep up at this pace, Destiny as you knew it will also change. Now, with the death of Aarol, all we have left is each other. This brother-sister thing we have better not stay that way forever."

Harlan put his own hands on her shoulders. He looked down at her magnificence, his voice cloudy, but his mind finally clear. "Napoleon, you've just suffered a major shock, in more ways than one. Physically, mentally, and emotionally. Think very hard before you make any major decisions." He could have done with a little more work on the words, however.

"That's not what I wanted to hear," she growled, her eyelids narrowing, her eyes glowing. Her tail switched back and forth like a metronome.

"It had to be said," Harlan maintained. "I had to say it."

Napoleon suddenly became casual, her arms still around Trigor's neck. "I'm a feline," she shrugged. "I've never been much for thinking. I follow my instincts."

"Yes," Harlan agreed, trying to be as circumspect as possible. No matter how painful the truth, he did not want to part with her. "You are a feline. And that's precisely why you had better think a little more."

Napoleon dropped her hands and whirled as if Trigor had slapped her. Her face looked perplexed, then hurt. Harlan could see his hint had gone all wrong. She was more mortified than he had ever seen her. She looked like a kitten who had just been spanked for the first time.

"You don't like me?" she actually mewed. "I mean, I'm not attrac— You mean like humans?"

Harlan felt the tightening in his chest and throat. He reached out to her, only stopping his hand when he couldn't decide whether the comforting came from personal desire or a Destinian soldier's natural paternalism. He couldn't afford to compound the misunderstanding. But while he could stop his hand, he couldn't completely control his voice.

"No, no, it's not that," he said quickly. Swallowing, his next sentence was calmer, more deliberate. "Napoleon, you are very beautiful."

Just as quickly as her composure had been lost, it returned with a snarling vengeance. "Then what is this?" she spat, prowling the bridge, then turning toward him. "Do you know I haven't felt truly alive from the moment I became aware? Do you have any idea the feelings Aarol awoke in me? He was old, he was battered, but he knew what I was."

She stalked back to Harlan until she was nose to chin with him. "Do you know?" she repeated heatedly up into his face, her voice a hiss. "Do you know that when I lay beside him . . . after all these years . . . the last of my race . . . all I could think about was you?"

Harlan nearly fainted. He felt heat and color boil up into his face, then drop out as if a sluice had opened in his neck. He had to blink to clear his vision, step back to keep his balance. All the feelings he had forced down when he had left her with the lion, all the emotions he had shut

behind his military veneer had broken free. But just for a
second. Just for an awful, endless second.

Napoleon misread his intent again. Before she thought
he was just trying to spare her feelings. This time she
thought he was almost horrified at the thought of her
desiring him. She marched away, then turned at her seat.
"Before," she spat at him, "when everyone in the solar
system was after my pelt, I didn't know what the attraction was. Well, now I know, Harlan Trigor. Now I know!"

Harlan stood quietly for a moment, facing the lithe
feline. He gathered up his scattered feelings, wadded
them in a ball, and swallowed them whole. Finally confi-
dent and sure, he approached the female, even though
her tail was lashing and her paws flexing. He only
stopped when their eyes were level.

"You want to fight?" he asked. "I will fight you. You
want to kill something? I will die for you. You want to be
loved? I will love you. I will always love you. I will do
anything you want me to, now or anytime. You mean that
much to me. I care for you that much." Napoleon's harsh
expression softened, nearly threatening to melt. She
knew what it meant for him to say this. He was a soldier,
but a Destinian first.

"But," Harlan announced, his voice steel. "I will not
pay homage to a whim born of frustration. You are not
afraid of what you have left behind. You are afraid there
is nothing more to find. I tell you there is. There always
is." He turned from her while he was ahead. Not bad for
a brain-cramped soldier. He sat heavily in his co-pilot's
seat, harsh reality yawning below him like a bottomless
pit. When she did not reply, he made his thoughts known.

"I don't want to hurt you," he said meaningfully,
helplessly. "You heard what the Last in Line said. Felines
cannot mate with any but their own kind."

Napoleon sank to the floor and curled up into a ball.
She buried her head in her arms, her breath coming in

tight wheezes. The sound of her tortured breathing filled the control room for minutes. Harlan finally rose, moved over to where she lay, and kneeled beside her. His fingers started with her neck and moved down her body until all the knots of tension were gone.

It took twenty-five minutes, but by the end of that time, Napoleon was breathing easily and a comfortable purr had started deep in her throat. She curled over, moving up his torso, rubbing his shoulders and curling her tail in his lap. She buried her head in his chest and they held each other for a few minutes more.

What else could they do? What more could they do? Now the truth was out: they loved each other. But the greater truth was that consummating that love meant death.

"That was really sweet," said Mess. They tried to ignore it, but that was a futile exercise. "Hey, you crazy kids," it called. "What happens now?"

"What do you mean?" Harlan almost yawned.

"I mean what do you want me to do while you work your way to heavy petting? I've got a few nice planets spotted that could make a darling little homestead. We could set down and it would be years, weeks, days, hours before you'd have to think about replication."

"Oh, no," said the feline from Harlan's shoulder. "You follow the coordinates I've already set."

"But that's uncharted space," Mess complained. "I don't have any information on that area. It might be dangerous. You might get hurt. I might get hurt."

"Just do it."

"It would be a shame to threaten this lovely alliance," it wheedled.

"We're going to do what we have to, Mess," Napoleon said with renewed deliberation. "I can't follow through on one thing, so I'm going to follow through on the second."

"Why? pressed the compubot. "It's useless. It won't change anything!"

"It's something I should do," she replied, jettisoning the rationalization of it's-something-I-have-to-do. She didn't have to do anything, but with her mating options closed off, the location and destruction of the Mantases was her only road to any sort of satisfaction.

"Revenge is useless," Mess intoned.

"Call it revenge if you want," Napoleon responded, unfazed. "I do have the memory of my entire race over me, but I'm not doing it because of that."

"Then why?"

"Because I can."

Mess made a sound like rubber being torn. "I can't change your mind?"

"No." But Mess wasn't giving up.

"What if I said it was stupid?"

"Nothing would happen."

"What if I said it was certain death?"

"I wouldn't care."

The compubot paused for a split second. "What if I said that three Mantas ships were on a collision course with us at this very moment?"

The feline was up instantly, her fur brushing Harlan's face. She leaped for her seat. "Relax, relax," Harlan said foolishly, more comfortable than he had been in light-years. "It's just trying to get a rise out of you."

"No, it's not," Napoleon said, eyes on the controls. "Mess doesn't kid about self-preservation."

"What?" Harlan boomed, jumping up. "Mess, what are you doing?"

"Don't worry," it said tersely. "I'll take care of it. Just waiting until they get in range."

Napoleon swiveled into position, seeing the tiny ships in one of the nine small VUs between the pilot's and co-pilot's chairs. The various tensor squares lit up according to category. In this case it was defense and attack. She turned on all the VUs so she could see everything around her.

"Unnecessary," Mess ruled. "I'd switch on any screen as it was needed."

"You're not in charge," Napoleon warned. "How long until they're in range?"

"Communications or weapons?" the compubot countered.

"Both," she snapped.

"Any particular order?"

"This is not a game!" Napoleon snarled.

"Don't worry," it soothed. "I was equipped with the finest weapons capable of production at the time of my resurrection. My niodes have been infused with the importance of your protection. Really, would I let anything happen to you?"

The pilots were aghast at the compubot's diffidence. On the *Black Hole*, it would have been screeching with paranoia. This newfound serenity was justly disturbing. "How do you know they're Mantas ships?" Harlan asked.

"I detect life forms capable of being only Mantases," it replied.

"Here they come," said Napoleon. Harlan studied the craft growing larger in the VU. They were long, triangular ships with a sharp point and screw-shaped bodies. The front ends bristled with blasters. Trigor spun out of his seat and strode toward his suit.

"No," the feline blurted, spinning toward him. He stopped, confused by her cry and her almost frightened expression.

"Mess," the feline called, "set up a communications link. Tell them . . . No, ask them to stop if they intend no attack."

Both were expecting some kind of balk, but all Mess said was, "Done."

"Are they stopping?" Harlan asked, anxious to get into his suit.

"No," said Mess.

"They're slowing down," Napoleon said, eyes intent on the screen. Seven sets of nine tensors lit up with numbers and corresponding digits detailing the range and speeds.

"Are they stopping?" Harlan almost whined.

"It seems so," Mess reluctantly admitted.

Harlan wanted to dive into his suit. The memory of the Finally Finished massacre was still strong in his mind. It made no sense for the Mantases to stop their attack. Unless they had something up their mandible sleeves. "Napoleon, I'm getting into my suit."

"Don't leave me," she cried. The plea brought him up short again.

"I'm just—"

"Please don't leave me." She wasn't even looking at him. Her paws were dancing across the tensors.

"There's nothing anywhere else," Mess complained in response to her tests.

"Napoleon, what is it?" Harlan asked in confusion.

"I don't trust boogers," she said, eyes and paws still intent on the controls.

"Neither do I," he replied with exasperation. "I should go out and check around. If you'd only let me suit up. . . ."

"I said don't leave me!" she yelled as the *Felidae* lurched downward. A flash of light filled the VUs and a concussion made the control room walls sing a drunken lullaby. Harlan was hurled up, but Napoleon held on to her console. The three Mantas ships had not moved. "Mess!" she shouted.

"They didn't fire!"

"They must have invisible weapons. Full attack."

"Done." The *Felidae* arced around in a semicircle, laying out a bank of white bolts toward the three stationary ships, now near enough to be seen clearly as pockmarked cones. The white light dissipated. Green lightning bolts followed, tearing at the pockmarks. But when they winked out, there was hardly any damage on the Mantas crafts.

The spinning *Felidae* continued to bath the blackness with green and white weavings, but they didn't stop the "invisible" Mantas blasts from getting through. Although none was a direct hit, the Destinian ship was continually buffeted by near misses.

"It was an ambush," said Harlan through clenched teeth. Even as they were banking madly, making a mockery of the interior gravity, he was crawling up his space bullet suit. Napoleon actually leaped out of her seat and grabbed him around the waist.

"Don't go!" she pulled at him, but he just kept climbing with her wrapped around his back. "Don't go."

The *Felidae* suddenly stopped, freezing the pilots in place. A sound reminiscent of a bead of water dropped into a long, thin well filled with oil came from the compubot's console, then things really began to get frenetic.

Coiled beams of red shrieked out from the edges of the ship, and deep blue beams hummed out of the very center of the tiger's eye. The entire ship was covered with deadly emissions, but when the dazzling display ended, the Mantas craft were unfazed.

Napoleon's tensor board was completely filled with flashing lights, colors, numbers, and letters. The feline suddenly bounced off Harlan and landed on the deck on all fours. "Mess, prepare to completely empty our weapon stores in their direction."

"That's ridiculous," the compubot scoffed stridently. "What will we do then?"

"Just let me at them," Harlan said triumphantly, climbing into the space bullet.

"No!" Napoleon shouted. "Suit up, but don't leave!" But—!"

"Harlan, this is a Destiny ship." She didn't have the time or need to explain further. Fighting the chills that threatened to engulf him, Harlan pulled the exoskeleton shell over his head and communi-linked with the compubot. Napoleon pulled open her spacesuit compartment in the back of her pilot's seat and started pulling on the skintight material.

"Keep them away from us," Harlan instructed the machine.

"You want to try?" Mess defended itself and begged at the same time. Trigor did take over, sending out a dizzying array of practically useless blasts. But he hoped that he did it in such a way that the Mantas ships were stymied and confused. He knew he couldn't hurt them, but he wanted to keep them thinking.

Napoleon had realized it before he had. The same assurance that had afflicted Mess had affected him. He thought Destinian weapons were invincible, but the Mantases had defeated the space bullets at the Mile Long Castle two years before. They had developed anti-Destinian weaponry, and while all the Destiny Mantases had been massacred, the insectoids shared psyches. Anti-Destinian weapons had to be on board the attacking ships. No wonder the *Felidae*'s sensors detected nothing.

"Hurry, hurry, hurry," Napoleon growled as she grabbed at the clear, open-bottomed globe attached to the bridge ceiling above her chair.

"The same to you," Mess said miserably.

"We've got to do this before they move in," she said, locking the helmet in place and striding toward the space bullet. She was just in time to see its awful, bland, slate-colored head screw into place.

"What are they waiting for?" Harlan worried. "Why haven't they destroyed us?"

"They're playing with us," Napoleon guessed angrily.

"They're talking to us," Mess said proudly. "I established a communications link, remember?"

The air was filled with the familiar, ominous hissing of a Mantas. " . . . And then you will know the meaning of strength. Then you will know the meaning of The Rule. But only for a moment. Only for a fleeting moment will you realize the futility of resisting the Universal Rule. We are all, all is us, we are everything, and everything is our source of strength. Each is all every . . ."

"Enough!" the feline shrieked, clamping on to the space bullet with all her strength.

"Hold on," she heard him instruct through her suit's communications link. "Mess, eject all the esc-globe eyes now!" Harlan did it with the compubot. The little balls popped out of the *Felidae*'s skin like bubbles from a swimmer's mouth. Under the ship's direction, they fanned out before the Mantas craft.

Napoleon flattened herself onto Harlan's back as a bolt from between the space bullet's "eyes" sliced open the bridge hull. The vacuum of space was like fingers which scratched, then tore at the cut. The air roared out and nothing roared in. Arms magically disengaged themselves from the space bullet's body and held Napoleon in place with breathtaking gentleness.

The esc-globes exploded in rapid succession as the Mantas ships' weapons swatted them like pesky flies. Hopefully, they were too intent on that to note the new hole in the *Felidae*. The space bullet floated off the bridge deck and drifted down until its head was facing the ripped opening.

"Wait!" Mess cried. "Wait!" Harlan drifted lazily away from the hole toward the slot in the compubot console with the red arrow pointing at it. "What about—!" Mess never got to say "me." Napoleon slammed a glove-covered paw on the slot and the niode-cirquid board that was Mess popped automatically into her palm.

Harlan shot into space and detonated the *Felidae* almost at the same time.

# TEN

There was no way to know what happened to the three Mantas ships. Harlan was going too fast for even him to gauge exactly the *Felidae*'s explosive damage to its adversaries. He'd like to think that the detonation destroyed the attacking craft. Whether they had Destinian defense weapons or not, there wasn't much they could do about tearing hunks of shrapnel spinning at them at super speeds. Harlan would certainly like to think that, at any rate.

But instead of knowing, he concentrated on undetectable escape and keeping Napoleon on his back. She put Mess' board in one of her spacesuit's pockets and took out a cord with which she made a makeshift rein around Harlan's space bullet head. They coursed through space that way, both suits feeding and cleansing them as they required.

But here on the *Shooting Star* there was no hunger. There was only the LOST and the many mysteries therein. Both considered their situation, environment, and each other. Finally the feline broke the smoldering silence. "Well?"

It was hardly the Gettysburg Address, but the two had developed an enviable psychic bond over the many months they had been together. A feline's senses were naturally heightened, while a Destinian's were genetically increased.

"Don't say anything you wouldn't want them to hear," Harlan suggested.

She smiled with mild sarcasm. "You think they're some sort of secret Comps, don't you?" Harlan had been introduced to Comps, the combination compubot/FM/TM police, on the old Earth.

Trigor frowned at her humorous derision. "I hadn't eliminated the possibility," he said with haughty defensiveness.

"You think uncharted space is crawling with Earthen officials just waiting to feed us a story like this?" It certainly didn't make much sense that such an outlandish tale would be used to lower their guard and get Harlan out of his suit.

He didn't honor her argument with a reply. Instead, "More importantly, how do we proceed from here?"

"Staying on board certainly isn't getting us any closer to our destination," Napoleon agreed. "They're stopping on already charted planets in mapped space."

"Not necessarily," said Muse. "Where do you want to go?"

Both the soldier and feline should have known that the *Shooting Star*'s compubot would be everywhere (Mess certainly had been on the *Black Hole* and *Felidae*), but her/its sudden intrusion still came as a mild surprise. But the nonmachines knew better than to complain. Harlan chose to question her/it instead, rather than answer directly.

"What do you mean, 'not necessarily'?"

"Well, charted planets to us may not be charted planets to you. Much has occurred since you three, I mean, two left Earth. More space has been mapped in the sixty years between our times, as well as the twenty years since we left."

Napoleon shook her head. "I'm getting confused," she warned.

"Come up to the bridge," Muse invited. "Let me show you something."

The halls were nondescript and narrow, making the vaulted bridge seem like a magnificent cavern. Roscoe was deep in his sunken chair by Muse's main console while Spot and Zero were off in a corner, cuddling together. The TM made no sound, but the two clones were cooing softly in turn. To Napoleon's surprise and slight disappointment, they ignored the hitchhikers. After all these years, she was used to and expected attention. She was the last feline, sexy, and a legendary Earthen criminal to boot!

A small speaker on the console softly told the two fugitives to approach, not wanting to disturb the others. On the top of the console, over the speaker, was a rectangular clocklike device that was continually changing in seemingly random patterns. "Here's The Thing," Muse said. "This is our one link to Earth. The technology wasn't sophisticated enough to keep us in constant vocal contact, so this has to do."

"What is this?" said the curious cat, pointing at labels reading "T.T." and "R.T."

"True time and real time," Muse explained quietly. "Real time is our time, the time we've spent in space. True time is Earthen time, that is, what year it is actually on Earth. Our tour was incompletely charted when we left, and new dates and new planets are fed into The

Thing as we travel. That's all one ECG U.W. Bro-ENCOM computer does back on Earth."

Harlan was relieved that the clock was the only thing communicating with Earth, but he didn't let the new information deter him from their original quest. "What does that have to do with our destination?"

"Shh," Muse hushed him, making Trigor glance into the padded chair where Roscoe obliviously toiled over a book. "We're traveling through what you think of as uncharted space. The new charts are in The Thing. We might know where it is you want to go and can drop you off there."

"Oh, no," Roscoe said calmly, eyes still on The Book, hands still moving across it. "Not today and not tonight. Maybe not even tomorrow. You know we're on a tight schedule, Muse."

"Roscoe, you know we're coming to the end of the tour," she/it reasoned. "There's no reason we can't take a short side trip between here and Meditar."

"Muse, Muse, Muse," Roscoe chastised, struggling out of the chair. When he had his feet on the deck and his clothes straightened, he continued, "You know Meditar is in between us and the Earth. You know it was designated closing night for that reason. I will not damage our perfect performance record for a joy ride." He glanced at the hitchhikers. "Legends or no."

"Aw, what'll it hurt?" Spot chipped in, suddenly at Pound's side. "It's been twenty years since we started. Larry knows how long on Meditar." She turned her wide eyes on Napoleon. "Where do you want to go?" she asked with exaggerated cheeriness.

"I said no," Roscoe sighed, frowning sadly. "We can't do it. Coven tonight, Meditar tomorrow, and Earth the day after that." Zero tenderly held Spot's shoulders in his hands. Harlan and Napoleon noted with interest that the girl was shaking. There was something like fear on her face. "I'm sorry, but that's what it has to be."

Roscoe should have turned heel and walked out after that pronouncement, but he just stood there. Thankfully, Zero had dramatic sense. He nuzzled Spot's neck and drew her away, back to where they had been sitting before. Almost as soon as they had sat, they started necking passionately. Napoleon looked away from the enviable sight. Pound immediately apologized.

"Our performance dates are locked into The Thing," he said. "We can't disappoint our public. Of course, you're always free to go, but . . ."

Harlan glanced at the feline. "But?"

"I was just wondering . . ." Roscoe started again.

"Yes?" Napoleon prompted. Maybe he wanted an autograph for his children. Or maybe his great-great-great-grandchildren. If he had any.

Pound's words were all in a rush. "Would you like to play Lord and Lady Macduff?"

Harlan stepped back, ready to move fast if he had to. "Is that a game?"

"No, characters in a play," Muse said. "In *Macbeth* by William Shakespeare."

"What?" Napoleon giggled. "Like on the VU?"

"In a way," Pound considered.

"Do I have to get raped or killed?" the feline asked, suddenly wary.

"No," said Pound, pointing at Harlan. "But he does."

"Ax in the head," said Muse.

Harlan backed up again, a mirthless smile stretching his mouth, and his mouth only. "You're welcome to try," he said flatly.

"No, no," Roscoe admonished, coming toward him. Harlan backed away until Pound stopped. "It'll all be faked. It's a play. Don't you understand?"

"A performance," said Muse. "For an audience."

Before the situation could disintegrate further, Napoleon interrupted. "You've been doing this for two decades. What do you need us for?"

"Precisely," Roscoe said disconcertingly. "I've got a load of rotting actobots backstage which can hardly get through all five acts. And there's just so much quadrupling up Spot and Zero can do."

"We've tried using local talent the last few planets," Muse continued to the befuddled fugitives, "but it was a disaster."

"Remember *A Midsummer Night's Dream* on Lepusia?" Roscoe shivered. "Whew. They just didn't get it."

"Come on," a returned and renewed Spot merrily extorted. "It'll be fun! I'll be Lady Macbeth."

"And I'll be Macbeth," a smiling Zero said to the redhead.

"Stop!" Harlan shouted, his hands up. "I'm completely confused."

Napoleon smiled upon him, a wide beam which showed most of her teeth. "Come on," she said. "It'll be fun."

Trigor didn't know what was going on, and he hated it when he didn't know what was going on. But it had been a long time since he had seen Napoleon smile like that, and he figured the only way he'd find out what was going on was to go along. And most anything would be better than zipping around uncharted space with a cat on his back.

"All right," he said. "On one condition." It was the others' turn to get wary.

"What?" Pound inquired.

Harlan motioned for Napoleon to give him what was in her pocket. "We have a friend," he said, holding up Mess' board, "who needs a place to live."

Roscoe looked at the console. "Oh, no, you don't!" yelled Muse. "It's not coming in here with me! I don't even know it."

Roscoe immediately soothed and comforted his com-pubot. "I wouldn't know how to install it anyway," he admitted to the hitchhikers. They were also stymied in that department. Larry had been the whiz. Napoleon even went so far as to acknowledge that Muse and Mess together might have been too much for any of them.

"Leave it here," Muse instructed haughtily. "I'll figure out somewhere to put it. In the meantime, you all have work to do."

So it was that Harlan found himself between Roscoe and Napoleon in a star-shaped esc-globe on its way down to the surface of the planet Coven. Roscoe had asked, and Spot had practically begged the feline to stay on the main ship, but she refused to be separated from the space bullet. She held his arm now like an eager girlfriend who had just gotten engaged.

"Nothing," Pound was saying. "We checked the book, but it was published before this region of space was charted. So we checked the thing, and again, nothing." He looked at his companions and, with a small smile, quoth: " 'The lunatic, the lover, and the poet are of imagination all compact: one sees more devils than vast hell can hold, one sees Helen's beauty in a brow of Egypt, and the poet's eye, in a fine frenzy rolling, doth glance from heaven to earth, from earth to heaven, and, as imagination bodies forth, the forms of things unknown, the poet's pen turns them to shapes, and gives to airy nothing a name.' "

"Nice," said a perplexed Napoleon.

"Who's Helen?" Harlan asked in exasperation. "What's Egypt? What is all that?"

"I have no idea," Roscoe told him. To the feline he said, "That's Shakespeare from *A Midsummer Night's Dream.*" To both he explained, "According to all our records, there was no planet called 'Coven.' The world that was catalogued in the thing for this location was a barren hunk of rock. But we had our premiere date scheduled. So here we are."

"Why go down now?" Harlan, as always the soul of practicality, asked.

"Recon prelim," Roscoe answered. "The planets joining the Brotherhood picked the play they wanted off a list that has no descriptions. They used to have one-line blurbs, but a lot of the worlds didn't know English yet and we certainly didn't know their languages. So most chose the plays from the sound of the title alone." Pound considered the planet beneath his feet. "I suppose that's better than capsulizing Shakespeare," he mused. "'*Romeo and Juliet:* two youngsters fall in love and accidentally commit suicide.'"

"Recon prelim?" Harlan reminded him.

"Oh, yes. Preliminary reconnaissance. We never know what the local customs are and how the play's content will affect them until we get there. My job is to meet with the proper authorities and get all the details worked out." He looked down at the strangely colored planet again. "They should be expecting us."

Harlan had an overwhelming desire for his suit, and Napoleon had one for her spitter, but both knew that, unless this was an astonishingly cunning Comp trap, it was wiser to leave them on the *Shooting Star*. To take the edge off everyone's nervousness, Napoleon asked about the Muse connection. She could understand why Mess was the way it was, but what was her/its excuse?

Roscoe admitted he could only guess. "It's an entertainment system. The U.W. scientists were no geniuses . . ." Napoleon could vouch for that. She had almost a dozen dead sisters as evidence. " . . . so I suppose they equated creativity with eccentricity. She/it's sensitive, manipulative, and jealous, but I'll tell you the truth. She/it's made the trip far more bearable than an emotionless compubot would have."

Napoleon had never thought of that, and appreciated Mess all the more for it. Harlan wasn't too sure he agreed. But before the feline could then plumb the depths of the clones' contributions during the trip, the esc-star passengers' concerns were redirected toward the planet Coven. Through wisping white clouds, they could see the rolling, rutted, magnificent surface. •

Roscoe's head leaned way down, making his long neck seem almost horizontal. His pointed jaw dropped and his high brows furrowed. Where naked rock should have been was a riot of clashing foliage. The ground looked like organic artwork. Textures, shapes, and colors looked as if they had jousted one another and the litter of their forms was the result. There was a swirl of brown and green, a jagged band of blue rising out of that, and all was interspersed with waves of red and orange leaves.

The sights beneath the clouds added to the LOST members' amazement. The vistas of rock which were there weren't featureless boulders created by nature. They were astonishing sculptures which ranged from formless abstracts to suprarealistic representations of crystals and squares. Roscoe hastily made communi-k (c) link with the ship.

"Muse, you getting all this?"

"In a manner of speaking."

"Any contact?"

"Beings have contacted," she/it said. "I put you right on the coordinates. They should be waiting for you."

"Are they intelligent?" Even Roscoe hadn't been able to eliminate all his TM conceit. Are they intelligent translated to "Do they speak English?"

"Only coordinates were sent," Muse answered. "But they're expecting you."

"All we have to find out now is who are they." Napoleon growled.

"Anything's better than Lepusians," Roscoe said, still

taking in the wonder. He suddenly looked at the feline, his expression thoughtful. "Giant bunny rabbits," he explained. "Earthen explorers named it Lepusia because it was overpopulated by six-foot rabbits."

"Coven?" Harlan murmured, following the logic.

No one was waiting for them when they touched down, but some things were. A line of large, gnarled, leafy trees stood in a line before the settled esc-star. Roscoe double-checked the atmosphere and gravity with Muse before they ventured anywhere. Much to the trio's consternation, the environment rivaled Earth in almost every way.

"'My story being done,'" Roscoe said to himself, looking around at the dense, beautiful abundance of Coven's nature, "'she gave me for my pains a world of sighs. She swore, in faith, 'twas strange, 'twas passing strange.'" Roscoe looked over to see Harlan and Napoleon staring at him. "*Othello,*" he said, explaining nothing.

The feline picked up one difference between Earth and Coven as soon as they broke the esc-star's porta-seal. The air temperature changed every few seconds. It was both warm and cool on the planet's surface. The light wind seemed to bear the changes on it as it moaned through the flora. It also bore the dusky smells of the rich fauna to the trio's nostrils as they surveyed different horizons for anything resembling inhabitants.

"Very nice," said Napoleon.

"Amazing," said Roscoe.

"Oh, I don't know," said the nearest tree. The feline and TM thought Harlan had said it. He thought Roscoe had said it.

They all became almost immediately aware of something new on the wind. It wasn't a smell or a sight; it was a word. A word repeated over and over again in a vague, distant chant. The three listened carefully. They looked at one another when the word became clear. It was the word "Coven" repeated over and over until it created a bass beat. "Coven, Coven, Coven, Coven, Coven, Coven, Coven . . ."

They whirled around when the trees started singing. Their knotholes were moving to create eyes and nostrils while their trunk bark opened as mouths. Four huge trees sang in harmony. Maybe it wasn't perfect harmony, but when four trees started singing, it hardly made a difference.

"What do you call something that can't be explained?
Just call it here where it's all the same;
So what if things can't be understood?
On another planet, we'd just be hunks of wood!"

The trees sang cheerfully, with great gusto, then each took a solo chorus line.

"There I'd have nothing to do,"
"Here I get to welcome you!"
"There forest fires rage full,"
"Here my bark is noncombustible!"

On that note they all joined in again for a rousing finale. "So when no other world suits, think of Coven: a place to . . . put . . . down . . . roots!"

The trees applauded themselves with their branches. Their rustling leaves sounded like laughter. "Very good," said the first.

"Ironic, biting," said the second.

"Satiric," said the third.

"Poetic," said the fourth.

"Thank you, everyone," said the first. And the trees fell silent.

The three visitors were motionless. Napoleon was so stunned that she didn't even wrap herself around Harlan.

"Passing strange," whispered Roscoe.

"Well, I'll be trigored," said the space bullet.

A huge set of cross hairs made of fire formed itself in the sky above their heads. The intersection of the two lines within the circle was directly over the singing trees. From the intersection came a narrow tornado. It swirled down to the ground, directly in front of the branched quartet.

This time Napoleon did retreat to Harlan's side, with a near screech. Roscoe dove back into the esc-star as the soldier stood between the feline and sudden storm.

The swirling unraveled and a man stood before them. The tornado slipped among the passing wind and disappeared. The fire in the sky winked out. The man's ground-length robe, long hair, and beard swirled in the remnants of the minor natural disaster. His hair was white, his robe was white with red detailing, and his facial characteristics were as deep as a river.

"Welcome to Coven," he said in a deep voice. "I am Merlin Master."

# COVEN

# ELEVEN

"Tomorrow, and tomorrow, and tomorrow creeps in this petty pace from day to day. To the last syllable of recorded time. And all our yesterdays have lighted fools the way to dusty death. Out, out, brief candle! Life's but a walking shadow, a poor player that struts and frets his hour upon the stage, and then is heard no more. It is a tale told by an idiot, full of sound and fury . . . signifying nothing."

Zero dropped his head to his chest. He stood in the middle of the stage, a single shaft of light, seemingly from the heavens, piercing the darkness to etch him from the surrounding curtain. Napoleon found herself holding her breath. She could hardly understand what he was saying, but she instinctively knew what he was talking about.

Zero had done the speech without flourish. He had spoken the words with import but without exaggeration or unneeded drama. He let the words' meanings (whatever they were) carry the weight of the emotion. The only thing different about him was his attitude. He was somehow taut, seemingly powered by a glow from within.

There was a slight pause.

"Signifying nothing," he said again, like a sigh.

There was a long pause.

"Signifying nothing!" he boomed angrily. Napoleon was thrilled.

"I said, signifying nothing!" he yelled offstage left.

A small, square robot on treads slowly crept out into the light, its two eye globes blinking. Zero was already throwing his hands up as the machine rasped out its line as if nothing was wrong. "Gracious, my lord . . ."

"He hasn't said his line yet!" Roscoe screamed from the dark.

The robot whirred until it was facing out toward the audience seats. "I'm sorry. Wasn't that my cue?"

"It says 'Enter Messenger,' doesn't it?" Pound demanded from a seat. "I only sent the message three times in big, blinking green letters, didn't I?"

"I don't understand," the machine complained. "I entered—"

"Late," said Zero angrily.

"I entered," the robot repeated, "and said my line."

Roscoe typed it out on his portoputer keys as he said it. "Just because you have an entrance doesn't mean you have a line!"

"I don't say it?"

"Just because you have an entrance doesn't mean you have a line *yet,*" Roscoe amended. "He has to see you and say, 'Thou comest to use thy tongue, thy story quickly,' first!" The robot said nothing. Pound could tell it was hopeless. "You see?" he called out to Harlan and Napoleon in the wings. "You see what I have to deal with? What parts were you assigned?" he asked the robot.

"The messenger, the English doctor, the Scotch doctor, a porter, an old man, a soldier, several lords, and a murderer."

"A murderer?" Roscoe said in disbelief. "Muse!"

"The first four can be reassigned," the compubot said smoothly. "It can still be one of the lords, however."

"I'll be the old man, the soldier, and the murderer," said Pound.

"Roscoe . . ." she/it admonished.

"It's not too much," the director defended. When Muse didn't answer, he capitulated. "All right, all right. What about Trigor's compubot?" Zero giggled. Every time anyone mentioned the feline's or soldier's name, he couldn't help thinking of them as profanity.

"What about it?" Muse coolly answered.

"You find a place for it?"

"Not yet."

"Well, find one! We need it!" Almost all the crew's previous civility and consideration had disappeared in the flurry of the rehearsal. "And you!" Pound yelled at the little square robot. "Get off my stage! Get out of my theater!" The machine squeaked and started to laboriously grind itself toward the darkness of the side curtains. Harlan thought it looked like a crippled old man limping away. Its pitiful demeanor was not lost on Pound either. "Besides," he called after it. "Your speaker is dirty. Robot, clean thyself!"

Zero stood on the edge of the spotlight's illuminated circle, his arms folded across his chest. "What now, R.P.?"

"Napoleon can play one of the murderers," suggested Muse. "I'll play Lady Macduff."

"Out of the question," Roscoe huffed.

"Why?" asked Muse. "She doesn't have to be seen on stage."

"And do Banquo's murder offstage?" Pound asked back incredulously.

"Well, that's the way it is in the original script!" Muse retorted.

Spot wandered over to where Napoleon and Harlan stood watching the insanity. "They go at it like this all the time," she said mildly.

"At the top of their lungs?" Trigor wondered.

"I thought he wanted me to be Lady Macduff," the feline said directly to the redhead.

"It changes all the time. We won't know who we are until near curtain. But that's all right," she said cattily, turning away. "We know the whole play."

"That's the reason I rewrote the original," Roscoe was saying. "What good is an unseen murder? It's out of the question. A robot can do a witch, but not Lady Macduff. We need blood and an emotional high here."

"What if I splash blood from offstage," Muse suggested. "It could be very effective."

"No, no, no!" Roscoe tantrumed, standing up and stamping his feet. "The witches aren't important anymore! Any thing can do a witch now. I need Lady Macduff humanoid and on stage!"

If Roscoe's rage wasn't justified, it was at least understandable. According to him, the hierarchy of Coven had eliminated one of the best Macbeth ingredients: the witches. Of course, their reason was completely understandable as Merlin Master explained it.

As hoary as the clichés were, it was all new to Roscoe, Harlan, and Napoleon. What did they know of Arthurian legend? So when the white-bearded, robed sorcerer appeared bearing the name of Earth's greatest wizard, it didn't strike them as unlikely in the least. Of course it helped that Merlin Master, the Sorcerer Supreme himself, was agreeable and ebullient.

"A small sign of welcome," he admitted humbly when asked about the singing trees. He had led them from the spot to a small sign with a strange shape on it. There were three straight vertical lines beside one another. A vertical line connected all three at the top. A slanted line went from the top of the first to the bottom of the second, then back to the top of the third.

"We will travel to my castle by Empty," Merlin said, motioning toward the sign.

"MT?" Napoleon echoed.

"Very good," the Sorcerer Supreme beamed. "Yes. Magic Transit." He walked to the sign and disappeared. Before the trio could get too shook up, he reappeared. "Follow me," he said.

It was not an unpleasant sensation. It was hardly a sensation at all. Napoleon walked to the sign, and then was walking away from the sign in another place. She turned but bumped into Harlan, who was right behind her. They both looked around at an impressive scene.

They stood before a castle. Simply put, it was a beautiful place, with spires, detailed rock inlay, and a drawbridge. No moat, however. The drawbridge fell onto a simple, flat road that was connected to a beautifully grassy courtyard. The only thing out of place in the scene was the big, pointed fangs which encircled the green as if a monster under the ground had tried to bite out the square only to lock his jaw.

Encircling the courtyard were more odd things. They were dwellings, mostly, but dwellings of completely different shapes and designs. There were barnlike houses, mansion-type homes, angular buildings, and one big gray ball with spikes coming out the top and bottom. They all sat in a nice little gulley, with forests and mountains going off in all directions.

"We are a small, quiet populace," Merlin Master said. "But we are very anxious to see your show. Please, come inside." He beckoned with an arm sweeping toward the castle entrance. "I would like you to meet my son and our BOP-ENSUB representative."

The interior of the place was odd, damned odd. There were some sections that were very impressive, as if the design work of unearthly minds and inhuman talents. But there were other sections, a majority of sections, in fact, that looked rough and unfinished. In some places, the atmosphere was positively stark. And the sectioning wasn't exact either. The castle interior looked like a once-healthy beast that was now sickly and diseased.

While Harlan and Napoleon were duly interested by this, Roscoe got down to business. "What was that?" He was having a hard time thinking of a description of what he was talking about. "What was that when we landed?"

"Please," said Merlin Master. "I will tell you everything. But first . . ." He led them into his throne room, a pretty expansive hall, except that it was afflicted by the same spottiness as the rest of the palace. It paled in comparison to Destiny's mile-long throne room.

The Coven throne itself was nice: thick, rich, woodlike, with a tall, padded back and wide, padded seat. On either side was a man. One was thin and tall (though not as tall as the Sorcerer Supreme). His hair was black and he had no beard, but his face was the same shape as Merlin's. The other was short, round, and potbellied. His hair was black also, and he had a thin mustache and pointed goatee. Both men wore robes; the short one's was red and the thin one's was black.

"This is your Brotherhood of Planets rep, Sparx the Elder," the Sorcerer Supreme introduced, pointing at the short man, who bowed smilingly. "And this," he continued, moving his arm to aim at the thin man, "is Merlin Masterson."

"Let me guess," said Napoleon. "Your offspring."

The old man smiled. "Right again." His son also smiled, his eyes on no one but the feline. He bowed, but his eyes did not leave her. Harlan's eyes did not leave him. Once they had been shown to seats around a large round table, Roscoe once again pressed on.

"All our information showed that this planet was just a nameless void," he said, with more directness than Harlan liked. "What happened?" The space bullet supposed the LOST manager needed to know that sort of thing for his troupe's well-being.

"There was no reason for anyone to think of this planet as anything else," said Sparx, of the bright, dancing eyes. All three Coverners seemed to really appreciate the LOST's arrival. "We import nothing, we export nothing. We have no industry."

"How do you live?" Napoleon asked. All Coverners looked at her. That required only two Coverners to change their eye directions. Masterson was looking at her all along. Harlan watched the watcher, not liking what he saw.

"Magic," said the Sorcerer Supreme. "All that you see, all that you have seen is the result of magic."

"You mean, like the singing trees?" Roscoe queried. It made a certain amount of sense, but not enough to hold on to.

Merlin nodded. "A minor spell to greet and entertain visitors."

"You mean it was an illusion?" Napoleon suggested. Again all six wizard eyes spotlighted her. Harlan was getting sick of it.

"Not exactly," Sparx hedged.

"Then it was a tangible creation," the feline surmised.

"Well . . ." Sparx hawed.

"Either it is or it isn't," Trigor said harshly. "Which?"

"Please, let me explain," Merlin soothed. "We, like so

many others, are descendants of Earthen refugees who left the planet in large numbers on vast ships to find new homes on other worlds, as did the original settlers of Destiny, I believe. Many of our people died investigating hostile environments, while many others died on the ship of old age. We were all dying, really. Even the ship was dying. It only had enough power to reach this place."

"You must have been surprised by what you found," the empathic Pound grinned.

"Oh, the planet was nothing like what you've seen," said Sparx. "It was what your records showed: a barren wasteland."

"But . . ." Roscoe said, more to himself than the others.

"Magic," Merlin repeated. "We discovered we could do magic."

"They ALL discovered it," Masterson said—his first four words. Even so, he still didn't lose his crooked-lipped smirk.

"What does that mean?" Harlan asked darkly.

"It means," Sparx said with a smile, "that everyone could do it. From the tiniest child to the most elderly of survivors. Whether they wanted to or not."

"What does THAT mean?" Harlan challenged, his patience growing ever thinner. The sooner he got Napoleon out from under Masterson's oily eyesight, the better he'd feel.

"We couldn't control the spells," Merlin reluctantly elaborated.

"They didn't know what they were saying," Masterson smirked.

"As near as we can figure," offered Sparx, "this planet's laws of nature allow magic spells to take tangible form. But our ancestors couldn't completely understand what constituted spells to the planet's laws of nature."

"Many more of our people died—experimenting,"

Merlin carefully relayed. The three visitors considered the ramifications of the statement. It explained the artful shapes of the plants and buildings they had seen. The Coverners must have dreamed them up. "Everything this planet is now was created by our illustrious ancestors. They created a world that would nurture and protect us."

Roscoe, ever the director, latched on to a telling hole in the story. "Gracious. Macbeth," he realized. "You mean even we . . . I mean, any one of us, if we put the wrong . . . I mean, the rights words together, we could . . . !"

"Oh, no," both Merlin and Sparx said at the same time. "No," the Sorcerer Supreme continued after a telling look at the BOP rep. "There is something else."

"Two something elses," Masterson leered. He seemed to delight in pricking pins into his father's regal explanations. The Sorcerer Supreme didn't seem (or deem) to notice.

"BS," said Merlin.

"I beg your pardon?" said Roscoe.

"Two BSs," said Masterson. Pound just looked at him. Merlin, in the meantime, looked at Sparx. This was too sticky for the planet ruler to explain.

"First, the Back Side," the rep detailed. "For every action, there is an opposite, but not always equal, reaction. The danger to our ancestors didn't come from the spells themselves. They came from the first BS." Sparx could see by the visitors' expressions that they weren't getting it. "It's like this. We see Coven's laws of nature as a long line of marbles. Whenever we move a marble, it sets off a chain reaction along the line until another marble is moved. But since we don't know which marble we hit or how hard, we don't know which other marble will fall."

"In other words," Masterson drawled, "one man would say a spell to create a stone wall and another person would suddenly grow an extra nose. The extra nose would subsequently take in too much carbon monoxide and the man would die."

"Or a witch would devise a love spell and a mountain would appear where a town had been," Sparx remembered sadly.

Pound's mouth was a small o, and his eyes moved from the speakers to the hitchhikers. "And the second BS?" he inquired squeamishly.

"The Big Spell," said Sparx.

"Coven's greatest wizards and witches banded together to protect the world they had so carefully created," Merlin intoned. "They couldn't risk an innocent child or an evil sorcerer from threatening the remaining populace. Together, over a period of years, they devised a planetwide blanket . . ."

"Like another atmosphere," Sparx added, garnering an irritated look from his leader.

" . . . to prevent errant magic. Now, whenever a spell is even innocently invoked—well, what happens is what happened when the trees sang." The visitors remembered the giant cross in the sky and the whirlwind depositing Merlin Master before them.

"That happens every time?" Napoleon asked incredulously.

"Every time," Masterson sardonically concurred.

"I am the Back Stop," Merlin proclaimed. "A third BS, if you will. It is my duty to protect our magnificent planet. The second BS prevents the spell from occurring, and I appear to counter the magician, if need be."

The three visitors looked at one another with expressions ranging from outright disbelief to deep concern. The latter emotion took the day. "Well, we have a fourth BS," Roscoe said. "Our Big Show. We're scheduled to perform the Coven premiere of the LOST production of *Macbeth* tonight. Considering what you've just told us, we have a lot to go over."

The three witches had to go, it seemed. Harlan watched Roscoe's scalp get whiter and whiter as the Sorcerer Supreme's face grew graver and graver when the men read the script. Soon it was all too much for Merlin Master to bear. He leaned back in the round table's head chair, putting his hands over his closed eyes.

"Sparx, please take care of all this. You know what to do."

"Very well, sire."

Merlin Masterson casually straightened and leaned over the table toward Napoleon. "Is there any way I can be of service?"

"No," said Merlin before Harlan could. "I need you here." Trigor looked at the Sorcerer Supreme, hearing something in his tone he couldn't immediately recognize but didn't like. What he saw there was a man anxious to keep his son with him at all times. Only the reason wasn't just paternalism. His eyes glancing off Harlan's stare, Merlin continued, "We must prepare the family for the performance tonight."

The ruler stood, creating the cue for everyone else to stand as well. He signaled for his son to follow, then marched from the throne room. Masteron practically walked backward to the far door, smiling upon the feline all the while. Finally, he too was gone. Napoleon watched him leave and then grinned over at the soldier, who was doing his best to be expressionless.

"So that's a prince, huh?" she said mildly. "What a creep." She covered her smile with a paw and used her other arm to dig an elbow into Harlan's side. "Cheer up," she said sarcastically, as Trigor couldn't prevent his relief from showing.

"Oh, yes," Sparx was saying as he approached Roscoe from around the table. "This will not do at all. I hardly dare read the witches' dialogue for fear their spells will be invoked. They must go. They must. Under no circumstances must they say any of these things tonight."

Pound couldn't reply. He was too busy thinking how he could amend that part of the play. In his mind, the witches were integral to the story. "Oh, fine," he finally mumbled. "No one understands Shakespeare anyway. With enough action, no one will notice. I must work this out with Muse. Show me where I can land the theater," he instructed Sparx.

The quartet moved out of the palace. "Would this do?" Sparx asked, pointing to the courtyard. Roscoe nodded.

"We could land the theater there," he figured. "I must get back to the esc-star."

Sparx showed them the way back through the Empty. "May I join you?" he asked once they had arrived at the singing-tree spot. "I can aid in your adaptation."

Pound was seriously preoccupied. "Certainly," he mumbled, "why not?" Harlan initially disapproved, only on principle, until he remembered he was just along for the ride as well.

They all piled in and the O'Neil Drive was instigated. The esc-star jumped off the ground as if the planet were a magnet of the opposite pole.

While they were speeding out of the atmosphere, Harlan finally gave vent to something that had been bothering him for a while. "So where is everybody?" It was true. The visitors hadn't seen anyone except the ruler, his son, and the BOP rep. Trigor was thinking that the Sorcerer Supreme purposely had the esc-star land away from the populace.

Sparx was unfazed. "In their homes."

The soldier checked, but Roscoe was still inside his own head. There was no evidence he had even heard the question, let alone disapproved. "In their homes?" Harlan pressed. "Just sitting in their homes?" It didn't make sense to him. Where were the children? Where were the birds, the animals?

"Doing magic," Sparx said, happily watching his planet dwindle below his feet. He didn't see the looks of surprise and suspicion on the hitchhikers' faces.

"I thought you said they couldn't do magic!" Napoleon disputed. Sparx looked to her in mild confusion.

"No, no," he corrected. "They cannot complete their spells. But they can still devise them. This is a planet of wizards and witches. We would be foolish not to take advantage of Coven's natural properties."

"But, but . . ." the soldier sputtered.

"If anyone creates what they feel is a perfect spell, they are free to present it to the Sorcerer Supreme. He and his GOBS."

"Guardians of the Big Spell," Napoleon guessed dryly. Sparx nodded with enthusiasm.

"Very, very good. You are extremely perceptive. I am just thankful you are not black. At any rate, the GOBS will examine and study the spell extensively to calibrate what Back Side effect it might have. Only when they are certain it is to the populace's benefit without causing wholesale destruction will they allow it to be cast."

"How long does that take?" Trigor inquired.

"A few years," Sparx shrugged. "No more."

They were aghast. Napoleon could only imagine the sorcerers' feelings after years of free witchcraft, to be yoked in this manner. It seemed humans were the same all over. It reminded her of old Earth's strangulating government controls. "Have any new spells ever been passed?"

"Certainly. The Empty was one such."

Harlan couldn't resist. "What was the Back Side to that?"

Sparx didn't blink an eye. "Every time it is used, someone sneezes."

Spot, Zero, and Muse welcomed them back with enthusiasm. No matter what the planetside results, they were about to embark on another great acting adventure. Pound gave them all a quick explanation, then hunkered down to work out the details during a run-through. It was during this rehearsal (or "reher prelim") that the robot problem cropped up. Pound demanded that Mess be re-created to take up the thespian slack.

" . . . Me!" the compubot blurted as Harlan secured the board inside a robot body. "What? What is this? Hey, what do you call this!" Mess "looked" at itself in chagrin. It could only see its interior by sending current through the aged connections. Harlan and Napoleon had to look at its outside.

They all sat in a long, narrow room crammed between the backstage area and the dressing rooms. Along one wall were thin metal arms which were Muse's waldoes. Along the other, within easy reach of the steel fingers, were spare parts. Muse had devised a cunning actobot for Mess to inhabit. It was two rectangles connected by a vertical pole.

The top rectangle was vaguely torso shaped and had two metal arms, much like the waldoes, one on each "shoulder." The bottom rectangle had ball-like wheels and special swinging metal sticks that spun in the direction the actobot moved. That was so, when a Shakespearean costume was draped upon the construct, the poking sticks would look like walking feet beneath the robes.

The niode-cirquid board went into a slot on the top of the oval steel head. Muse had given it two ball sensors for eyes, a metal triangle for a nose, and a long, horizontal speaker for a mouth. Mess was mortified.

"I can only see forward!" it blurted. "I have to turn to see behind me! Whose idea was this?"

"Mine," said Muse. "Ingrate."

Harlan wasn't going to allow this to escalate. He shoved a portoputer before Mess' ball sensors. "Memorize this."

Mess' hand came up to awkwardly grip the thin ledger. "What . . . what is this thing?" it complained about the arms. "This isn't one of my manifestations."

"You'll get used to it," Muse promised coldy.

"Where am I?" Mess bleated. "Who is that?"

"I am the stage manager," Muse informed him. "And you are Fleance, Young Seward, Macduff's son, a messenger, and one of the mystics." She/it obviously thought of Mess as unwanted competition. She/it would have been very happy to play the roles the new compubot was getting.

"I'm which?" Mess squeaked.

"Read," Napoleon commanded. "And memorize."

Mess' head creaked around until its sensors flashed on the feline's face. "Who are you?" it asked as if it had never seen her before.

"The other robots are playing all the lords, gentlemen, officers, soldiers, and attendants," Harlan said brusquely, concentrating on his own portoputer. "Napoleon and I play anything with names. So far, I'm King Ducan, Banquo, Siward, and Macduff. I think."

"Better find out," said Napoleon nervously. "We go on tonight."

"Don't worry," said Muse. "This is Shakespeare. Nobody really knows what's going on anyway."

# TWELVE

Roscoe was still working when the audience started filing in. His work would continue throughout the performance. He would edit and amend the scenes to make the drama hold together no matter what happened. As the sorcerers filed in, the atmosphere backstage rose to a hair-thin crescendo, and stayed there.

For the first time since Harlan and Napoleon had come on board, Zero and Spot were staying away from one another. Like Roscoe, they seemed engrossed inside themselves. The feline had watched as both looked at the floor and moved their lips. Occasionally they would gesture. Mostly, they stayed in their dressing rooms.

Napoleon wondered if theirs were anything like hers. All the rooms were architecturally the same; each had an entrance that connected to the bridge and another that connected to backstage. But the feline's was full of costumes, one for each of the characters she was to portray. Her major roles were to be the gentlewoman, an apparition, and a murderer. There were others, but they were minor.

For those, she could read off the lines from the paw-sized portoputer Pound gave her. Muse would see to it that the proper line would scroll out at the proper time. Memorizing wasn't as easy for her as it was for Mess or seemed to be for Harlan. He said that he was used to this sort of thing. Ceremonies on Destiny were even more ornate and ritualized.

Napoleon had always secretly harbored the belief that she could do as well as any VU star on Earth, but now that she had to make good on that claim, she wasn't too sure. But she'd be larried if she let that snot Spot get the better of her. If that—catty FM could do it, so could she.

"What do you think you're doing?" asked Muse in her ear.

"Just taking a look at the audience," said Napoleon, unfazed. She stood at the corner of the stage, peeking between the curtains.

"That's very unprofessional," Muse sniffed.

"They can't see me," the feline promised. To her disappointment, they didn't live up to Merlin Master's example. The Sorcerer Supreme himself was in the front row, center seat. He was decked out sumptuously and by the looks of it, he was ready for a ripping good time. He kept rubbing his hands together and pursing his lips in a long smile. Strangely, his son was nowhere to be seen.

Everyone besides the royal family seemed dowdy in comparison. Instead of being regal and majestic, they mostly looked like dotty eccentrics trying to look regal and majestic. Everyone was overweight and hairy. Their robes and accoutrements were garish and unwieldy.

"Still, it is just not done," Muse reprimanded. "Go back to your dressing room. We'll be starting soon."

But Napoleon was feeling frisky. She turned away from the curtain, but didn't go back to her dressing room.

Instead, she did a little dance in her first costume, the multicolored tatters swinging around her like waving fingers. She moved before the giant painted backdrop, which covered the stage's rear wall. The artwork pictured a palace expanse, complete with Coven-like foliage. In the corner of the work was a signature which read "Muse."

"Please," pleaded the artist, "clear the stage."

The feline went back to the bridge area. Roscoe and Muse had landed the *Shooting Star* perfectly in the square, using the O'Neil Drive so the grass and dwellings wouldn't be damaged. Then the theater's outer walls were unsealed and swung out, revealing a public entrance to the seats. All must have been in readiness planetside because Sparx stayed with the troupe.

The small sorcerer approached Napoleon now, his lips spread in a wide, understanding smile. "Don't worry," he advised. "You're going to be wonderful."

"Thank you," she smiled back. "Aren't you going to join your friends? You've been with us for hours. Why don't you eat something before we start?"

"Don't worry," repeated the warlock. "I'll eat later. With my friends."

"There you are," said Harlan, approaching. Sparx smiled at his placid countenance, then moved away. The soldier was wearing his first costume, as Banquo. It was a brown tunic with pants and a rich red vest. On his arms were shimmering gray sleeves. Muse had promised him that the sleeves and the tight body stocking beneath would turn shiny white when he became Banquo's Ghost. It was all in the lighting, Muse had said.

"Get ready for a long night," Napoleon advised.

"What makes you say that?" Harlan asked dryly, pulling at his bulky costume.

"Looks like a very dry audience."

"You've seen them?"

Napoleon nodded and Muse clucked, "Very unprofessional." Harlan asked for, almost demanding, a description of what she saw. When the feline saw his expression, she wanted to know what was on his mind.

"I'm not sure," he said intently. "But I've spent too many years as a soldier not to follow my instincts. For some reason my stomach muscles are clenching."

"Oh, that's just stage fright," Muse laughed. "Once you get going, they'll go away, believe me. Just follow your instincts and you'll do fine. Uh-oh." The compubot paused. "Get ready," she reported. "We're starting."

"Where's Mess?" Napoleon asked.

"In the actobot area," Muse informed her. "It's going through the spare parts, repeating, 'That's no good,' over and over."

The three Earthen fugitives reunited offstage in the company of several other actobots. Across from them were Spot and Zero, alone on the other side of the stage. To simplify matters, the two "stars" always entered stage left, and everything else entered stage right.

Roscoe had also cut the first two scenes and most of the third to eliminate the witches. Nobody wanted to see what would happen if their line, "Posters of the sea and land thus do go about, about; thrice to thine and thrice to mine, and thrice again to make up nine," was said.

Instead, they heard the strange sounds of the audience. At first it sounded like a great rustling, but then they realized it was many people sneezing in turn. "They must be coming from all over the place to get here," Napoleon figured.

Harlan was secure in his memory of every line of the play. Any man who could control the encyclopedic functions of a space bullet could handle a lousy little five-act play. Instead, he thought about the face of Merlin Masterson as it leered at Napoleon. He thought about all that had been said and all he had seen. And his stomach wouldn't stop clenching.

Napoleon's low, kittenish chuckle interrupted his reverie. It was starting. Muse was working her own magic. The stage was bathed in colors and the front curtain started rolling up. He looked down to see the portoputer in his hand flashing "BEGIN."

Harlan resisted the temptation to stick his head out. He knew the lights would blind him to the audience's faces, and to the third-level glass Roscoe sat behind, controlling the entire affair. He looked instead to his companions. Napoleon's features were lit with excitement and a touch of self-doubt. Mess said and showed nothing.

The soldier found himself thinking, "Poor thing." Muse had hammered into it the meaning and importance of the stage presentation. If Mess screwed up here, it'd have her/it to answer to. And she/it had made Mess' new body. She/it was a third deity to Mess now, right behind Palsy-Drake and Larry.

"So fair and foul a day I have not seen," Zero said. It was the new first line of the LOST's *Macbeth*. It was also Harlan's cue. He joined Mess and another actobot on stage. The other robot (playing Ross) got the ball rolling.

"The king hath happily received, Macbeth, the news of thy success. . . ."

Napoleon was thrilled by Harlan's first line. "What? Is this true?" The line was originally, "What? Can the devil speak true?" but everyone thought it best to eliminate all references to devils and demons. No one wanted the fellows showing up.

Still, the feline was delighted by Trigor's ease on stage. Pound had simplified things enormously, having the leads stay on their side of the stage and everyone else staying on their own side, but the drama of the Macbeths' plan to kill the king had impact. Even Mess was no problem. It said its words with the import they carried. All had worked with different languages for so long that Shakespeare's tongue was relatively easy pickings.

That only left Napoleon's own entrance. The scenes rolled on while the feline became more and more concerned. As scene four went on, with all the actobots, Harlan, and Zero blathering about the Thane of Cawdor (whatever it was) and the Prince of Cumberland (whoever he was), her heart beat faster and faster. For a moment she thought she couldn't speak at all. She had to mew just to make sure she still had a voice. But no amount of swallowing could eliminate the dryness in her throat.

Then scene five started and Spot came on. Napoleon dodged the exiting actobots and took Harlan's arm. "I've got to change," he whispered. "I'm the king in scene six." She reluctantly let him go. She watched him nimbly and silently make his way to his dressing room where Muse's waldoes waited to lift off one tunic and drop another, on.

Harlan instinctively understood the theatrical semantics involved. They were putting on a show, so it wouldn't do to talk normally offstage or lumber around while Spot and Zero were emoting. He assumed that the only way for an audience to enjoy a presentation like this was to play it straight and hard. He had been at enough boring presentations on Destiny to understand that. And, of course, a space bullet was fearless.

Sadly, the same was not true of the Mandarin feline. She just got more and more nervous. What if she forgot what she was supposed to say? What if she couldn't see the lines Pound was putting on her portoputer? The only thing that distracted her from her paranoia was Spot's first lines. The SM had come sweeping out on stage in a gorgeous gown, the top of her breasts gleaming with ethereal light, her hair curled out in a grand mane, opened her mouth, and spoke directly to the audience.

"They met me in the day of success. While I stood, there came missives from the king, which hailed me. This have I thought good to deliver thee, my dearest partner of greatness. . . ."

At first Napoleon rationalized that Spot was supposed to be reading a letter. That was why her tone was so flat. But then Lady Macbeth finished the letter and sank into her actual lines.

"It is too full of the milk of human kindness to catch the nearest way. Thou wouldst be great. Art thou not without ambition? But without the illness that should attend it?"

The constriction that had wrapped around Napoleon's chest dissipated and the feline's face broke out in a wondrous realization that made her whole evening. "By Cheshire!" she breathed. "She's lousy!"

The remainder of the first two acts went by the feline in a whirl. The murder of King Duncan was the best. While Zero hacked at the stage-blood-spouting dummy, Spot lay in a regal bed, naked, Muse's lighting making the SM's creamy skin glow. Napoleon finally got on stage as a lady in attendance, but she didn't get to speak until act three, when she played one of the murderers.

Harlan watched the scene roll by, filled with a pride he was surprised he felt. He watched Napoleon lay it on thick, hissing and spitting her murderer's speech out with more than a little realism.

"I am one, my liege, whom the vile blows and buffets of the world have so incensed that I am reckless what I do to spite the world. I am so weary with disasters, tugged with misfortune, that I would set my life on any chance, to mend it or be rid of it."

The audience was with her too. To the whole cast's surprise, the sorcerers proved to be an enthusiastic lot, who both applauded and were vocal in their support. They gasped and laughed in almost all the right places.

Then the first scene of act three was over and the feline came bounding offstage and right into Harlan's arms. There was something about performing that flushed a person with enthusiasm.

"Better go get the ax," Harlan whispered in her ear. The third scene, Banquo's murder, was coming up. Napoleon, as the first murderer, had to swing the weapon at Harlan as Banquo while Muse shot blood all over the place. " 'Safe in a ditch he bides,' " the script said of the death. " 'With twenty trenched gashes on his head.' "

Napoleon went to where the ax should have been, on one of the prop tables, as Spot and Zero did scene two. The weapon was not there. "Muse?" the feline called quietly. "Where's the ax?"

"You took it," the compubot replied hastily.

"I did not."

"I saw you. Where did you leave it?"

"I didn't. Where is it?"

Muse said nothing as she/it made a hasty circuit of possible locations. She/it hated to be perplexed. "I don't have time for this. Get back to stage right."

Napoleon stood her ground, tail slashing. Then she hurried back to Harlan on all fours.

"Treason has done its worst," Zero was saying to a diffident Spot. "Nor steel, nor poison. Malice domestic, foreign intrigue, nothing can touch him further. Duncan is in his grave."

"The ax is gone," Napoleon told Harlan. "Muse said I took it."

Trigor had to think about it for only a moment before the stomach clenching returned as one long clench. "Taplinger-Jones," he cursed. "Merlin Masterson is not in the audience?"

"Not when I looked."

"Mess," Harlan beckoned. "You're Banquo."

"I can't be," it bleated. "I'm Fleance." Banquo's son.

"Fleance doesn't have to be on stage," Harlan said, already moving.

"But the party scene's after," Mess complained. Napoleon shushed the compubot's loud tones. "Everything'll be on stage!" it said in a lower tone.

"Take my lines," Harlan said over his shoulder as he went to the prop table.

"Where are you going?" Muse demanded. "You're Banquo and Banquo's Ghost!"

"Where's the ax?"

"The feline took it."

"She did not."

"I saw her!"

"Are you sure?"

"Of course! Wait—oh, no!"

"For now I am bent to know," Zero said on stage, "by the worst means, the worst."

"There were two," Harlan said for her/it, already moving into the bridge area, and not meaning the axes. "Find it!"

"I am in blood," Zero said. "Stepped in so far that, should I wade no more, returning would be as dangerous as continuing."

"Roscoe?" Muse called. "Roscoe!"

Harlan raced around through the side hall. Just on the other side of the wall was the audience. At the end of the hall was a left turn which led to Pound's booth in the back. The soldier could practically smell the odor of his target and feel the heat of the enemy's footprints on the floor.

"Strange things I have in head that will to hand," said Macbeth. "Which must be acted ere they may be scanned."

Harlan hurled open the plain booth door. There, before him, Roscoe Pound lay sprawled across his console table, blood covering his head. And behind him stood Harlan's feline companion with a crimson-dripping ax.

# THIRTEEN

The eerie light from the control board was the only illumination in the tiny room. The fur-covered feline reared back, the ax in its paws. Harlan moved forward with blinding speed. When his blurred body was focused again, his right palm was straight out from his torso, having smashed into the false Napoleon's chest like a sledgehammer.

The cat flew back, hitting the wall hard. The ax jerked out of its paws. Harlan caught it in midair, and only a tremendous effort of will kept him from cutting off the feline's head with it. Instead, he stepped forward, making sure the cat remained where it had sunk to the floor. Before his eyes, the feline disappeared.

Sparx the Elder cringed in her place. His eyes held no shame, embarrassment, or even chagrin at being caught. The eyes were red, filled with only frenzy. He leaped up, grabbing for Harlan's hair. Trigor's right upper cut was so devastating that it sent Sparx' head into the booth ceiling. As the sorcerer fell, Harlan swept his arm into the man's chest. Sparx slammed back into the rear wall.

Harlan's expression was barely controlled rage. The vague disquiet he had been nursing since joining the LOST bloomed into certain disgust. He made sure Sparx was unconscious (sorcerers were human still) and checked Roscoe. To his slight relief, the human's eyes fluttered when he was pulled off the console.

Harlan tapped Roscoe's face and the brown eyes snapped completely open. Then he grabbed for his head. The soldier plucked the man's wrists in midair so his fingers couldn't do any more damage. "What happened?" Roscoe moaned.

Harlan had always hated that cliché. "Sparx the Elder was attacking you," he answered anyway. "Do audiences always do this?"

"Sparx? No, Napoleon . . . Napoleon attacked me!"

"No," Trigor said. "Sparx was disguised as the feline." He studied Pound's wound. Thankfully it was not deep. But the blood had made smeared red channels all over Roscoe's head.

"Sparx? But . . . what?" The soldier ignored the man's confused mutterings. Instead, he instantly made some assumptions. The sorcerer had risked a Back Side to change into Napoleon in order to approach Pound without suspicion, even when holding an ax. But the ax? Why not stab him or choke him or hit him with something else?

The sorcerer's eyes had been maddened. He had chopped Pound's head at the crown. He had torn at Harlan's hair. He had wanted to get to the tops of their heads. Either of their heads.

Trigor looked over Roscoe's drooping skull to the glass partition and beyond. It was the party scene, act three, scene four, with the entrance of Banquo's Ghost. "Pray you, keep seat," Spot was saying flightily. "The fit is momentary. Upon a thought, he will again be well."

The audience didn't seem to be listening to her. They were moving in their seats. Harlan quickly checked the door. He had torn it from its moorings. It would offer the director no protection.

"Roscoe," Trigor said, grabbing his arm. "Come on." He dragged the groggy man into the hall. He had almost made it to the first audience door when Merlin Masterson lurched out.

Harlan threw Pound back. The director stumbled and fell on his side, red dotting the floor. The soldier moved himself back, to put room between him and the hunched, thin man in the black robe. Harlan's hands were at his side, open, ready for whatever. "I knew it would be you," he said.

Masterson's head rose. His eyes were orange, seemingly burning. "No," he said torturously. "My father . . . !" Harlan suddenly realized that the sorcerer was not in a crouched position of attack readiness, but in the contorted posture of a man possessed.

"Masterson, what is it?"

"My father," he grunted. "Tried to keep me . . . but I . . . escaped."

"What is going on?" Harlan demanded. He now knew that each word had to escape Masterson's clamping mind as well as his writhing lips.

Masterson laughed, trying to break the supernatural prison inside his skull. His mirth created a crack for a clue to get out. "The planet nourishes and protects us," he quoted his father. "Have you not seen food? Have you not seen the children?"

The words hit Harlan like surf. For all the declarations of welcome, no food or drink was ever offered them. And Napoleon had described an audience of only adults.

There was not a single child among the sorcerers, not even Merlin Master's son.

An ugly truth began to take shape outside Harlan's head. He felt it start crawling into his mind on long, hairy legs.

"The Big Spell," Masterson choked, hardly able to keep his feet. "The Back Side!" He stumbled forward, his hands up like claws. His eyes were now completely red. "Stop me! Please!" Harlan stepped in between the sorcerer's clutching hands and drove the young man's jaw back with his fist. A sharp snapping sound echoed down the hall and Masterson dropped onto his back.

"Ooh," Roscoe groaned, having dragged himself onto his knees, his hands holding his ears to keep them on his head.

"Pound!" Harlan snapped. "Is there any safe place on the ship? Anywhere you can lock yourselves in?"

"What?" he replied, not looking up. "Locks? No . . . not really."

"Trigor," Muse called warningly. Harlan turned back at the sound of other people in the hall. At the opposite end were three male Coverners. Harlan could tell by their expressions, and the thick wands they held in their hands, that these were the guards Merlin had left to keep his son imprisoned.

The sticks held no fear for the Destinian. He had been trained with the bow and staff on his home planet. Instead, he watched their eyes, gateway to their brains, and the signal to the control of the Big Spell's Back Side. He swept among the charging trio, his hands shooting out to deflect the weapons and his legs sweeping up to trip and kick them.

His first move pushed one against the wall, tripped another and dropped the third onto his back. Harlin hit the first hard, bouncing his head against the wall he was sandwiched against, and then threw him onto the tripped second. While he was pinned by the first, Harlan kicked him in the head. Then he spun and took two giants steps toward the third, who was just getting up.

He was searching for his dropped wand, so his back was to Trigor. Harlan's foot met his rear and he was catapulted into the side of the doorway. His head made a nasty cracking sound, then he slid to the floor and lay still. Harlan spun in time to see Sparx come roaring around the corner. He raced right for the kneeling Pound.

Harlan scooped up a wand and threw it like an under-hand javelin. It caught Sparx in his open mouth. The man's head seemed to crackle and he jumped back while still moving forward, causing him to spin upside down in midair. When he crashed to the floor, Harlan had already collected the stunned Roscoe and was beating it to the stage door.

"I didn't know," Muse babbled. "I can't see into Ros-coe's booth!"

"It's all right," Harlan barked. "Get the others offstage."

"Avaunt! And quit my sight!" Zero shouted to Ban-quo's Ghost. "Let the earth hide thee! Thy bones are marrowless, thy blood is cold, thou hast no speculation in those eyes which thou dost glare with!"

Napoleon looked down at her blinking portoputer. In big, green, flashing letters, it said "RUN."

"Run!" Napoleon said, thinking it a new line of dialogue.

Spot did a double take at what she thought was the feline's ad lib, then went on with her speech. "Think of this, good peers, but as a thing of custom. 'Tis no other. Only it spoils the pleasure of the time."

"No," said Mess. "It's not a line. It's a stage direction. Run."

Spot and Zero ignored it. "What man dare, I dare,"

the FM Macbeth continued, inwardly cursing the amateur help.

Harlan left Roscoe on Muse's console and raced for his suit. He didn't even slow when he was debating whether to collect Napoleon first. If she was in any trouble, it would be best that he was in his space bullet first, rather than both of them having to fight back to it.

With one bounding leap, he was off the floor of his quarter's entrance and soaring in the air toward the open top of the granite statue. A red-eyed Coverner came roaring out of the neck opening, its clawing fingers clutching for Harlan's head.

Trigor pivoted in space. He landed (like a cat) on the shoulders of the suit and angrily tore the Coverner from his precious armament by the throat. He grabbed and jerked once, hurling the sorcerer from his hiding place like a goldfish plucked from a fishbowl. The sorcerer smashed headfirst into the wall, his limbs flopping around him like a stepped-on spider.

Even before he hit the floor, Trigor was in his suit with the exoskeleton over his head. The suit practically leaped into life, Harlan's anger fueling it. With an incredible effort of will and a large depletion of its standing power source, he got it hovering off the ground and the head screwing on. But before that turning fixture locked in place, a single white bolt cut a hole in the sorcerer who had dared to trespass.

The space bullet became horizontal and floated into the hall. It sank lower and lower until it was five inches off the floor. The standing power source was not fast enough. Harlan hovered vertically again, then disengaged the suit's legs. The Destinian stone's amazing properties allowed two leglike limbs to appear from the solid base and slide the suit toward the stage.

"What should I do?" Muse cried inside the suit.

"Protect Roscoe any way you can," Harlan ordered.

"And tell the others!" He slid as fast as the suit allowed him toward the backstage door.

"Approach thou like the rugged Russian bear," Zero was saying to Banquo's Ghost, who kept telling everyone to run. "The armed rhinoceros, or the Hyrcan bear. Take any shape but that, and my firm nerves shall never tremble. Or be alive again and dare me to the desert with thy sword. If trembling I inhabit then, protest me the baby of a girl. Hence horrible shadow! Unreal mockery, hence!"

The houselights came up. The actors looked down at a red-eyed audience which was crawling on stage, led by a horribly grinning Merlin Master. His slithering manner and the expression on his face immediately spoke to Napoleon's heart, mind, and stomach. There was the timeless second when she just looked at the sea of bodies coursing toward her, but then her mouth was open and her feet were moving.

"Run!" she howled. She ran right into Harlan's space bullet. He didn't have to scoop her up. She climbed onto his shoulders with two pulls. Zero grabbed Spot's arms and threw her behind him. He whipped out his stage sword and faced the mob the way the Thane of Cawdor would.

"We're acting artificials!" Spot wailed. "We don't know how to deal with this!"

"Then act like you're fighting for your lives!" shouted Napoleon. "Act very realistically!"

Zero swung his prop blade at the first thing that came at them. It smacked against a sorcerer's head, knocking the attacker back. But the next attacker grabbed Zero's wrist. And the third grabbed his hair.

Bam. Bam. Two off-white ovals snapped into being against Zero's attackers. They were thrown along the stage and into the side curtains by the shattering force of the space bullet's finger blasts. Spot looked to see a right

arm had detached itself from the suit, and a forefinger
was pointing from the hand.

A lightning bolt cut a half-inch channel in the stage in
front of the crawling sorcerers. They didn't even slow.
"No warnings shots," Napoleon hissed. "Where's my
spitter?"

Harlan's second lightning bolt went from stage left to
stage right, dancing across the foreheads of the leading
magicians. They were all sent into the sorcerers behind
them. They made a big pile off the end of the stage.

Spot was crying in terror. "What is this?" Zero yelled
at the feline.

"Everything has a Back Side!" Harlan answered for
them all. "Even the Big Spell!"

"This is it!" Napoleon realized. "WHERE'S MY
SPITTER?"

Zero quickly helped Spot to her feet and pushed her
back toward the bridge. The sorcerers were uncoiling
themselves from the pile and climbing onto the stage
again. Muse dropped the curtain on them. "Get back!"
she/it called.

"What do they want?" Spot wailed.

"Our heads," Harlan told them. He started to slide
backward.

"Into the bridge!" Muse cried.

"Go!" Harlan instructed the feline. She sprang off his
shoulders and landed on all fours several feet ahead of
the artificials. She ran that way into the bridge area
where Roscoe was slumped in his chair. She kept going
until she reached her dressing room. From her magster
she pulled her spitter and strapped the beamer to her
back.

Muse dropped all the hanging scenery flats onto the
sorcerers as they snaked across the stage. Harlan was the
only one left, but the weighted stage-sized paintings
couldn't hurt his suit. That was more than could be said

for the wizards and witches. The huge tarps broke their skin and some bones. Whoever dodged the falling canvases got a finger blast in the chest or head.

"Protect Roscoe," Muse pleaded to the feline. "Protect the actors. Trigor can take care of himself!" Spot didn't chortle at the mention of Harlan's name this time.

"What about me?" Mess screeched, leading a bunch of actobots onto the bridge deck.

Muse only paused a millisecond. "Get in here!" A flap on her/its console popped open. Before Napoleon's startled eyes, the compubot rolled to the console, bent its head down, and slapped the top of its "skull" into the opening. She saw the niode-cirquid board shoot out of Mess and into Muse.

She returned her attention to the TM, FM, and SM. The compubots must have been in silent communication for Mess to know what to do. Or it had been instinctive, like metal sex. Muse's following single exclamation of "Oh," certainly gave credence to that theory.

The feline instantly saw that her/its suggested strategy was no good. "I can't leave Harlan out there."

"Wait," Muse grunted. "Please. Just a ... moment."

"He won't come back here," Napoleon said. "He won't risk the sorcerers getting in here. He'll defend the stage doors." She realized it as soon as she said it. She was already whirling around to face the dressing room doors. She swept a band of spitter ammo across the openings as the sorcerers started to pile out. The pole beams chopped them down and drove them back.

"Zero!" Napoleon yelled. "Do you know how to use a beamer?"

She knew the answer even before he said, "A what?" An FM was never allowed to touch a weapon. "Put the switch at the base to yellow, then point it at the dressing room door. Oh, what's the use!" She kept firing the spitter with one paw and pulled the beamer down with the other. She lashed her tail around the dial and swung it to a wide aperture. Then she brought the barrel up.

A beam of light bathed all the doors at once, anesthetizing everyone there. The bridge was suddenly, awfully quiet. Napoleon stood, slightly crouched, her hair on end, both weapons aimed at the side doors. Zero stared fearfully at the open backstage door. Spot desperately clung to him, her head tight against his neck. Roscoe Pound suddenly came crawling out of his chair on all fours.

"The BS," he mumbled. "The BS. Everything has a back side, everything."

"Yes," Napoleon growled. "We know. Now what?"

Harlan echoed the sentiment. He blocked the backstage door, watching in amazement as the sorcerers began to scale the sides of the theater, crawling along the balconies and lighting fixtures. Some had even reached the halfway point when a lightning bolt from the space bullet electrified the metal framework, sending sorcerers screaming off the metal bars.

The smoking bodies hit the stage and bounced. Before they settled, other sorcerers leaped on them, tearing at the corpses' heads. They crawled to other bodies whose skulls had been cracked open by the falling curtains and scrims. Some others even tore at the skulls of fallen actobots. The still living witches and wizards dug into the dead people's heads, pulling out hunks of brain.

Harlan distinctly saw them rip a tiny bean-shaped nodule from the skulls and pop it in their mouths. They fought like wild animals over who would get to eat it, clawing at each other and whining. The space bullet pounded at them with his blasts and bolts. They flew away as if a grenade had detonated under each group. The dead bodies flopped in place like Muse's theatrical dummies.

Harlan couldn't help but wonder how many other visitors had been welcomed by singing trees, then had their brains sucked out. But the operative question now was, what were they going to do about it? Spot had an immediate suggestion.

"Kill them! Kill them all!"

It made a certain amount of sense to Napoleon. "We can eradicate what's here, then take off," she said.

"They're all over the ship by now," Harlan advised.

"We don't have interior weaponry," Roscoe groaned.

"We could hunt them down," Napoleon suggested.

"They're on board? They're on board?" shrieked Spot hysterically. Zero put a hand over her mouth and dragged her down to the floor, speaking intently in her ear. She kicked and flailed away from him, still screeching.

"Be quiet, Phyllis!" Roscoe shouted and then moaned in pain. Spot almost instantly stilled, standing in place like a chastised child.

Harlan watched as Merlin Master's head appeared at the edge of the stage. He had just untangled himself from the initial pile. There was a large black stain across his forehead. Much to the soldier's distress, the red-eyed face began speaking.

"Patience," he said. "Patience, my loves. Quell your hunger. Calm yourselves until the red desperation courses from your body." It had a promising start, but a horrible finish. Merlin seemed to look right into Trigor's eyes.

"Then use the magic, my children," he said. "Use your magic to get your meal."

# FOURTEEN

Harlan slid into the bridge area and slammed the back-stage door closed as sorcerers poured in the door from the *Shooting Star* hallway. Napoleon whirled around as the space bullet sent a bolt right through the bodies of the first three wizards scrambling through. The feline sent spitter bolts into the fray, killing others as they tried to claw by.

"Napoleon!" Zero yelled. She turned back as more sorcerers leaped through the four dressing room doors on the opposite wall. A beamer blast felled most of them, but two got through. Harlan blasted one. Napoleon spitted the other. It slid on the floor to her feet.

"Get to the middle of the room," Harlan ordered. The actors ran over to Napoleon. Roscoe crawled on all fours, his face a mask of red stripes. "Muse, get the actobots to circle them." The compubot did not reply.

"Muse!" Roscoe bellowed in pain.

"Please," her/its weak voice pleaded. "Please...."

"Muse, no!" Roscoe barked, his vision clouding. "Muse, intensify, centralize!"

Everyone looked at the wounded man in confusion until the compubot voice they recognized returned. "Understood," she/it snapped. The robots started moving toward the people.

Napoleon couldn't help but wonder what that conversation meant, but she didn't have time to dwell on it. None of them did. "Harlan, what are you doing?" the feline demanded.

"The sorcerers are about to use magic," he said as the space bullet's feet slid him across the deck. "BS be larried."

"Magic?" Spot gasped. "They could do anything to us!"

"What are you going to do?" Zero shouted. "Kill everyone on the planet?"

"If we have to," Napoleon said grimly. She started to move toward the dressing rooms between two approaching actobots, fully expecting Harlan to head back to the stage. She felt certain he knew what had to be done. Neither of them were strangers to slaughter.

"You're not thinking," he reprimanded, continuing to slide toward them. "We wouldn't stand a chance."

Napoleon stopped dead. "But we could die fighting!" she flared.

"For what?" he countered.

Roscoe misunderstood. "He's right. What's the use?" he mourned. "We can't fight magic."

"Yes, we can," the space bullet announced. "But we only have a few seconds while the sorcerers prepare."

The image of comatose sorcerers was too much for Napoleon. "Kill them! Kill them now!"

Harlan's stone arm reached out to take the feline's. It was an unbreakable grip, but a tender one all the same. "I can't risk it. They could be ready at any time. We can't afford to be divided. If we die, we die together." Napoleon looked up at the blank slate face, then returned to the group, biting her lower lip and swishing her tail.

"Mess, Muse, it's all up to you now," Trigor called. "The magic of this planet can be discovered in its laws of nature. You can harness it through spells and incantations. Those are based on numerals and letters that lock into natural powers." Harlan only wished he could be as certain as he sounded.

"Intensify, centralize," Roscoe repeated. "Protect us."

The space bullet slid up to the feline. They stood back to back. Harlan took in the backstage and dressing room doors. Napoleon watched the hall door. They waited, weapons at the ready, for the appearance of Coven's human monsters.

They didn't have long to wait. New surges of sorcerers appeared in the doors within seconds. Napoleon took a last look at Muse's silent console and pulled both triggers. The wide beam had narrowed to a dark orange bolt which seemed to fold the attackers wherever it touched them. The spitter continued to perforate the bodies with aqua-smoked punctures.

Harlan just kept blasting the demons back. Three fingers had appeared on the hand of his right arm. The off-white ovals seemed to slam into the air itself, creating a combination wall and battering ram. The sorcerers would surge forward and then be hurled back. They flew off their feet, their arms and legs askew. They crashed into the hall and against the dressing room walls, breaking arms and legs and necks.

The bolts from the space bullet head arced to the backstage door, making the sorcerers dance in place before collapsing. It had a macabre power in Spot and Zero's eyes, as the pathetic-looking, hairy, overweight people in the loud robes jerked their waists, shoulders, knees, and elbows before dropping.

Harlan and Napoleon fought intently and professionally, without anguish, just waiting for Coven to swallow them up with witchcraft.

Spot's lips moved back off her clenched teeth. Zero held her tighter and pulled her head to his shoulder. He felt her mouth moving against his shirt. At first he thought she was babbling, but then he began to hear the words. Soon he recognized them. Then he was saying them along with her.

Macbeth. Act four, scene one.

"Double, double, toil and trouble; fire, burn and caldron, bubble." Roscoe looked up, blinking the dried, flaking blood from his eyes. His eyes widened and he almost smiled. If they were to go down, then they would go down fighting—fire with fire. "Fillet of a fenny snake, in the caldron boil and bake. Eye of newt and toe of frog, wool of bat and tongue of dog. Adder's fork, and blind worm's sting, lizard's leg and howlet's wing. For a charm of powerful trouble, fire burn and caldron bubble."

The ceiling of the bridge disappeared. Everyone but Harlan couldn't help but look up. "Taplinger-Jones," the feline snarled. "I don't know about this."

"Who did that?" Roscoe blurted.

"If fire rains down from the sky," Harlan said, "they did. If not, we did. Keep going, we've got nothing to lose."

The hitchhikers fired between the protecting robots, and the actors kept chanting, "Scale of dragon, tooth of wolf, witches' mummy, maw and gulf. Of the ravined salt-sea shark, root of hemlock digged in the dark. Liver of blaspheming Jew, gall of goat and slips of yew. Slivered in the moon's eclipse, nose of Turk and Tartar's lips. Finger of birth-strangled babe, ditch delivered by a drab. Make the gruel thick and slab, add thereto a tiger's chaudron. Cool it with a baboon's blood, then the charm is firm and good."

A sorcerer's forefinger popped off. Another's side tore open. A nose ripped off one's face, and the lips of another. Finally a fifth sorcerer's head burst off its neck. Although all of these things happened to already felled sorcerers' bodies, the sights and sounds were ugly. Guts poured across the bridge deck. Spot buried her head on Zero's shoulder, Zero turned his head, and Roscoe nearly retched.

"Is that the spell or the Back Side?" Napoleon wondered, still firing. The sorcerers before Harlan started slipping in the grue. He blasted them as they dropped, keeping a space bullet "eye" on the sky. It was Coven's sky and the Coverners might drop anything on them from it.

"What difference does it make?" he grunted.

"By the pricking of my thumbs," Spot sobbed, "something wicked this way comes." "Act one, scene three!" Roscoe called out from his knees.

"I myself have all the other," Zero started before Spot joined in, their voices growing in strength. "And the very ports they blow all the quarters that they know. I the shipman's card. I will drain him dry as hay. . . ." A sorcerer's guts began to pump out from his open mouth.

"Don't look!" Roscoe pleaded. "Keep going."

"Sleep shall neither night nor day." Only Zero could continue. "Hang upon his penthouse lid, he shall live a man forbid. Weary nights nine times nine, shall he dwindle peak and pine. . . ."

They all heard the screams from outside the walls. They could imagine some sorcerer dwindling.

"Though his bark cannot be lost, yet it shall be tempest tossed. . . ." A sorcerer's skin torn from its body?

"Here I have a pilot's thumb," Zero just managed to say between gagging. "Wrecked as homeward he did come." He had to stop, imagining the pop of another sorcerer's digit.

"How many of these creatures are there?" Napoleon exclaimed. "I'm running out of ammo." What she really wanted to know was when the enemy would fight back with their own magic and whether the LOST's own deaths would be this simple to cause.

"Coven is turning on its own," Harlan guessed. "It has to be. The spells must strike them first. We are aliens to this world. They have to create a spell that will redirect the planet's power toward us."

"Muse," Roscoe begged. "Protect us. Protect us, my love!" The console started to hum. Roscoe reached out, his fingers shaking. The metal was warm to the touch. "Hold on," he called to the others. "Just a little while longer."

Napoleon dropped her spitter. There was no more ammunition in it or on her tail band. She took the beamer in both paws and kept feeding the backstage door with debilitating light. She had to turn the intensity down. She couldn't afford to run dry too soon.

As soon as she thought that, the sorcerers began to run through the light unscathed. "Har-lan!" she shrieked. The space bullet immediately pivoted and another arm sprang from his side. He stood, arms out, blasts coming from three fingers on one hand and two fingers on the other. The charging sorcerers were thrown back but not stopped. They hit the floor and walls, then struggled up to charge again.

The beamer had no effect anymore. The finger blasts were just pushes to them now. It started to rain.

Napoleon howled and howled as the cold water doused her, matting her silky fur. She turned the beamer all the way up, until its shaft of light was hair thin. It simply stopped at the sorcerer's bodies. They stopped too, making faces as if they had indigestion, but then just kept coming on. The beam hit the stage wall and cut a tiny hole right through it.

The space bullet's lightning danced in a circle around the LOST, eradicating the sorcerers' feet. They fell on their faces and slid toward them. Napoleon smashed each one in the head with the butt of the beamer, swinging it like a club. Spot and Zero huddled on the floor. Roscoe stayed on all fours but raised his head to the rain to wash the blood from his face.

"You!" the Sorcerer Supreme boomed. They looked up to see him above them, his arms wide. "You are the most precious. You are the most rare. You will have the most vitalizing effect. And we will hunger no more. First you shall die and then we shall feast."

The thunderbolt exploded directly in Merlin's middle. It shot from Harlan's head so quickly its path was not apparent until it struck. It seemed to disintegrate the sorcerer, but then Napoleon saw him fly backward over the far wall. The space bullet had struck it as hard as it could with the feline in proximity. If the LOST had not been there, she didn't doubt he would have treated it like an Earth Destroyer ship.

"They almost have the key!" Trigor seethed. "Climb on me."

When no one moved, Napoleon started snarling. "You heard him! Get on. Grab on to him anywhere you can get a hold." The feline pulled a screaming Spot up and vaulted her onto Harlan's crooked left arm. She sat on it like a tree branch. Zero needed no further encouragement. He did the same on the right arm. The feline helped Roscoe up onto the suit's shoulders and then she grabbed it around his waist.

"Hold tight," he instructed. "I'm going to have to blast to lift off."

It was at that moment that the acid began to fall and the magic got them.

Complete description was utterly impossible. Things as outlandish as the very fabric of existence being torn had resonance. First there was the burning pain of tens of burrowing dots across their bodies. Then came the attack on their beings. Until then none knew the reality of souls. For eternity after, they could not separate it from themselves. It was the ultimate falling sensation—the pain that attacked the nerves, the mind, and the psyche. It was forever, but if it had lasted any longer, they would have come back hopelessly insane.

Instead, it was as if they had ridden the rubber band. It had stretched out over damnation, then snapped back. Their minds were teased with barely comprehensible horror, then swung away. They returned to burning life with the words of a woman in their ears.

> "Hum hum hum
> Keys of the kingdom, spilled blood by Tegalon
>     insuperable
> onus of sea tide chosen light
> the wandsbearer
> by pride of the Estagoth
> and treasure in most holy portions
> night secret's torn
> arcohannigan arkohannigan narkaganiafin
>     pelosarus."

"Muse!" Roscoe cried thankfully. But she/it/they weren't hearing. She/it/they were beyond that now. Harlan fed a space bullet link in, but he could only start to understand what was happening inside the console. But he knew this much. First defense. She/it/they had to stop the acid and keep it away.

> "Hum hum hum
> let the red splendor
> diamonds of the hidden source

seen by eyes of Raimando of Xxormuccik
and swollen with the rains of Xxormuccaccon
bride to the sacred eleventh level masters
Amasind
Baarsalos
Kapheermene
Dap
Biit-Naquerloos
Rahal
Agsindsamund
tear the veil
rend the curse
by night or day
heaven storm earth anger."

The LOST lay crumpled on the deck floor, their hair
smoking, their skin bruised by dots of burning pain. But
while the rain had not stopped, the acid had. The water
now cleansed their wounds. Still, they huddled from it, an
ache washing over their exhausted bodies.

Inside the console the compubots clicked. They dove
deep into their memory banks, digging, collecting, align-
ing. They sucked in Coven air and Coven earth, analyzed
and organized. They shuffled it with past facts to achieve
future predictions. They drove the results through their
connections and into verbal form. Her/its voice droned
on, gathering in certainty and strength.

"Hum hum hum
surasolep nifainagakran ninnagohokra
    naginnhocra
as at the black sun's
blasted of ravaged moon
broken light

> by the stones
> made blessed in the book
> of Estagoth
> his word
> his will as well
> his wish
> scepter-bringer
> water giant
> moon wielder
> keys of the kingdom
> spilled blood by Tegalon insuperable
> this be done
> hum hum hum."

The rain stopped. The clouds did not part and the sun did not come out, but at least the rain stopped. Harlan stayed linked with the console, awaiting the next stage. He felt the electricity surge through the connections as her/it retreated and he/it attacked. For next, it was the magic. The magic had to go away. The LOST had to have its own Big Spell, no matter what the Back Side.

The magic was based on nature. Nature was based on math. The spell was sculpted from numerology. Mess, its mind dizzyingly powered, spat out the calculations.

> "PHASE ONE:
> $721.056 +/- .005$ C.
> 22.595 of planetary rotation
> as 3.14l59265881324 logarithm
> past largest star equinox
> OR
> $721.056 +/- .005$ C.
> 22.595 of planetary rotation
> as sine midwave of gravitational pulse

in galactic plasma
duration of tone as follows:
5243.973647281 kilocycles
748300857.11115 db
projecting:
laser or other photonic source
.000000003547869 tons particle mass
Spectrum violet (559543.003344567927
megacycles)
15.1065 seconds."

Nothing happened. There was no apparent change in their plight, but, as Harlan reasoned, at least they weren't all dead either. Before he could think of anything else, Mess tried again.

"PHASE TWO:
721.932 +/− .005
38.629 of planetary rotation
as 3.14159265881324 logarithm
past largest star equinox
OR
721.932 +/− .005
38.692 of planetary rotation
as sine midwave of gravitational pulse
in galactic plasma
duration of tone as follows:
5466.81459238 kilocycles
748317642.87542 db
projecting:
laser or other photonic source
.000000000225873 tons particle mass
spectrum blue (36428955.281774365 megacycles)
15.1065 seconds."

Harlan felt it. She/it/they had linked with what they felt sure was the magic source of the planet. And although he exulted with them, the fear was that the world wasn't having any of it. It was like a numerology wrestling match. Mess would hurl it to the mat, but Coven would slip out before he/it could pin it. Mess kept the sorcerers reeling (he/it was practically spinning their brains), but he couldn't quite unplug them.

"Caution," he/it said. "Shielding for phase three required. Self-destruction of photonic source better than seventy percent probability. Succeeding radiation half-life two forty-four point nine three two plus or minus point oh eight five billion solar years!"

Harlan didn't understand or hesitate. "Do it!"

"855.9222 +/− 0000002 C.
1.11562 of planetary rotation
as 3.14159265881324 logarithm
past largest star equinox
OR
855.9222 +/− 0000002 C.
1.11562 of planetary rotation
as cosign midwave of gravitational pulse
in galactic plasma
duration of tone as follows:
44812764379.003416 kilocycles
.00000000000553 db
projecting:
laser or other photonic source
971.5643 tons particle mass
spectrum white
.0000004 seconds."

It was done as it was said. They felt nothing and saw nothing, but the planet rolled over. It gave up the shield to the visitors. They had their cone of safety. The sorcerers could not get to them with practiced magic. They knew it, she/it/them knew it, and Harlan knew it. He trumpeted it to the others. The others were hardly in any condition to celebrate. Only Napoleon managed to get to her feet, and even then she fell heavily against the space bullet.

"Let's . . . kill them," she gasped.

"No, wait," Harlan said.

"We have to," Napoleon pressed as the magicians started to get to their own feet. "They can't use their magic, but they can still attack. We have to get them before they get us."

"Mess, Muse," Harlan signaled. "Keep going. The last step."

"What do you want?" Mess whined. "Isn't this enough?"

"No!" boomed Merlin Master. The Sorcerer Supreme remained hidden, but his voice came from everywhere. "Do you think you can counter hundreds of years of witchcraft that easily?"

"We just did!" Mess taunted.

"No! I say again, no! Your miserable, paltry shield cannot protect you for long. This world rails against your machinations."

"That's true," Mess mumbled.

"Our minds gather as one," Merlin warned. "Our powers unite. We shall smash through your protection. We shall reach you."

"Muse?" Roscoe called feebly.

"Come on," she/it called to he/it. Harlan felt them sink into themselves again. She/it instinctively knew the last step. They had to reach the core of the problem and solve it. They had to break the Big Spell itself.

Napoleon watched as the sorcerers stood. Whether they had gash wounds or were missing hands or heads, they stood. They stood in lines and in groups where they had fallen. They stood all around the cowering LOST, just staring at the circle of actobots which were shoulder to shoulder around the humanoids. The sorcerers just stood and stared.

It was not being able to see or hear any hint that was horrible. There was no hum, no murmur, no outward threat, and no movement. Napoleon knew that they all struggled to reach through the numerology shield, but she saw and heard nothing as warning. It was like standing over a trapdoor blindfolded. One never knew when one was going to drop into the darkness. One never knew what one was going to drop *on*.

"Harlan," she said desperately. His head spun open, he tore off the exoskeleton skull covering, and vaulted out of the suit. She dropped the beamer to embrace him. They held each other tightly, their eyes closed, her tail wrapped around his right thigh. Neither had to speak. They could die like this.

"I need a human of no sexual experience who has never taken the life of any organism within its genus," Muse blasted out in a monotone.

All eyes turned directly to the director. "Ros-coe?" Spot wailed in increasingly higher tones.

"Get over here," Muse spat. Roscoe walked stiffly, with increasing speed, toward the console. Another square on its surface popped open. "Take the wire there," she/it instructed sternly. Pound reached into the console. "No, not that one. No. Yes. No. Yes, that one. That one, take it." Roscoe pulled out a wire topped with a small metal ball. "Swallow it," said Muse.

Merlin Master flew in above them. "Prepare yourselves!" he laughed.

"Swallow it!" Muse screeched. Roscoe stuck the ball-topped wire deep into his mouth. He pushed and gagged. "Swallow it. Keep it in your throat." Roscoe choked and almost coughed it up. "I said keep it in your throat!" Muse chastised.

"Your time has come!" Merlin Master proclaimed.

"Shut up," Zero muttered.

"Pull on the wire," Muse told Roscoe. Harlan started for the director to help him, but Muse told him to keep back. "He has to do it. Pull it an inch. Good, now keep it there. Relax. Relax!" Pound started to shake. "Sit down," Muse snapped. "Go, sit down in your chair." He moved quickly to the deep seat while Muse fed slack to the wire to keep it in place. "Lean back. Close your eyes. Under no circumstances close your mouth. Do you hear me? Nod if you hear me."

He nodded.

"We have you now!" Merlin boomed.

"Shut up!" Zero shouted.

The sorcerers began to shamble forward.

From the pit of Roscoe's chair came a strange voice. They all looked away from the approaching creatures when the words started. Roscoe's own eyes popped open when he heard it. It was a strange amalgam of Muse's and Pound's voices. No . . . it was Pound's voice with Muse's inflections and tone. She/it was controlling his vocal cords with the ball-topped wire.

> "One o'clock
> two o'clock
> two o'clock
> three
> the bird in the woods
> is singing to me
> fly away
> fly away
> fly away home
> if I get home first
> his song is my own."

Napoleon couldn't help herself. She scooped up the beamer and bathed the sorcerers with orange light. It didn't slow them in the slightest. She kept firing until the beam faded and went out. Harlan held her back when she dropped the weapon. If she had not been declawed on Earth, her nails would have shredded his skin.

"Monday
Tuesday
Wednesday too
look at the clouds
they look at you
the grass is green
the sky is blue
open your eyes
see what's true
last to close
is Thursday's fool
first to open
isn't afraid
Friday to Sunday
he can play."

The sorcerers reached the actobots while Merlin Master laughed. The robots slammed at the creatures with their metal arms, but even though the magicians' skins were ripped open, they didn't fall. They grappled with the actobots, overwhelming them by sheer numbers.

Harlan had to clamp his jaw hard and hold on to Napoleon to keep from scrambling into his suit. He was sure they wouldn't be able to get to him in there through any method but magic, but he also knew that he would not be able to protect the others effectively while in there. The sorcerers were too close to their victims now. And he couldn't place Napoleon inside. The suit responded only to his touch.

Better to die with them than watch them die.

Roscoe started to talk real fast.

"A is for Apple, B for Ball, C for the Castle that
  stands so tall
D makes Daddy, E his ear, F the Flute we love
  to hear
G is the Goodness we ought to give
H the Heaven we then shall live
I is for me, I'm telling this rhyme
J for the Jewels that brightly shine
K stands for Kitten, L for Lips
  I use when I give Kitty a kiss
M is for Mother, N for Nose
O is for older as each of us grows
P is the pillow, soft for sleep
Q for the Quiet little ones should be
R is the Rose, S its Stem, and T the Thorn, its
  one defense
U Ukelele, V Violin
W the whisper and the whistle of the Wind
X is for X-ray, the healing light
Y is the Yes that means we're right . . ."

Roscoe's voice became hushed and deliberate as the sorcerers' bloody fingers touched the humans.

" . . . and Z is the secret
we'll never tell
the magic letter
that completes this spell
Z."

The sorcerers fell. Merlin Master, the Sorcerer Supreme, only had time to recognize his doom and scream before he fell from the sky, smashing into the deck face first.

Spot sobbed deliriously in Zero's arms, kissing him all over. Napoleon grabbed Harlan's head in both her paws and kissed him too, his beard and her fur mingling. Muse slowly pulled the wire from Roscoe's throat. It slithered out of the chair and across the floor like a bleeding snake. When Pound was finally able to struggle out of the seat's recesses, the LOST was there to cheer him.

"I don't understand," he managed to get out as they hugged him, clapped him on the shoulders and back, and shook his hands. Harlan Trigor smiled down at him, saying the one thing he knew was more true than anything else in the universe.

"If it works, you don't have to understand it."

# FIFTEEN

Coven was a vastly changed place when they stumbled out of the *Shooting Star*. The magic shield seemingly covered the alien ship as well as the aliens. All the Back Side effects, save the roof-raising one, pummeled the planet rather than the theater.

That was not to say that the theater itself was in any great shape. All the magic-powered sorcerers were now unleashed from the tyranny of the Big Spell. Those that were dead stayed dead, but those who were wounded felt all the pain and lost all the blood.

Merlin Masterson, who succeeded his dead father as leader of the populace, called an immediate emergency meeting of the greatest wizards and witches. His first action was to send away those who, like his late father, had resisted change.

Merlin Master had been a slave to the planet. He too felt that if it worked, he didn't have to understand it. He had allowed Coven's magical properties to keep him alive

forever without procreation or nourishment, other than
the occasional felial gland from the human brains of
visitors.

He had loved his son, the last child created naturally
on the world, but hated Masterson's rebellious nature.
The young man kept his emotions in check, but secretly
fermented revolution. He was only driven to open insubordination after meeting the recon-prelimming LOST
members. He couldn't stand the thought of seeing the
feline murdered in a blood frenzy.

The LOST stayed in the ship, repairing the damage
while the newly formed SOBS, the Survivors of the Big
Spell, tried to institute a new order. Many of the
wounded sorcerers died as the SOBS doublechecked
spells which might heal them. Those that survived were
soon repaired, although all suffered colds as a result.

The next order of business was to create a more natural life span and lifestyle. The SOBS gave the populace
back their sexual systems and ages. Although a new
mountain range appeared as a result, at least it didn't
appear on them. Finally, the new Sorcerer Supreme got
around to figuring out a spell to get the *Shooting Star's*
ceiling back on, much to Mess' disapproval.

"We do all the work, and they get all the credit," it
complained. It had not been the same since, one, joining
Muse in her console, and, two, finding everyone congrat-
ulating Roscoe when the Big Spell was broken.

Muse, her/itself, was sullen and distant as she/it sent
the actobots around to mend the ship. "My stage," she/it
grieved. "My beautiful, beautiful stage."

The ceiling that finally returned was domed and the
wrong color, but that was all the Back Side effect that
was evident, so everyone called it quits. The populace
that remained to see the troupe off was pathetically
small, and as Masterson said good-bye, it was apparent
that their work was far from done.

"We're still working on a new Big Spell," he revealed. He shrugged upon seeing Napoleon's horrified expression. "It must be done. There'll be children soon, and some of our elderly might be too set in the old ways. We must again protect ourselves from innocent and evil witchcraft. Only this time time we'll attempt to differentiate between good and bad magic. And we will not proceed until we know what the Back Side effect actually is.

"Still, we have much to thank you for. I have been allowed—entreated, in fact—to offer you a single wish each that is within my power but not in yours."

"Is that wise?" Harlan asked.

"We are willing to take the risk," said Masterson, "at my discretion. Mr. Pound?" They were all amused by the ancient title of respect.

Roscoe raised his hands. "Thank you, no," he said quickly, looking at the once acid-rain-filled sky. Zero shook his head even before the Sorcerer Supreme spoke his name.

"I want to live beyond my time," Spot said in a rush.

Masterson smiled sadly. "None of us can do that," he said gently.

Napoleon turned toward the SM, fully expecting her to ask for something else just as egocentric, like eternal youth, but Spot bit her lip, looked down, and shook her head as Zero put an arm around her shoulder. There was something very sad, small, and afraid in her actions. The feline dismissed her sympathy by thinking that Spot selfishly didn't want to lose her good looks.

"Mr. Trigor?"

Much to Napoleon's surprise, the space bullet actually gave it serious thought. But, "I'll keep it under advisement," is what he finally said.

Merlin Masterson smiled down upon the feline. "Mr. Napoleon?"

She didn't hesitate. "I'm looking for a planet called Nest. Where is it?"

The LOST troupe looked at her in various degrees of amazement. Spot looked mildly confused. Roscoe looked like he had swallowed a live frog. But Masterson pondered the question for several moments.

"I do not know where it is," he ultimately said, "and I know no sure way we can find out." Napoleon was crestfallen. A fat lot of good this wish-bestowing was turning out to be. "However," the Sorcerer Supreme added, "There is a method wherein you could gauge its location."

"All right, fine," said the feline. Harlan put out a hand to stop her, then thought better of it. He opened his mouth to warn her of possible problems, but thought better of that too.

Merlin Masterson stepped back and spoke to the world and her.

"To achieve what you must do,
to yourself you must be true;
Where ever you go, no matter how far
the nearer you get, the more you are;
You reach the place, you reach your core;
You will have found what you're looking for."

# MEDITAR

# SIXTEEN

Harlan Trigor bit at his thumbnail. The *Shooting Star* moved through space toward its next destination (it had to go at its fastest speeds to make up the time it took to repair the damage on Coven). But the faster-than-light speed did nothing for the tiny bit of extra flesh at the edge of his thumbnail. He himself could pull it off without unduly affecting the performance of his space bullet suit.

The aftermath of the Coven adventure still resonated throughout the ship. At first they had all been deliriously happy that they had survived. But when they had to clean up the blood and guts, a certain philosophical depression set in. Seeing dead bodies wasn't that mind-shattering in and of itself, but this was a theatrical lot who thought continually about the nature of life and death and then waxed eloquent about it.

Add to that the long days of space travel, with nothing to do while Roscoe worked on the new recon prelim and the crew grew distinctly testy. So Harlan chewed on his thumbnail. Occasionally he would make a face and rock his head back and forth. A bit later he would make the same face and mumble something. A little while after that he got some actual words out. "The more you eat, the more you grow; the closer you get, you stub your big toe."

Harlan shook his head again, doing an exaggerated heebie-jeebie. "You eat too much, you get fat; bite your tongue, you silly . . ." He stopped, shook his head, and muttered.

"All right already!" Napoleon growled from her cross-legged position on the bridge floor near the VU Port (tm). "It was worth a try!"

She knew he was irritated by both the risk she had taken to ask the location of Nest and by the resultant answer. Masterson would only do the spell, not explain it. No matter what they asked, the Sorcerer Supreme would only smile and nod knowingly. Harlan hated that. She had had to hold him back from unscrewing Masterson's head and looking for answers down his neck.

Truth be known, Napoleon was irritated also. She was no closer to knowing the location of Nest now than she had been years before . . . or so she thought. She was also annoyed by her overwhelming desire to clean herself. She had to keep stopping herself from licking her paws. Every few minutes she found her arm coming up and her tongue coming out. She forced it down, and the other in, with ire.

Harlan directed his bad temper at her. She directed hers at the artificials. She looked over to where they lay in the opposite corner, making all sorts of sticky, wet noises. Although they were both in another set of ornate costumes, they were practically making love right in front of her.

"Will you two stop that?" Napoleon complained. "Let's have a little consideration for Lil, huh?"

The clones stilled. Spot's head appeared from the black-and-yellow folds of her new, revealing dress. Her cheeks were flushed, her eyes bright, and her lips wet. "Who's Lil?"

"I'm Lil, plaything. The Last in Line. The last of my kind."

"Really?" Spot bleated. "So?"

"So I don't have anybody to make out with, stupid!" Napoleon snarled. "You two are torturing me over there." Zero's head appeared from the mound of arms, legs, cloth, and torsos.

"What about him?" Spot asked of Harlan. "He's cute."

"Thanks," Harlan smiled without humor. "But I'm not her type."

"I saw you kissing before!" Spot tattled. Zero tried to quiet her, but she was a spoiled child.

Napoleon rolled her eyes and shook her head. Harlan leaned his elbows on his knees. "That's all we can do," he said gravely.

Zero tried to pull her down again, but Spot was having none of it. "Well, so what? I can't have babies either."

It was Harlan's turn to roll his eyes. Napoleon looked over with narrowed eyes at the bubble-headed cutie. "Sex would kill me," she said purposefully.

"Oh," said Spot. And then, when the full import of the statement hit her: "Oh!" Regret set in. "Gee, I'm sorry."

Regret began to creep into Napoleon as well, on several counts. "That's all right," she answered and apologized. No one said anything for a couple of seconds (not even Mess, who was still infuriated that Merlin Masterson hadn't offered a wish to either it or Muse).

"Do you, I mean, do you want us to leave?" Spot asked in a small voice.

"That's all right," Napoleon reiterated, looking down

at her legs. They looked pretty dirty. "Just lighten up on the lovemaking, that's all.

"No, really," Spot offered tearfully.

"Well," Napoleon sighed. "Maybe it would be better if you two did go to your quarters or something." But Spot was already on her feet, hurrying out of the room before starting to cry in earnest.

The feline watched her go with disinterest. She shrugged slightly and continued to clean between her toes with her paw. Again she had to actually keep herself from leaning over to lick them clean. Zero's posture and expression caught the corner of her eye. She looked over to see him sitting on the floor, one leg bent, one leg out, his chin cupped in one hand. He was looking back at her with a scowl. She couldn't be sure whether he was angry or just examining her.

"You don't know, do you?" he said.

"What?"

"About us."

"I know you like each other," she said defensively. "A lot." Even she was surprised by her bitchiness.

"You trying to say something?" Zero challenged.

"I just did." The feline's back went up, some fur standing on end.

"Well, come right out and just say it."

"I just did." The FM looked away from Napoleon's steady glare to Harlan, but there was no way the soldier was going to get involved in this.

So Zero just shook his head and shrugged with sardonic resignation. "Sure, all right, so we don't love one another. We both know it. She's a flighty brat and I'm just"—he frowned—"nothing. A living nothing. Zero."

Napoleon made a noise of complaint, half growl, half whine. She stretched her back and scratched her head. "Oh, come on!"

"Listen," Zero said. "You're not the only one with a

tough life. But at least you've got a full one. You'll live to whenever you're going to live to. But we're artificials, pussycat. Our made-day was the day this ship went into space. And our term-day is the day it returns."

Harlan inhaled very deeply. Napoleon was shocked to attention. "They're going to terminate you when the ship gets back to Earth? Roscoe wouldn't do that."

"Roscoe probably doesn't have anything to do with it," Harlan offered.

Zero shook his head. "You don't understand. He won't have to. They won't have to. We were made so that the moment we complete our last performance we will simply . . . turn off." The FM climbed to his feet. He spoke as he walked toward, then right by, Napoleon. "Maybe now you'll understand why we act the way we do." He left the room in search of Spot.

Mess couldn't resist the temptation. "Really," it clucked. "How thoughtless. And after all that time with Larry too."

"Aw, damper," Napoleon whined, getting up. "I don't believe it anyway. The U.W. scientists weren't good enough to build in obsolescence that exactly."

"It's sixty years between your departure and theirs," Harlan reminded her.

"I don't care," she maintained. "They wouldn't have been able to do it in six hundred years. They've been lied to. All the TMs did that. It was part of the behavior modifications. The TMs would say anything to break our spirit."

Harlan did not judge. "Well, at least that explains their behavior." He remembered Spot's fear of finishing the tour and her request for life beyond her time. "But it doesn't explain yours," he said to the feline pointedly. She just scowled back at him. "You've been behaving strangely ever since we left Coven."

"You should talk."

"That . . . !" Harlan started angrily, then forced himself to calm. "You're right," he agreed. "I'm sorry. The entire affair was very unsettling." He waited for her to apologize back, or at least reply, but she said nothing. All she did was stare at the floor. "Are you all right?" he asked. She kept staring intently at the floor, her tail lashing. "Napoleon?" he called. She still didn't react. "Napoleon!" he called sharply.

She hopped into the air and mewled. She looked at him in blinking surprise. "What? What is it? What do you want?"

"Are you all right?"

"Fine," she snapped, as if she couldn't be anything but.

"You were looking at the floor."

"So? I thought . . ." She stared thoughtfully at the spot two feet in front of her feet again. "I thought I saw something," she mused.

Harlan looked and saw only the deck. "It's just the floor," he said.

Her head snapped up. "I know that!"

Harlan was going to ask what she thought she saw, when Roscoe came blustering in, his hands filled with portoputers and the Book. "The kitchen is filled with feathers," he said. "And Muse won't clean it out." He dropped his things in his seat and turned to the fugitives with his fists on his waist. "Must be another Back Side effect." After the Coven fiasco, it was hard separating the spells from the side effects. The full ramifications of the Big Spell—Breaking Spell Back Side effect had yet to be discovered.

"Maybe just a practical joke to dispel the boredom of space travel," Harlan said glumly.

"Better this than the alternative," Pound said with assurance, leaning on Muse's console. "After that last experience, I'm going to be deliriously happy with a life full of boredom."

"Is it true Spot and Zero will automatically terminate after the next performance?" Napoleon asked.

Roscoe shrugged. "That's what we were told."

"Do you believe it?" Harlan asked.

He shrugged again. "I didn't come here to talk about them," he said with a strange calm. "I wanted to talk about you." If he was expecting a pointed reaction, he was disappointed.

"What about us?" Napoleon replied easily.

Pound was not giving up. "Not about you really. About Nest." The reaction was slightly stronger this time. Harlan stirred. "Getting involved with sorcerers was bad enough. I don't want to mess with Mantases."

"The legend of Nest is well-known on Earth," Pound continued when the fugitives said nothing. "The Mantases were exiled from the planet shortly after you three, I mean two, left, but their reputation still remains. You obviously don't want to visit their planet just to sightsee."

Harlan put up his hands. "The less you know about this the better," he said. That statement was hardly soothing.

"We owe you a great debt for saving our lives on Coven," Roscoe said nervously. "But—"

"Don't worry," Napoleon said flatly, with a slightly condescending tone Harlan could have done without. "We have as little interest in returning to Earth as you have in meeting Mantases."

"Tell you what," Harlan interrupted. "Give us some time to think this out."

"I don't want to force you to leave," Roscoe said with remorse, although he was practically doing just that. "You've been a great help. . . ."

"We'll stay until you reach Meditar," Napoleon decided for everyone. "We'll help you put on—what is it?"

*"The Tempest,"* said Roscoe.

*"The Tempest,"* she repeated. "Then we'll be on our way."

The *Shooting Star* continued through the cosmos, oblivious of the confrontations, growing nearer and nearer to Meditar (which lay between Coven and Earth). As they neared the planet, everyone on the ship except Roscoe felt greater and greater dread. The clones were certain that they were flying to their deaths, and the fugitives didn't feel so different. It wasn't so much the danger that bothered Harlan, but the fact that they were no closer to the problem (let alone the solution) than they had been when they left Finally Finished. And Napoleon kept acting weirder and weirder.

"The records say that Meditar is a type-two planet," Roscoe told everyone after gathering them together for a production meeting. Type one was a planet made up of a groundlike substance capable of sustaining their weight. Type three was a gaseous planet. Type two was everything in between. "And they've asked specifically to see *The Tempest*."

Trigor looked down in consternation at the feline who was rubbing herself against his side. She didn't stop when she saw his expression. "I'm cold," she explained.

"It's a beautiful fantasy," Muse was saying, unable to remain uninvolved any longer. For her/it, the play was the thing. "About a man named Prospero . . ."

"Played by me," said Roscoe.

" . . . who lives on an enchanted island with his daughter Miranda . . ."

"Me," said Spot.

" . . . along with a fairy sprite called Ariel . . ."

"You," Roscoe said to Napoleon.

" . . . and a misshapen monster named Caliban."

"You," said Napoleon to Harlan. Everyone laughed. Once they had started work on the production, all the previous real-life dramatics were forgiven, if not forgotten. Such had it always been and such would it always be for the Light Orbit Space Theater.

"There's a shipwreck," Muse continued with feeling, "stranding members of the royal court who had exiled Prospero initially."

"Mostly me," said Zero.

"And me," Mess reminded them.

"Miranda falls in love with the son of the king, Ferdinand."

"Definitely me," Zero said.

"And all's well that ends well."

*All's Well That Ends Well* was a comedy and *The Tempest* was an adventure, but the LOST had distinctly tragic overtones as they neared Meditar. During the subsequent rehearsals and meetings, Spot dragged herself around as if one leg had gone to sleep. It eventually got so bad that Roscoe had to remind her they weren't doing *Richard III*.

Thankfully, Spot was still an actress. The magic of the theater soon possessed her and she was hurling herself into her roles with hysterical abandon. The mess on Coven was practically forgotten as the entire crew threw themselves into preparations for the final presentation. As fearful as the clone actors were, they knew that this, their last performance, had to be special. After all, it was their swan song.

Harlan also busied himself in the rehearsals, using them to temporarily forget his own inner agonies. Napoleon was becoming more prickly and eccentric with each passing moment. For the first time in their relationship, their conversations were getting strained. He was afraid it was all because she was desperate to destroy Nest, and, ultimately, he wasn't too sure if they should anymore.

"How?" he had pondered. "We're going in blind. How

do we get in? How do we get out? How do we destroy it? What in the name of Destiny do we do?"

"How should I know?" she hotly contested. "What else can I do? I can't go to some other planet and be a religious leader or a tourist attraction. I'm the last of a race destroyed by these monsters. I must get my people's . . . *my* revenge." Harlan had looked at her sadly. Who his sadness was for neither of them could be sure. "Harlan," she had practically begged, "try to understand. How would you have felt if the Mantases had succeeded in taking over your planet?"

He remembered and he felt empathy with her situation, but it wasn't enough. He had to find some way to explain. "Do you want to know the reason I left my planet to travel with you?" he asked her. "I know I said I had no real future on Destiny and that much is true, but—"

"You said it was because you had lost as much as me," the feline mewed.

"That and more," he admitted. "I followed because I felt for you and didn't understand—"

"Didn't understand why you felt for me?" she mewed again, the hurt in her cat voice obvious this time.

"No, why the Mantases did it. This Universal Rule they keep selling; what is it? Is it just more religious absurdity or is it tangible? Why do they follow it?"

"Does it matter?" Napoleon growled.

"Of course it does! We're going to Nest to face this Universal Rule." The feline turned and marched away from him, scowling.

"We are going to destroy the Mantas race," she said vehemently.

"I'm tired of destruction," Harlan sighed. "Even so, it doesn't make practical sense." The feline turned on the exhausted soldier.

"Would you listen to yourself?" she accused. "How do

you change the Mantases' minds? How do you alter their beliefs?" She crossed her arms and mimicked his tone. "The choice between social change and total annihilation is an easy one. The latter is simpler and more effective." She wasn't quoting him. She was simply playing soldier.

"And would you listen to yourself?" he said helplessly.

Napoleon's face closed shop. "I'm afraid this is logic." She spoke precisely. "Tell me; how did you feel when the Coverners came crawling on the stage? The only difference between that and my quest is that you had no choice but to fight back or die. I have a choice. I can confront the thing that destroyed my people or I can go away and make believe it isn't important. You tell me. What should I do?"

Harlan Trigor had looked her straight in the eye, his own expression wounded and worn. "I just hope there'll be another way," he said flatly.

"I don't," Napoleon had said.

"It's a tale told by an idiot," Harlan now said. "Full of sound and fury and signifying nothing."

"That's *Macbeth*," Muse scoldingly interrupted. "We're doing *The Tempest* now. Don't confuse your lines."

Harlan snapped back to the ship's immediate needs. He spent most of the time after that infamous conversation ensconced in his space bullet suit. It made for a marvelous, shambling, misshapen Caliban costume, and it made a wonderful sanctuary for him. Inside he was in his own sparkling world of soothing comfort, cut off and superior to the rest of the universe. Outside it, he was just another masterless soldier, little more than a mercenary. Inside he was practically a deity, the center of his own solar system.

"As wicked dew as e'er my mother brushed," Harlan said his entrance line carefully. "With raven's feather

from unwholesome fen drop on you both! A southwest
blow on ye and blister you all over."

And so it went until they reached Meditar. Only then
did Trigor emerge from his nurturing supershell. The
space bullet man strode into the bridge. In front of him
was the collected crew of the *Shooting Star* with Napoleon on her haunches. In front of them was a sight that
never failed to be breathtaking in its many forms, a new
planet slowly turning before them, flanked by several
satellite moons. Beyond that was the system's sun, blazing in the background with a fierceness that could intimidate even a Destinian.

Roscoe Pound turned when he heard Harlan enter. He
beckoned, smiling. Meditar looked like a white, puffy
planet, its exterior a globe of clouds. "The performance is
scheduled for tomorrow," the director said. "We just
made it in time. I'd better go down for a recon prelim
immediately. Muse, start implementing type-two
procedures."

"Right," she/it said.

"I'll go with you," Harlan volunteered.

"Not with all the parts you have to learn," said Pound,
looking toward the console.

"Alonso, Sebastian, Stephano, and Caliban," tattled
Mess.

"You've too much to do. Napoleon can accompany
me."

"I really don't know," Harlan worried, but that only
succeeded in getting the feline's dander up.

"Don't concern yourself with me!"

So it was that Harlan watched the clear star of the
vehicle leave the ship. Everything had gone smoothly
except when Napoleon suddenly lurched in front of the
craft just when it was starting to move. She had skittered
away on all fours, hitting the wall with a thump. Dazed
and blinking, she had then proceeded to scratch her ear

with her back foot. Harlan was about to go help her when her expression stopped him. She looked like a frightened kitten. A frightened kitten?

From Harlan's observation area, it looked as if two people were dropping calmly into a gigantic foam bed. He watched them disappear into the foam and remained looking at the place until they had disappeared for several minutes. A placid misgiving tickled the edge of his consciousness. Things were seemingly peaceful, but Harlan's every breath was caught with foreboding. He resisted wishing Napoleon well, even mentally. He didn't want to jinx her, considering that Merlin Masterson had jinxed her enough.

Trigor reluctantly left his vantage point and moved through the hallways to the theater. On stage the robots were unfolding clear, thin costumes. Spot and Zero were standing nearby, looking into their portoputers. "What are those things?" Harlan called.

Spot didn't look up. "Our portoputers," she whined.

"I know that," Harlan replied patiently. "Not those. That."

"Those are our seasuits," Zero answered without taking his eyes off his lines. "It's the way we perform underwater. Slows things down considerably, but we don't drown."

Harlan jumped onto the stage and examined the outfits. There were grates behind the head, at the waist, at the wrists, and at the feet. He imagined the costumes pulled oxygen from the water and used the liquid to power the actors' limbs. If there was one thing Harlan knew, it was specialty suits. He longed for his own. He quickly shook the longing from his brain. On top of everything else, he didn't need an addiction to the safety of his suit. Instead of remaining a self-contained armament, it was becoming an escape. He'd have to watch that.

Meanwhile, Napoleon shook herself at the same time as she hovered in the esc-star over the wavy Meditar surface. She felt as if tiny mice were in her brain, kicking at the nerve endings and laughing at her reflexes. She forced her mind off the desire to lick or scratch herself and concentrated on the new planetfall.

Up close, Meditar was not the shiny liquid ball it had appeared to be from the upper atmosphere, which was breathable, thankfully. It was a big light blue sea filled with spinning squares and dots of flickering yellow.

"It's beautiful," she almost lied. Although she should have found its serenity wondrous and the endless ballet of the graceful yellow specks grand, the sight of all that liquid was making her crazy.

"It's not $H_2O$," Muse reported curtly.

"What is it, then?" Pound inquired.

"I have no way of knowing," she/it huffed. "That's what you're down there for."

"What am I supposed to do?" Roscoe argued. "Stick my toe in it?"

"Ew" shivered the feline. "Don't say that."

"Get a sample," Muse suggested.

The idea was too much for Napoleon to bear. "Mess, what do your sensors show?"

It paused before replying. "My sensors correspond with Muse."

"Muse?" Roscoe called.

"According to our findings," she/it said frostily, "the Meditarians should be in viewing range."

"I suppose you concur, Mess?" Napoleon said sarcastically.

"It's all the same equipment now," it replied chivalrously.

"Is that all they can say?" Pound complained to Napoleon. Then, scanning the liquid's surface: "What are they? Invisible?"

"We can gauge intelligence and react to certain programmed stimuli," Muse informed him with a chill. "We're only as good as our programmers. If you want shapes, go get yourself a raynar."

Before Pound could bark back at her/it, Napoleon tapped his shoulder. "What?" he tensely reacted.

"I think they've been here all the time," she said, pointing down. "Waiting for us."

Roscoe saw a huge clump of yellow-flecked water growing into a fist beneath them. It reared back and just as it was about to slap the vehicle, the liquid flattened and the yellow spot formed a word: "HERE."

As soon as the LOSTers registered their surprise, the liquid column collapsed and the Meditarian surface was relatively level again. "Was that you, Muse?" Roscoe said hopefully.

"NO," the yellow specks spelled out beneath him.

"Why don't they speak?" Napoleon wondered aloud.

"PAIN," the flecks spelled.

"Incredible," Pound fretted. "They control the water."

"I think they *are* the water," Napoleon guessed.

"NO."

"I stand corrected," Napoleon said before turning to Pound. "You're not going to get much applause from this group."

Two liquid hands took shape before them. They smashed together, bathing the side of the esc-star with yellow flecks. They each twinkled and vibrated, then fell back to the sea. Inside the vehicle came a long rustling noise—the sound of no hands clapping.

# SEVENTEEN

Sandwiched between the white of the sky and the light blue of the water was the *Shooting Star*, floating peacefully above the waves at a height rivaling the O'Neil Drive craft Pound had initially visited in.

"Things change here," Mess had informed the crew. They had all gathered on the stage after Pound's return to put the final touches on the physical production of their final performance. "When humans first visited the planet, they were transformed by the water into the yellow things."

The more poetic Muse took over. "They broke down into components; their ideas, their feelings, their language, and their memories all flowed into and through the liquid. The shared consciousnesses of many peoples blend and frolic down there beneath the waves."

"I'm getting seasick," Zero said dryly.

"You mean," said the more practical, now paranoid

Spot, "that if any of the water touches us, we'll change too?"

"The Meditarians seem to think so," said Roscoe cautiously, not wanting her to panic any more than she already was. "They can communicate through comm-links with great effort, so they warn others away when they can. Otherwise, they do nothing but survive down there."

But Spot was not put off by Pound's attempt to elicit sympathy. "So even if our seasuits get a tiny rip, we'll change into those things?"

"Thousands of them," said Mess. "Even if a drop hits you."

"How are we going to perform then?" Harlan briskly interrupted.

Roscoe only smiled and strode over to the stage door. He swung it open and shouted, "Ready when you are, Muse!" To only the fugitives' surprise, the audience seats sank into the theater floor and the back walls began to swing out. Stretched before them were the waves of Meditar. With the O'Neil Drive keeping them on an even float, the compubot had turned the place into an outdoor arena hovering majestically fifty feet over the planet.

"So we start at the appropriate time?" Napoleon asked with a smile.

"Yes," Pound announced with relish. "The show will go on!"


"Five minutes," said Muse. "Five minutes to curtain."

The actors were in their seasuits which were supplemented with multicolored cloth from the costume department just in case. The suits turned out to be skintight except for the helmet which looked like an upside-down beaker. Communication devices were part of the helmet's material, so no gridlike speaker blocked the actors' or audiences' view. Walking, however, was like being wrapped in adhesive tape.

"These were made for underwater performing," Muse had told Napoleon. "The air supply is taken from the atmosphere by a filter in the back, so don't worry about breathing. And don't fret about the jets either. They only work in water."

So now Harlan, Napoleon, Spot, and Zero moved anxiously about the dressing room they shared. "I hope this will work," said the feline.

"We've been through worse before," said Zero.

"Oh, yeah?" Spot countered testily. "Where?"

"Remember Perald?"

"Oh." Spot giggled. "Yes."

"A gas planet," he explained to the others. "And the mist kept changing thickness. We were doing *Romeo and Juliet* and the robots had to keep pulling us back to center stage. We finished the love scene half a mile away from each other."

Spot laughed, a freckled hand before her face. "That was so long ago," she remembered quietly. "It's almost impossible for me to believe we're about to start our last performance. . . ." Suddenly both her hands came up, smacking hard against her seasuit helmet. Zero hurried over to embrace the shaking figure but not before the other two saw the actress crying. "Oh, Zero, what are we going to do. I don't *want* to die!"

"Now, listen," Napoleon said flatly, more irritated than anything else. "You two are human beings. If you were developed and raised in a U.W. lab, so what? So was Larry. And he's living happily on Destiny. No one's going to turn you off or take you away at the end of the show. These fears are all in your mind."

"No, I can't help it," the SM squealed. "What are we going to do? Oh, what are we going to do?"

"Places, everyone," came Muse's even voice. "Places."

Zero looked at her evenly. "I'll tell you what we're going to do. We're going to deliver a magnificent performance."

Napoleon waited for Mess to say it, but when he/it didn't, she thought it: "I think I'm going to be ill."

Like the good trouper she was, Spot's tears dried and she struggled to plaster a pleasant expression across her tragedy-ridden face. Napoleon only scowled at her. Harlan thought it was about time the fugitive contingency offered a little support. "Good luck," he said. Spot just stared at him before crying and running away. "What did I say?"

"It's bad luck to say good luck," Muse reprimanded.

Napoleon waited for Mess' inevitable interjection, but once again it did not arrive. "That's stupid," Napoleon herself said crankily. Mess was practically getting polite in its old age. It must have come from living with someone/thing else.

Harlan flashed the feline a disapproving look before asking her/it, "Will she be all right?"

"She has some time before her entrance," Muse assured him. "She'll be fine by then. But as for you two . . . curtain!"

"Come on, Nap," said Harlan. "We're on first." She hopped on over, the excitement of acting overriding all her aggravations. The two slid open the watertight door to the stage. It was a magnificent sight. The first scene called for a storm at sea and the Meditarians were up to it. Waves crashed all around in a gloriously chaotic fashion.

Whatever their problems and worries, the call of curtain freed the LOST's minds and souls. They could feel the thrill in their stomachs like a whirling gem growing brighter and brighter until its glow infused their entire bodies. On stage that night, they could forget their own dreams and nightmares. They would live Shakespeare's.

With a flash of artificial lightning, the final play of the troupe's twenty year tour was officially under way.

"Boatswain!" Harlan boomed, leaping from offstage. Napoleon was right behind him.

"Here, master! What cheer?"

He whirled around, wind tearing at the costume strips over his seasuit. "Speak to the mariners!" he shouted at her. "Fall to it, verily, or we run ourselves aground! Bestir!" With that, he pushed past her and back into the dressing room.

Napoleon moved on, the wind pushing her forward to the very edge of the stage. Looking into the deep, choppy blue, she felt that fear again. The liquid filled her with a dread that went beyond rationality. It seemed to touch something in her primordial psyche. She staggered back, letting the play's words lift her away from the fright.

"Cheerily, my hearts! Cheerily, cheerily, my hearts! Take in the topsail! Tend to the master's whistle! Blow till thou burst thy wind, if room enough!"

And the wind did blow, so much so that Napoleon wondered whether Muse was completely in charge of the situation. She turned to find Harlan behind her in his Alonso persona, along with Zero as Antonio and the little, forgetful robot as Gonzalo. They made quick work of the dialogue, establishing that Alonso was king and the boatswain would fight the storm. Napoleon quickly exited, followed by Harlan who immediately started changing back into the guise of "shipmaster" for a new set of lines.

"I feel terri— strange," she gasped to him. "Terribly strange."

"Hold on tight," Harlan suggested, completing his costume change. "Let's talk after our ship sinks." With that, they both leaped onto the stage to face some very storm-tossed robots. "All lost! To prayers, to prayers! All lost!"

"The ship has split!" Napoleon cried. "Oh, farewell, my wife and children!" She prayed that the Meditarians had a firm grip on the fact that this was all playacting.

"We split, we split!" Harlan raged. "Farewell, brothers!" He pulled Napoleon to his bosom and fell back into the dressing room. The robots scattered as Zero delivered his lines to the blinking robot.

"Now would I give a thousand furlongs of sea for an acre of barren ground. Long heath, brown furs, anything! The wills above be done! But I would fain die a dry death." Seconds later, the FM actor came crashing back into the dressing room.

"What an exit," Spot breathed, slipping by him to sneak on stage. The second scene went off without a hitch. Pound was already at center stage when Muse created the atmosphere of Prospero's peaceful island.

"If, by our art, my dearest father, you have put the wild waters in this roar, allay them," said Spot in her role of Miranda. On cue, the sea instantly diminished. Napoleon, for one, sighed in relief while absentmindedly scratching her ear.

"You've got an itch?" Harlan asked seriously.

She suddenly realized what she was doing and snapped her paw down. "It's nothing," she said.

"I don't think so," Harlan replied, kneeling before her with narrowed eyes. "How are you feeling?"

"Fine," she said defensively.

"Think about it," he suggested. "How are you actually feeling? Do you feel all itchy and filthy all of a sudden?"

Napoleon felt the irritation that was all too common recently as it rose back into her throat. "What are you getting at?" she spat, but his expression cut off any other sarcasms. She could see a man she loved: caring eyes, capable mind, strong body, warm heart. All her erratic irascibility left her mind and she could finally think clearly. "Well, now that you mention it . . ." she mewed.

" 'To achieve what you must do,' " he quoted, " 'to yourself you must be true.' "

At first she thought he was going over their lines, but then she remembered as well. " 'The nearer you get, the more you are. . . .' "

" 'You reach the place, you reach your core. . . .' "

"The spell . . ." she realized.

Harlan nodded. "You wanted to know where Nest was. They gave you a way to find out. You've been scratching and licking yourself. You've been rubbing against things and sleeping erratically. You've been seeking out warm spots and purring."

"Cheshire," she gasped. "What have they done to me?"

"They've made you a feline Nest detector," Mess guessed. "The closer you get, the more catlike you'll become."

"But, but, but," she stammered, her expression shifting from calculating hope to anguished fear. On the one paw, she now had a way to find the Mantases' home, but on the other, she could see the yawning pit of cat insanity. Like a person thinking about upcoming senility, she could practically feel her intelligence slipping away.

"Harlan," Muse interceded, "your cue for Caliban is coming up. Napoleon, you too." The feline began to change into her guise as Ariel the spirit while Harlan climbed reluctantly into his space bullet suit.

"For now, concentrate," was all he could suggest from under his exoskeleton.

"Done," she said with preoccupation. Rather than think about Coven, she'd focus on the play at hand.

"Fine apparition!" Roscoe called. "My quaint Ariel, hark in thine ear."

Napoleon made the jump from offstage to his side with fine feline style. She rolled over to him then rose slinkily up to place her cat ear near his mouth. "My lord," she told Pound, "it shall be done!" Then she leaped, rolled, and sprang back into the dressing room. Harlan passed her on his way out, tatters of oily looking gunk hanging from his suit.

"Thou poisonous slave," Pound called. "Got by the devil himself. Upon thy wicked dam, come forth!"

"As wicked dew as e'er by mother brushed," Harlan said with feeling, "with raven's feather from unwholesome fen drop on you both! A southwest blow on ye and blister you all over!"

Thus the play continued. The actors navigated the outdoor set well, careful of the edges while expansively performing the magic comedy. The high point came when a robot and Zero playing the two sodden sailors Trinculo and Stephano get Caliban drunk. Harlan's hiccups were a great favorite of everyone's.

But, finally, they reached the final act, act five, and the finale of the grand work. Prospero collected all the characters before him on a loaded stage. The dressing room and backstage were empty as the entire Light Orbit Space Theater faced Meditar. Harlan was back as King Alonso. Napoleon was Ariel. Spot and Zero were Ferdinand and Miranda.

Pound swept himself around, his arms wide, and delivered the last speech to all the world, all the galaxy, and all the universe. "I'll deliver all! And promise you calm seas, auspicious gales, and sail so expeditious that your royal fleet shall be cast far off. Be free and fare thee well!"

The last word rolled across the waves. A tremendous crash followed and before everyone's eyes, the stage tore open.

Hunks of wood and pieces of the poor machines flew everywhere, followed by a gray, bitter, fast-moving cloud of acrid smoke. The concussion threw the actors to their faces as the robots arced in the air. The feline slid across the floor on her stomach, coming to rest with her head over the edge of the floating stage. She saw the little absentminded machine drop, its treads spinning and a horrifying wail coming from its speaker. She watched it hit the water and quickly sink, curling down like a cork-screw.

The stage began to rock sickeningly. Pound skittered over the edge, holding on for dear life with his fingers. Napoleon heard the rip as one side of his seasuit tore open. It was all she could do to hang on herself. He was beyond her reach.

But not Harlan's. His double-jointed limbs smartly snapped into use, his feet propelling him toward the fallen director like a crab. The ship swung up, throwing Pound back onto the stage like a rag doll, then down again, hurling Pound forward over the waves. Harlan's strong legs vaulted him up and his iron fingers clamped on Pound's left wrist. He threw both himself and the terrified director back onto the stage.

The ship began to spin sideways. Spot and Zero had become a single crumpled heap in its center, the clouds giving the couple an ethereal glow. But as Napoleon watched, the halo was blotted out by a looming shadow which broiled over them all. Out of the clouds, beyond the actors, came a spaceship. A large, triangular space-ship. A Mantas spaceship.

Napoleon pulled herself up, shrieking in the desolate ruin of the theater. "Where did those things come from?" Harlan held Pound, whose mouth was open in a silent scream. As they watched, the single attacking ship sent a bolt blasting at the artificials. Shrapnel splinters flew everywhere. Napoleon sank to all fours and skittered toward Spot and Zero. She dodged through actobots who rolled to protect all the actors on instructions from Muse. They rallied valiantly, but they were too slow to avoid the Mantas guns.

The ship rocked again, throwing the clones past the feline. They fell on either side of her in the angry, clapping chaos of the assault. They tumbled directly for the gaping hole in center stage. Napoleon grabbed Zero's leg and looked over her shoulder just in time to see Spot somersault over the pit's lip. Zero twisted forward to pull his torso over the hole and grab her wrist.

Napoleon held him and he held Spot as she kicked over the Meditarian waves. The feline gritted her teeth and tried to pull back as the Mantas ship sent a bolt into Zero's back. Red flecked the feline's face as the man's back smoked and bubbled, but his grip did not loosen. Even after he was dead, he held on to his love.

Then Harlan was there, reaching down and grabbing Spot's other wrist. Both he and the feline pulled, bringing the dazed girl back to the ship. Trigor bundled the girl and Pound into his strong arms and hustled to the stage door. Napoleon was on his heels, dragging Zero. They threw everyone into the dressing room, Harlan vaulting over their writhing forms and into his space bullet suit in a single motion.

As the feline dragged the prone actors out of the way, Harlan went right past her, his "arm" becoming ninety degrees from the torso, a granite forefinger pointed directly at the Star Nosed Mole.

The bolt came from both his finger and his forehead. They mingled in front of his neck and danced on the Mantas ship's point. It had the same effect as slapping a dog. The spaceship ducked and retreated. Meanwhile, Harlan's feet kept sliding toward the stage edge. Napoleon watched him dive off the end and fly toward the Mantas ship like . . . well, like a bullet.

Napoleon leaned forward to shut the stage door. Maybe if the Mantases couldn't see them, they wouldn't kill anyone else point-blank. But as her paw gripped the door edge, the Star Nosed Mole let off another blast. It tore open the floor from the previous pit to just under the feline's feet. Her legs pumped, but to her own disbelief she saw Roscoe's shocked face fall up. She walked in space, feeling only air. Her brain finally informed her that she was falling. Toward . . . all that water.

She screeched and clawed and kicked but nothing saved her. She hit the surf with a jarring splash. On Earth it would have knocked her unconscious, but the liquid was different here. It was like hitting a feather mattress, but one which swallowed her up. She contorted, landing on her feet, naturally, and the clear, yellow-flecked ooze dragged her down.

It wasn't that bad after all. The sky above crackled with angry fire, but here was a soft new world of dancing colors. The seasuit automatically began extracting the air from the oxygenated water to pump it into her helmet. The water jets were working as well, propelling the feline deeper into the depths of Meditar.

The panic quickly subsided and she felt warm and secure. This new environment was flushed with light. The nearby sun illuminated the liquid, keeping her vision clear. She dropped into a seemingly bottomless pool of beauty, with the yellow specks actually showing her the way. As soon as she gained control of the water jets, she was almost enjoying the silent, lulling experience.

It was not silent for long. Out of the murkiness came a familiar form. The space bullet propelled himself toward his ill-fated mate. "Some curtain call," Trigor grunted.

"Harlan!" Napoleon cried, overjoyed until she remembered why they both were here and what was above. "What happened?"

"It was a trap," he said through their comm-links needlessly. "The Mantases must've been tracking us since Finally Finished. They were probably hoping that the Coverners killed us. When they didn't the boogers waited until we were all out in the open."

"How? How could they without our knowing?"

They have Destinian and Earthen antiweapons," Harlan said with certainty.

The feline grabbed hold of him as he passed. They started to rise, but a million tiny voices suddenly tinkled against her helmet. "ENEMY," they said. The feline looked up, but the ocean distorted her view. "MERGES!" the tiny voices cried in a chorus of billions.

"Nap," Harlan called. "Hold on." He turned and moved deeper into the planet. As she watched, the Meditarians cleared the way to the surface so she could see what they had been talking about. It was a sight she was not to forget. The Mantases, the obsessed, unbelievable Mantases, were streaming out of their spaceship. They were leaping from an airlock, without any sort of protection, into the water.

They fell hundreds of feet without parachutes or motor drives. When they hit the surface they seemed to explode into thousands of yellow tensors which drifted lazily toward her. The monsters were trying to reach her through the planet. But the planet was having none of it.

The sea broke in whirlpools of darting, quivering, undulating cells which turned on each other, creating little cosmos of light and deadly tortuous designs. As one yellow creature defeated another, the loser's luminous interior stretched into a shaking snake form. It's lifeforce winked out and was then completely consumed by the victor.

Although dozens of Mantases had made the kamikaze drop, millions of entertained flecks rallied around the space bullet and feline. They made a yellow trail for them to follow. They gathered behind Harlan's feet to propel him and his charge toward safety. He followed them away from the fight to the surface, where he blasted into the air like a fired missile. Napoleon wrapped herself around his neck as he shot straight for the Star Nosed Mole's underbelly.

The feline buried her head against Harlan's neck as his finger blasts smacked the enemy ship's stomach. The bolts ricocheted off the alien surface like snow off ice. All his fingers suddenly extended as the Destinian weapons assailed the Mantases' ship. They seemed to burst there, but instead of jagged tears, the outside walls were left with only green shadows.

Harlan blasted at the ship in frustration, but nothing seemed to work. He sailed through his own shrapnel to head for the lurching *Shooting Star*. Napoleon held on for dear life as he swung in toward the now closed stage door. The partition swung open and Roscoe reached out. "Get off," Harlan told her.

"No!" she suddenly screeched, holding tighter like a drowning woman clutching a lifeguard.

"You're blocking some of my armament," he said reasonably. "Get off."

"No!" She climbed away from Pound's fingers.

"Nap, get inside."

"No! You're not leaving me!"

"We'll all be killed if I don't do something!" He tried to shake her off.

"No, I know what's going to happen!" she cried. "You're going to do something crazy!"

"Get off me!"

"No, no, no! You're going to do something suicidal!" She felt the acid tears gathering behind her clenched eyes. "Let me come with you!"

"Get her off me!" The electric shock and the metal arm came at the same time. The shock peeled her from him and metal hand gripped her wrist. The space bullet was gone and Mess' manifestation pulled her inside.

Muse sealed the stage door and sent the ship through the clouds as Napoleon threw a tantrum. She/it sent the

*Shooting Star* away from the Star Nosed Mole at her/its fastest speed. Spot was sobbing over Zero's ruined form. Roscoe was gasping for breath by the door. The feline was slamming her paws on the compubot console. "He can't do this!" she wailed. "He can't leave me!"

Mess slapped her across the face. She stopped hitting the metal and blinked at his blank head. "Think," came Harlan's voice from the robot's speaker.

"We can't escape the Mantas ship," Pound choked.

"We have no weapons," said Muse.

"We're not fast enough," said Mess.

"And Harlan's suit has no effect on them," Napoleon whispered. "What does he think he's doing?" The naturally cunning feline mind took over. She put herself in the Destinian's place. What could he do? What was the only way to save them all?

"Hold on to something!" she yelled at Pound while running to Spot's side. She took her arms in her paws. "Come on, you have to secure yourself." The girl shook her off. Napoleon suddenly realized how Harlan must have felt when she wouldn't let go. "He's dead, Spot" she said harshly. "The Mantases killed him. But you have to live. You can't let them kill you too. He died to save you."

"No," Spot said tearfully. "He died on the last line." It was no use arguing with the grieving girl. Instead Napoleon grabbed *Zero's* ankles and dragged him to Roscoe's chair. Spot hysterically ran after them.

"Mess," the feline called. The manifestation raised an arm in salute. "Protect Pound." Uncharacteristically silent, Mess rolled toward the numb director. The man embraced the machine as it locked its wheels. Napoleon hurled herself over Muse's console to land on all fours. She then pressed her back against the stage wall and the soles of her feet at the console base. Now, if only Harlan's plan worked.

The Mantas ship started after the LOST ship as

Harlan zipped around it. He was a superman looking at his own blood for the first time. It was choking him, blinding him. His suit had been invulnerable forever. He had been all-powerful all his life; the best of the best. Nothing had ever stood in his way, not space pirates, not invading hordes, and certainly not alien armies.

But now this one miserable little pipsqueak was taking his most powerful blasts and bolts at point-blank range without a flinch. Raging inside the suit and himself, Harlan gave it everything he had. Every nerve, every muscle, every inch of skin was moving, making the man-shaped granite stone an eruption of cosmic light. He looked like an exploding rainbow.

The chunks, lines, circles, orbs, tubes, and arrows of light bathed the Mantas ship. Harlan dove through the dazzling wonder to soar out the other side. Not a single weapon had the least damaging effect on the Star Nosed Mole.

Outside, the suit looked placid and undaunted. Inside, Trigor was panic-stricken. The only reason he wasn't terrified was that he didn't know the meaning of it. Claustrophobia clutched at his throat. His home had become a prison. The suit had stopped being his savior and was threatening to become his tomb.

He had to get out from under the Star Nosed Mole's sights. They obviously had anti-Destinian defense devices. Since that was the case, they probably had anti-Destinian offense devices as well. They could not only defeat him, they could destroy him like a human hand crushing a graham cracker.

Harlan put on all his suit's speed. He zoomed away from the Mantas ship and directly toward the floundering *Shooting Star*.

In the tunnels and corridors of the Star Nosed Mole, the Mantases scurried to their appointed tasks. The creatures themselves would never admit it, but there was a discernible excitement in the air. After years of tracking and months of plotting, their objective was finally in sight. Their antennae and mandibles touched the tensors that readied the weapons "borrowed" from Destinian and Earthen technology. They readied the adapted technology to wipe the LOST ship from the skies.

"You are certain the feline is on the ship?" asked Sellag.

"We have seen her leave the planet of sorcerers" answered Kannex.

"She has not slipped away?"

"We have tracked her."

"She did not detect you?"

"We are invisible to Earthen and Destinian sensors."

"She will not escape?"

"The Rule will destroy her."

"She will not fight back?"

"The Rule will protect us."

The voices paused as they came to understand the futility of fighting the Universal Rule.

"What will happen?"

"She will join her ancestorsssss."

Harlan surged toward the *Shooting Star*. He did not slow as he neared. To the Mantases, it appeared as if he would collide directly with the ship. And no Earthen craft could withstand the might of a space bullet. He would tear through the vehicle like an arrow through rice paper.

The space bullet shot into the LOST ship. He went right into the O'Neil Drive grate on the bottom of the construct. His suit expertly sought out the engine's power source. His life took place before his mind's eye as he aligned himself with the engine. It didn't pass before his eyes; it was simply all there for a second before winking out.

He then remembered his early training to become a double-jointed warrior with almost total control of almost every muscle. He remembered how Larry had been given the same sort of power by his creator, Weinstein-Hubbell. He remembered how his own OD had been adhered, seemingly by magic, to the back of his suit back on Destiny.

Magic . . . the experience on Coven tweaked his recollection of his own escape from Mantas treachery on his home planet. He remembered how he had added the extra OD to power his suit away from his own people, his own brother space bullets. He had double the normal space bullet power. Two engines . . . two incredible engines inside his space bullet suit. . . .

His eyes seemed to flicker and his skin seemed to quiver as certain muscles flexed and certain digits moved in a specific, blindingly fast pattern. The pattern of engine transference was set up. Then, suddenly, the space bullet suit was part of the *Shooting Star* engine.

"Mess!" Muse's console cried as the power surged through her/its niodes.

"Coming!" the manifestation called back, leaving Roscoe to fend for himself. It wheeled crazily toward the panel which had flipped open before. It flipped open again and Mess smashed its robot head against it. Pound clearly saw the cirquid board sink into the machinery.

"No!" the man shouted as he fell to his face. The floor wasn't below his feet anymore.

The Mantases ordered Harlan and the Earth ship eradicated. A bolt went out but it hit empty space. The *Shooting Star* was no longer there.

The VU Ports (tm) went out, as did the lights. So it was totally black inside the ship as Harlan added untold speed to the craft and the compubots struggled to deal with it.

The Mantases struggled to deal with it as well. As soon as the theater troupe had zipped away, the Star Nosed Mole gave chase. But Harlan had gotten the jump on them. Both ships went as fast as they could, but both remained equidistant from each other. They coursed through space is a straight line, in an unchanging pattern, the *Shooting Star* just out of range of the Mantases' weapons.

The trip was agony.

"Muse?" Roscoe called pathetically from the darkness. In reply, one or two dim lights flickered on. The bridge was bathed in gloomy illumination. Shadows made the area ominous and moody. Still no starlight came from the VU Port (tm). "Muse?" Roscoe called again, starting to rise from his position near the stage door.

He could just imagine what the stage looked like. Or, rather, what it didn't look like anymore. Most of it had probably been destroyed by the Mantas blasts. The rest was probably ripped away in the first desperate escape attempt through the Meditarian upper atmosphere. What had been left was now most certainly decimated by the jump from single to triple OD power. Unless, of course, the O'Neil-invented speed had somehow freeze-dried the remaining tatters of the LOST's once proud stage. Who knew with FLIT (Faster than Light Travel)?

Roscoe stumbled past the hexagonal console where Mess' manifestation lay on its "face," its head yawning open. "Muse?" he asked a third time. But there was no reply. The director walked on stiff, weak legs, the horror of the Mantas attack numbing his brain. This was even worse than Coven. On Coven, none of them had been hurt.

He grabbed on to the side of his chair for support. He

could just make out the twin shapes of the figures inside.
"Spot?" The SM sat up. She came into the gray light to
Roscoe's everlasting regret. She was covered in Zero's
blood from her neck to her knees. Her eyes were wide and
empty. She had been covered in blood before, but that
had been Shakespeare's blood. This was not the same.
This was horrible.

"He died on the last line," she said.

Roscoe choked back the bile that crawled up his
throat. "Come out of there," he managed to whisper. She
did not move. She looked somewhere between the corpse
and the director. "Come out," he choked. He reached for
her. She screeched and clawed at his hand. He snapped
his arm away and backed into Muse's console.

"What's the matter?" he heard the feline say softly,
flatly.

"You shouldn't have put her in there" he whispered,
not turning.

"There was no time to argue," Napoleon said. "I
didn't."

"It's driven her mad!" he said, turning. He gasped,
choking off the words. Napoleon was lying on her stomach on the top of the console, her paws out, her legs
tucked under her haunches, her tail up, her eyes glowing
gold in the dark. Her shape had a satanic sensuality and
her face was more alien than it had ever been before.

"I've got my own problems," she said cruelly, her voice
silky, purring, and pained. "Harlan?" she called sadly.

"How . . . how can you say that?" Pound demanded,
getting over the shock. "Poor Phyllis needs help."

"She was slowly going insane the entire tour," Napoleon spit back. "Or hadn't you noticed that? The tour
itself did it. The lies the TMs told her did it. Her mind
was snapping when the Mantases attacked. Harlan!" She
writhed on the console. "Why doesn't he answer?"

"Savor." Roscoe gulped.

"What is that?" the feline said slowly.

"The compubots are in savor," Roscoe told her weakly. "It's a state of bliss. It started to happen before, when your compubot first joined mine, but I called her/it out of it." Napoleon remembered. Roscoe swallowed again. "They revel in their own cirquids. They're overwhelmed by their own niodes. They're feeling . . . alive." He couldn't swallow now. His throat was dry. "The speed has pushed them over the edge."

"How do you know?" Napoleon challenged irritably, scratching her back against the console.

Harlan almost smiled apologetically. "It's a fairly common complaint among creatively programmed boards."

"I'm hungry," said Napoleon. "Harlan!"

"He can't get through the comm-links yet," Roscoe said to the air.

"The ship is on automatic. The compubots are shut down for all intents and purposes. He can't talk to us."

"The Destiny Mother I can't," Trigor's voice cursed.

"Harlan!" Napoleon cried.

"You obviously haven't heard about space bullet abilities," he scolded Pound. "We're better than that. Hold on, Nap. The compubots are dormant. I have to take over."

"What are you going to do?" Roscoe demanded tightly.

"Don't worry. I have to keep basic ship functions going. Then I'm going to see if your special effects equipment can be adapted as weapons."

"Where are the Mantases, Harlan?" Napoleon asked stridently.

"Still on our tail," he said, making hers swish forward. "They're not gaining, but they're not backing off either."

"How many?" she asked.

"One," he answered.

"One!" both the feline and director exclaimed.

"One?" Napoleon repeated. "It doesn't make sense. If they had double or even triple teamed us, we never would have escaped. One ship to kill two of their greatest enemies?"

"My thoughts exactly," Harlan said, ignoring her unconscious egomania. "We're on the right track, Nap. Something is obviously taking precedence over eliminating us."

"Nest," Roscoe realized.

"Exactly." Napoleon grimaced. "They must be ready for the birthing. Most of their ships have to be protecting their home planet."

Harlan heard her tortured tone. "How are you feeling, Nap?"

"Not good. The Coven spell is working, but it's making me sick."

"Then we're getting closer," Trigor said supportingly. "Pound, where are we going?"

"I'm not sure," the man admitted. "Better check the cirquids."

"I did," Harlan shot back. "I couldn't tell the destination from their positions and heat, but I do know that Muse didn't set any new coordinates."

"Then it has to be . . ." Roscoe trailed off, realizing the truth.

"What?" Napoleon demanded, frightened that she already knew. The dread made a wave across her fur, making all her hair stand on end.

"Earth," said Roscoe Pound.

# DOOMSTAR

# EIGHTEEN

Napoleon was beside herself. Harlan wanted to crawl out of his suit and through the engine to get her, but he had to remain to sustain the *Shooting Star's* life-support systems. Meanwhile, she bounced around the bridge. That description was not as facetious as it sounded. It started slowly, with the feline staring at her tail as if it were an alien worm. Then she started batting it with her paw. Then she started chasing it in circles. Finally she leaped into the air, writhing and racing around the bridge with wild abandon.

Roscoe held his head in his hands while sitting cross-legged on the floor. Finally he couldn't take it anymore. "Napoleon!" he yelled sharply. She skidded to a halt, tumbling end over end. In spite of everything, Pound had to laugh. Napoleon herself relaxed with a goofy grin and licked her right paw.

"Cheshire," she swore. "This is weird." Neither Pound nor Trigor deemed to comment. "It's like . . . I'm a spectator in my own head. I feel distant, not quite separated from myself. It's not like I'm being shut out so much. More like . . . someone else is moving in. There are two of me in here."

"You're in savor," Roscoe smiled.

"Concentrate," Harlan advised, but he had his own troubles. He was just managing to keep the labyrinthine ship going through the compubot's dormant connections while carefully investigating ways to fight the still pursuing Mantases.

"It's getting worse," Napoleon complained like an addict going cold turkey. "But how can that be? Earth isn't Nest. And Nest can't be in the same solar system . . . can it?"

"You'd think not, wouldn't you?" Harlan mused, preoccupied.

"Oh, if only Muse were here," Roscoe fretted.

"Tell me about it," Harlan echoed.

"It's all your larried compubot's fault!" Pound finally exploded. "She/it was doing all right until he/it came along!" The director sounded like a father whose treasured daughter had run off with the neighborhood scumboy. Or, even worse, he sounded like a jilted boyfriend. The accusation did little to soothe Napoleon's addled psyche, but it helped get her mind off it. There but for the grace of Cheshire went she.

"Grow up," she snarled.

"There's just too much imput," Roscoe fretted, stung.

"They're . . . enraptured now." Napoleon sank miserably to the floor. How long would it be before too much cat input enraptured her?

She didn't have long to consider it, thankfully. "They're making a move," Harlan reported. "It's futile, but they're shooting at us." The Star Nosed Mole was pouring blasts at the *Shooting Star*, all of which crackled into nothingness just beyond the LOST's tail.

"What do they hope to achieve?" Napoleon wondered. "They're only draining their own supplies."

"Indeed," Harlan agreed. "As for us, the special effects equipment is virtually useless, so I'm trying to take over the navigational controls."

"Why?" Roscoe asked.

"When we reach Earth," he said as calmly as possible, "we'll automatically slow down."

"And if we slow down," Pound realized.

"They'll get us," Napoleon finished for him.

The two ships coursed on, neither giving nor taking a light-inch from the distance that separated them. But the Star Nosed Mole continued to fire upon the LOST ship, seemingly out of frustration. Harlan dared not move for fear of putting the *Shooting Star* in the insectoids' clutches. Instead, he desperately sought to override the compubots' savored control of their fate. Meanwhile, Napoleon scoured the ship for more ammunition for her empty spitter and beamer. When that proved fruitless, she took apart the weapons and put them back together. Several times. Then she lay them on the floor in a variety of pleasing patterns and started playing with them.

Roscoe did his best to ignore her. He got some food-stufs and brought them to his chair. "Please," he asked Spot. "Have something to eat."

Napoleon slid over to the seat. "It's no crime to keep on living."

"He died on the last line," a tiny, weak voice said from the depths inside.

"So?" Napoleon countered cheerfully.

"I didn't die," Spot replied, seemingly not hearing the feline's tone. "I don't understand."

The feline shrugged elaborately. "What's to understand? You were lied to. The Mantases killed your lover before he could realize that. So now you keep living . . . unless you want to kill yourself."

Roscoe was aghast. "You *have* to live on," he pleaded with the girl.

"Why?" Spot wondered.

"Because," Roscoe stammered. "Because . . ." He *had* to think of something. "Because I need you to." Napoleon looked at him in astonishment. A TM saying that?

Roscoe's amazing show of consideration seemed lost on the despondent girl. "To be or not to be," she mumbled.

"Full fathoms five thy father lies," Napoleon interrupted, quoting from *The Tempest*. "Of his bones are coral made. Those are pearls that were his eyes, nothing of him that doth fade. But doth suffer a sea change into something rich and strange."

Roscoe grabbed the gauntlet and ran with it, refusing to let the feline's intervention ruin things. "Our revels now are ended," he said as Prospero. "These, our actors, as I foretold you, are all spirits, and are melted into air, into thin air. And, like the baseless fabric of this vision, the cloud-capped towers, the gorgeous palaces, the solemn temples, the great globe itself. Yea, all which it inherit, shall dissolve. And, like this insubstantial pageant faded, leave not a rack behind.

"We are such stuff as dreams are made on, and our little life is rounded with a sleep."

Somehow the words didn't make anyone feel any better. To make them feel much worse, Spot took Zero's dead hand and spoke for both Ferdinand and Miranda from act three, scene one. "Here's my hand," she said for the corpse. And then the girl's reply: "And mine, with my heart in't." Spot bowed her tear-soaked face and cried again.

It was at times like these when Napoleon really missed Mess' obnoxious manners. It could irritate the Cheshire out of her, but it could also defuse situations like nothing else. But it was sunk in savor, so the feline took over. "Nice try," she said to Roscoe before trotting off.

Pound simply looked at the devastated girl and the dead boy and realized how much he cared for them. "O brave new world," he quoted softly to keep from joining Spot's sobs, "that has such people in't. My ending is despair."

"We're slowing," Harlan announced tightly. Napoleon sat up and wailed like a lost kitten.

"Quiet," Roscoe scolded, marching to the still-empty VU Port (tm). "Are we nearing Earth?"

"We must be," Trigor answered dryly. "But not close enough. We're just slowing a fraction. It's the beginning of our descent."

"Can't you maintain the speed?" Napoleon almost begged.

"Only my own. I can't control the ship's engine." He didn't have to color in the picture. The once seemingly invincible space bullet had granite feet of clay. He couldn't destroy the Star Nosed Mole and now he couldn't even gain control of a savored compubot.

Napoleon was suddenly on her hind legs and screeching to the ceiling. "Don't you dare! Don't you try it! Don't even think it!"

"What are you babbling about?" Pound accused angrily.

"There's only one option," she snarled for both the director's and Trigor's benefit. She wanted the Destinian to know she knew. "He could try to distract them, or delay them, or create a diversion. But don't . . . you . . . try . . . it!"

"Don't concern yourself," he said blandly. "Even if I did, the *Shooting Star* wouldn't have enough power to escape or even maintain an atmosphere. Looks like you're stuck with me."

Roscoe kicked the compubot console. "Snap out of it, will you/it?"

"Too late," Harlan said. "Nap, I'm coming up."

The feline misunderstood. "Don't you . . . !"

"I want to be with you," he said and disengaged from the ship's engine. He didn't bother to add the inevitable "when the end comes."

The *Shooting Star* slowed. The Star Nosed Mole shot by. Harlan flew out of the engine over to an airlock. The Mantas craft turned. Trigor entered the LOST ship, tore out of his open-topped suit, and raced toward the bridge as the enemy craft cautiously approached the meandering theater vehicle.

Napoleon's mind cleared when she saw Harlan's face. Her troubles were forgotten when she saw his expression of anguish. He was the superhero who had lost his powers. His life was meaningless because he had failed his friends and his love. He was a cripple who couldn't comprehend his own handicap. He was a soldier who had loved but had lost everything. She embraced him fervently.

"Escape," Roscoe choked. "Go the way we found you."

Harlan shook his head, his lips set. "It won't work this time. There won't be the element of surprise this time. They can outrun and outgun me. They'll destroy me. . . ." A new thought struck him. "But maybe not you. Come on, Nap!" He grabbed her hand and ran back through the halls. They grabbed her spacesuit on the way to the airlock. By the time Pound had caught up to them, both were sealing their protected exteriors.

"Good-bye, Roscoe," the soldier said. "There should be just enough power to keep you alive. And maybe they'll leave you alone once they get us."

"No!" the director cried. "What . . . what about your compubot?"

"Better it should be happy," Napoleon said vacantly, climbing onto the space bullet. "Get out of here, Roscoe."

"Please," he begged, overwhelmed by the reality of tragedy.

"At least this way we all have a chance," Harlan said with as much comfort as he could muster. "But there's no chance if you don't leave the airlock."

Roscoe backed away, gasping out Shakespeare's words. "Good night, sweet prince. And flights of angels sing thee to thy rest."

Napoleon smiled grimly as the door closed in the man's face. "Misery acquaints a man with strange bedfellows," she quoted sardonically to Harlan.

"I would fain die a dry death," he returned as the air was sucked out and the outer door opened.

The cat-saddled space bullet shot out of the ship and cut through space at Trigor's top speed. He wanted to put plenty of distance between him and the *Shooting Star* so the LOSTers wouldn't catch any part of the Mantas death blast.

"Napoleon," he whispered to her. "I love you."

"Harlan," she whispered back. "Look."

The two stopped and stared off into space, dumbfounded. There was no Star Nosed Mole. The Mantas ship was no longer there. In its place were hundreds of hunks of Mantas ship. Star Nosed Mole debris spun off in all directions. The only thing besides the theater craft that was whole was a simple, severe, dark-blue-metal, rectangular spaceship lined with VU ports (tm). Its markings were unmistakable, however, as was the language of the earnest voice coming over their comm-links.

"Doomstar Ship *Hartman-Barker* here," said a human voice. "Are you all right?"

That was only the first surprise. Another came when Harlan and Napoleon finally set foot and paw back on the *Shooting Star* bridge. After all, what else could they do but return? Where else could they go? For Harlan, it

made practical sense; if the ship could eradicate the
Mantas craft, it stood to reason it could also make quick
work of the space bullet. As for Napoleon, she was
curious.

"What did I tell you?" was the first thing they heard.
Roscoe said it to the six nice-looking men who stood there
while he motioned at the newcomers.

The next surprise was how the half-dozen men fell to
their knees and bowed their heads. It was Finally Finished all over again. The power of Lil was back at work.
The tableau remained that way, the men bowing and the
fugitives motionless, until a familiar voice spoke up.

"Nice to see you back," said Mess. "Remember me?"

"Mess?" Napoleon cried happily.

"Oh, so you *do* remember my name!" it replied sarcastically. They had left it behind and it wasn't about to
forget or forgive.

Harlan, an expert in redirection, didn't take the bait.
"What happened out there? How did the Mantas ship
get destroyed?" The men shifted on their knees but none
said anything.

"Their ship just blasted it," Roscoe said excitedly.
"When our ship slowed down, the compubots came out of
savor and the VU port cleared. I saw it all!"

"How did you do it?" Harlan asked the kneeling men.
"The Mantas ship was impervious to our weapons."

One man looked up, then quickly looked down again.
"We simply fired on it—sir—and it imploded."

Harlan looked at Roscoe with a raised eyebrow.
"They're from Earth," Pound related. "A world
which . . . worships you."

"Don't ask me why," Mess sniffed. The two ex-fugitives looked at one another with combinations of pleasure
and surprise.

"Thank you," said Napoleon to the kneelers. "Please,
get up."

The men looked at each other and then stood, all smiles. "Is it really you?" the first man asked the pair. Napoleon examined the men carefully. They were like tousled-haired young men, not the smug, superior True Men with the proper Real Human factors. So, still a bit leery, she nodded.

"It is her!" another cried happily.

"Of course," said Mess with some of the missing RH factor. "How many last felines from Mandarin do you think there are?"

The men ignored the compubot's interruption. "It's been so long!" one gushed. "The Hitcote said you'd return, but I never would have believed it if I hadn't seen it with my own eyes!"

"The hit coat?" Napoleon instantly wondered. "What's that?"

"Who," the man corrected. "He's . . . well, he's the Hitcote, that's all. You know, the Hitcote." Before the ex-fugitives could say they didn't, the man went on. "Wow. After all this time you three come back and we six, of all people, actually save your lives!"

"You know us?" Harlan finally asked, unable to get a real good grip on the entire thing.

"Sure!" said the man. "Everybody on the planet knows you." The men laughed.

Harlan laughed with them. "Oh, I see," he baited. "You were expecting the *Shooting Star* and just happened to . . ."

"What?" said the man. "We were waiting for what?"

"The *Shooting Star*. The LOST ship."

"What's that? Oh, is that this? Your new ship? I guess the *Black Hole* must've been destroyed, huh? What did you call it again? The *Lost Star?*"

Roscoe finally had to step forward. "Wait a minute. You mean you haven't heard of the Light Orbit Space Theater?" He glanced at the ex-fugitives to see Harlan

silently advising caution. Trigor turned to get the feline's
soundless input, but Napoleon was staring out the VU
port (tm) with her eyes wide and her mouth hanging
open. Soon all the LOSTers were doing the same. Slowly
drifting by were huge space-rock letters: R, A, T, S, M,
O, O, and D.

"Great," said the man. "We're getting close. We've
been in touch with the *Lost Star* ever since we destroyed
the other ship. We took it upon ourselves to link compubots to bring you in."

"Muse?" Pound called.

"True," was all she/it cryptically said.

"Oh, this is so great," the man practically bubbled.
"It's been so long, and we're so happy to be bringing you
in!"

Let me get this straight, Harlan thought to himself.
We left an Earth which was hopelessly corrupt and per-
verted, not to mention physically disintegrating. Several
True Men were killed to do it, which was Earth's ultimate crime. We left behind an Earth which was building
a new home for itself which was called "deux ciel," or
"second heaven." Only the army of FMs which were
actually building it nicknamed it Doomstar.

But now there were giant rock letters spelling the FM
name in orbit and the fugitives' murders not only seemed
to be pardoned, but worshiped. Adding the fact that these
fellows seemed to know nothing of the LOST, there could
only be one general explanation. Unfortunately, the
ramifications of that explanation threatened to brain-
cramp Trigor again. All he could think to do was wade in
deeper. "Bringing us in?" he said vacuously.

"Sure," said the man. "Everybody'll love to see you
three. They'll absolutely love it."

"Three?" said Pound. "But—"

"Sure," said the man. "Napoleon." He pointed to the
feline. "Harlan Trigor." He pointed at the space bullet.

"And Larry." He pointed at Roscoe Pound. "We worship you. You are our deities."

"What about me?" Mess cried.

"You're a damper down," Harlan warned. He checked on his love. She was his greatest concern. By the looks of it, she was beyond comprehension. Whether it was from these revelations or the Coven spell was a moot point. "Isn't this nice, Larry?" he said pointedly to Pound, who shut his mouth tight.

"I don't get it," said Mess. "What's going on here?"

"The revolution," said Muse, who had gotten the story from the *Hartman-Barker* compubot over her own niodes.

"Sure," said the man. "Everybody knows the story."

"Except us," said Harlan. "We've been away, remember?" The man's constant chipperness was beginning to get on his nerves.

Dawn finally reached the man's face. "Of course," he realized. "It all happened after you left. Please forgive me. Let me introduce ourselves. I'm Stan, that's Jerry, that's Louis, that's Bob, that's George, and this is Julius."

"Another Julius," murmured Napoleon, coming out of her fog. It was the name of the clone she and Larry had known so many years ago. "You're all FMs."

The six men chortled. "I guess you'd say so," Stan smiled. "We don't use such terms anymore."

"Why not?" Harlan asked pointedly.

"After *we* killed the TMs," Mess said pointedly, having been filled in (in more cirquid ways than one) by Muse, "they instituted the NAO."

Harlan would have been happy to hear the story straight through and fill in the blanks then, but Napoleon was fearless. "Who's 'they'? What's the NAO?"

"The other TMs," said Stan with a big, incongruous grin. "The Noah's Ark Operation. They killed every-

body." That reminded the feline of the piles of SM and
FM corpses littering the Denver Plateau Spaceport
where she and Larry had fought to reach their esc-globe.

"Then they made a whole new race of clones," said
Muse, "but from the same cell banks they had used
originally."

"They thought they could take up where they left off,"
said Mess.

"They continued to brainwash and drug us," said Stan
pleasantly. Harlan realized that when Stan said 'we,' he
meant it. Every new clone was a copy of an old one. Stan
must have gone back generations. "Only they didn't
know about the RIM."

"The rim?" Napoleon immediately questioned.

"Reincarnation Image Memories," said Stan. "We
remembered the massacre, you see. We remembered
everything the True Men had done to us ever since we
started." He looked back at the five others. They were all
smiling and nodding.

"The FMs and SMs did exactly what the TMs were
afraid they would," Muse related. "Once they discovered
what you—"

"We," Mess reminded them.

"Did," finished Muse.

"We killed them," Stan said mildly. This confession
had all the tension of a back rub.

"How long ago was this?" Harlan questioned.

"Oh," mused Stan, "I don't know. A hundred years or
so."

"A hundred!" Roscoe blurted.

"Two hundred?" Stan asked him.

"Two?" Pound echoed.

"Maybe five hundred," Stan reconsidered. The LOST
director looked helplessly at Harlan, and Trigor knew
why. According to Pound, he had left Earth sixty years
after they had. But according to the diffident Stan, the

FMs and SMs had turned on their Real Human masters by then. Harlan nodded knowingly to Roscoe. FLIT had scrambled time for all of them, giving the theater troupe enough time to leave before the clones murdered the TMs.

"That doesn't explain the stone letters," said Napoleon, taking a new subject right out of the air.

"Sure it does," said Stan.

"No, it doesn't."

"Sure it does."

"No, it doesn't!" Napoleon maintained.

"We built the letters out of sight of our TM managers," said Stan.

"As a show of defiance," said Muse.

"To work off their frustration," said Mess.

"That explains it," said Napoleon.

"Sure," said Stan. The other five all nodded.

"Doomstar landing procedures under way," Muse reported.

"DOLP," Stan agreed.

Her/its brisk announcement garnered a curious look from Roscoe, who joined the others at the VU port (tm). All conversation was temporarily postponed as the six eyes of the director, feline, and space bullet took in the impressive view.

Earth was gone. At least, it was essentially gone. The Earth the fugitives and the director had known was gone. The planet called Earth was gone. Instead of the big blue marble, there was a small red ball, which served as a companion to a small white ball, both of which revolved around a big brown rock.

Napoleon looked at Harlan. Harlan looked at Napoleon. Roscoe looked out the VU port (tm). And they all knew. The red ball had been Earth. The white ball had been its satellite, the moon. And the huge stone was the result of all the FMs' labors; that old devil, Doomstar.

"But there's no oceans, no foliage," Roscoe mourned. "It's just a barren landscape."

"The world is inside," Muse informed him in a crisp impersonal manner. "Doomstar consists of levels between a heat/power source and a frozen water supply. The exterior wall of the planet houses a distribution system that balances the ecology."

"We're chaperoning you to our lowest, most exclusive level," Stan revealed proudly. They could now see the tiny ports all over the world's surface. Soon, no doubt, they would see a low-lying dot open just for them.

"How are you holding up?" Harlan whispered to Napoleon.

"I'm about to crawl out of my fur," she admitted through clenched teeth. "The nearer we get to this place, the more I feel like chewing on my thigh. I'm scared, Harlan. Something must be wrong with the Coven spell. This *can't* be Nest!"

"No, it can't," Trigor reminded her. "You're still able to make full sentences. If I understand the spell right, Nest is where you'll totally revert to feline form." He eyed the new world's two moons. "It isn't Nest."

"Then it's got to be Cheshire close!" Napoleon seethed.

"What about me?" Roscoe had entered the whispering fest. "I don't want to be Larry. Why can't we tell them who I am? Or, at least, who I'm not."

"Idiot," Napoleon growled. "You're a TM. They killed all the TMs. Would you rather be treated as a returning hero of the revolution or the last of the slavemasters?" That shut Pound up, but couldn't distract the feline from her inner plight. "Harlan . . ."

"Hold on, Nap. Concentrate. I'm here."

Doomstar loomed larger and larger in the port. "Approaching outer atmosphere," Muse announced.

"Automatic Landing Procedures understood. Automatic Landing Procedures engaged."

"ALP," Stan said happily.

"Contact with *Hartman-Barker* broken. Outer atmosphere breached."

Stan, Jerry, Louis, Bob, George, and Julius fell heavily to the floor.

Harlan, Roscoe, and Napoleon whirled around at the sound of the FMs' faces and heads smacking into the deck. The clones lay still, bleeding. The three LOSTers stared in astonishment. Trigor carefully stepped over to the bodies and methodically checked each one.

"They're all dead," he said evenly.

"Is it my breath?" Napoleon asked blankly.

# NINETEEN

As soon as the initial shock wore off, Napoleon spit and backed to the far wall, her back arched and her hair on end. All the blood left Pound's face, and Mess started babbling.

"Boy, I'm glad they didn't find out about me! Why do you think I was left out of your legend anyway? Those guys sure acted freaked."

"Freaked?" Harlan asked deliberately.

"Another drug term," Muse told him. "From Palsy-Drake days." She/it suddenly knew a lot about the *Black Hole* and *Felidae*'s compubot. Trigor continued to search the corpses.

"What are you looking for?" Roscoe asked nervously.

"Anything to explain this."

"You think they killed themselves?"

"I don't think anything. I mean, I don't know. Napoleon!" The feline had started to sniff at the dead men's feet. "Concentrate!"

"Muse," Pound called. "Do we have to land?"

"ALP is set," she/it answered distantly. "There's no turning back."

"Yet," Harlan added. "Prepare to take off as soon as we land."

"Who is he talking to?" Muse wanted to know icily.

"Must be me," soothed Mess.

"Well, it certainly can't be me," continued Muse. "I do not take orders from him."

"I don't really either," Mess assured her/it. "I only do it as a favor to my resurrecter."

"Stop that, Mess!" Napoleon demanded, shaking off the Covenisms. "Don't let her intimidate you. Be an. . . . it."

"Really!" huffed Muse.

"Do as they say!" Roscoe shouted.

"Then I'll just do it as a favor to my master, shall I?" Muse said quickly. Harlan felt like adding some choice words of his own, but a hiss from Napoleon brought his head around to face Roscoe's chair. The feline stood before it, pointing a paw. Roscoe was there first. He saw his actors still in their macabre embrace, only now Spot was dead as well. Harlan put the truth together instantly.

"All the FMs and SMs died as soon as we entered Doomstar's outer atmosphere."

"Oh, my stars!" Roscoe exclaimed. "Then Doomstar *could* be Nest!"

He was right. No one knew what lay inside the planet now. Harlan got two steps toward his space bullet suit before he realized that it was useless against the enemy. Napoleon just stood there, dumbfounded, unsure whether to collapse in a leonine heap or start climbing the walls.

"Doomstar's not responding to comm-link," said Muse.

"Oh, my larry, what have you gotten me into?" Roscoe moaned.

"Calm down," said Harlan, quickly going through their options. It was very quick, since it turned out that they didn't have any. "You'd be in this with or without us."

"I didn't even want to come here!" Napoleon whined.

"Everyone damper!" Harlan boomed. "Status, Muse."

"Completing ALP. Manual override ineffective." Pound ran to the VU Port (tm). He saw the entry port yawning open before them. He saw the plain dull silver hangar inside. He saw some small dark figures moving around. He turned away, unable to consider their possible fate. Instead, he ran to one of the tables.

"Hey," he said. "I'm picking up VU programs." Sure enough, the tabletop was lit with identifiably human images. It showed rapid-fire scenes of violent battle, complete with graphic special effects. Much to Pound's surprise, the sequence was very similar to the sort of fare he had left behind twenty (or sixty or several hundred) years before.

There were big close-ups of naked, sweaty women chained to dungeon walls in torturous positions. Sickening devices were clamped all over, under and onto their gleaming forms. The only noncaptive female was a woman in a fur coat with a blazing rifle. Beside her was a tall man in a bulky purple suit whose own blasting gun ripped into a mob of contorting fighters. Liquid of every color was splashing on the walls, floor, and the ceiling.

"Let's get out of here!" the girl in the orange fur coat cried.

"Not until we find Titu!" the man shouted back.

"Oh, where's Larry when we need him?" the woman wailed.

"Hey," said Harlan.

The scene switched to a dank cell where a beautiful, naked, black-haired girl lay bound and gagged to a plank which hung tenuously over a pit of thin, long, copper-colored spikes. On her stomach lay a small ticking explosive device taped to her sides and back. Behind her was a craggy-faced, handsome, sandy-haired man who was tip-toeing through a mass of sleeping apes.

"Just hold still, Titu," the man whispered earnestly. "I'm a pal of your brother's. I'll save you."

"Hey," Harlan said louder this time.

Back on the VU screen, the sandy-haired man tripped and the rifle slipped from his shoulder. He tried to catch it, but he was a klutz. It wound up bouncing off an ape's face, then falling to the stone floor with a loud, persistent clatter. All the apes' eyes snapped open and everyone stared at the embarrassed hero. "Oops," was what he said.

"We'll be right back with 'The Cat and the Clone' after these vital contingencies," said a VU voice.

"Hey!" Harlan boomed, stalking over to the set.

He was in time to see a beautiful, naked woman holding up a bottle of green liquid. "We've worked hard on new Tonsit," she said brightly. "But we worked so hard that the price nearly went up. But we, the great people at Mindwind, wouldn't do that to you. We knew that you couldn't afford to get your morning and meal-time rush if we made everything compatible with the BOPS-AGH's regulations. So we refused, then passed on the savings to you! Now you can get Tonsit tight for the same low price as ever!"

The woman's face was obliterated by small print and a voice on the soundtrack intoned: "New, not improved Tonsit, for your morning, mealtime, midnight rush."

Harlan's Destiny-trained eyes picked up all the words that flashed on the screen. "Use as directed if possible, read instructions if possible, the BOPS-AGH have discovered that point oh four two percent of the carrrigan dioxparagentacide is hazardous to an average person, an average person being among the sixty-five thousand three hundred and thirty-seven people tested from the highest planetary level in a general age range averaging three months sixteen days ten hours and thirty-two minutes. Ingestion is not advised, although not prohibited. Based on a thrice-daily usage of no more than ten milligrams and no less than three milligrams. Some restrictions might apply, given level regulations. Mindwind companies are in no way responsible for the use or misuse of this or any other product of any other company in any way, shape, or form, nor are they liable for any actions by anything anywhere. Tonsit is not be be mistaken or confused with any other product of this or any other company or individual, living, dead, sick, or comatose, retarded, autistic, or certifiably insane when certification relates to general consensus, common knowledge, or official sanction or decree. Personal effect may vary, but no state of mind or party can be attributed to this or any other product, ingredient, or waste material anywhere within the sphere of any Mindwind company, factory, individual, or that individual's property, when property includes anything within that individual's experience, living, dead, sick, or comatose."

These words disappeared from the screen in less than two seconds and were replaced by images of two young people running, laughing, eating, playing, and finally, having sex. Bouncy, lilting music played on the soundtrack. There was a close-up of the lovers' smiling, sweaty faces, and then a sonorous voice proclaimed: "These images have almost nothing to do with Gulpease Brand Tonics, but we have found through research that showing our Gulpease Brand Tonics is not as effective as giving the impression that Gulpease Brand Tonics are somehow associated with acts of personal pleasure."

The lovers went out of focus and the Gulpease bottle with a tall, sparkling glass labeled Gulpease came into focus. "It's a great life," said a woman's sultry voice.

"Why not *live* it?" Then images of a climber falling off a beautiful mountain, a swimmer drowning in a crystal sea, and a well-dressed couple getting hit by an OD vehicle flashed in Roscoe's and Harlan's eyes.

"Hey," said Pound, who was getting uncharacteristically thirsty. "Did you see that?" Trigor nodded, also having seen the tiny letters saying "subliminal messages in use" at the bottom of the VU screen.

"Gulpease Brand Tonics," said the male voice. "Gulpease Brand Tonics. Gulpease Brand Tonics."

Gulpease Brand Tonics," said the woman. "Gulpease . . . Brand . . . Tonics. Gulp . . . ease . . . Brand . . . Ton . . . ics."

This time Harlan was already carefully watching the bottom of the screen, but even Roscoe could read the words that appeared. "Guaranteed Cumulatively Fatal. Latest Findings: five uses/nausea, ten uses/illness, fifteen uses/chronic disease, twenty uses/catatonia, twenty-five uses/death. Your results may vary. Loquacious Liquids renounces and rejects its customers."

Then it was back to the thinly disguised adventures of Larry, Napoleon, Harlan, and his sister, Hana, who they had renamed Titu. Roscoe looked meaningfully at the real Trigor, who could only begin to make sense of what he had just seen.

"Doomstar responding," Muse announced calmly.

"Turn that off," Harlan snapped, tearing his eyes off the hypnotically ugly images. "Muse, status."

"ALP complete. AT (Automatic Takeoff) unresponsive. Doomstar port lock secured."

"What does that mean?" Roscoe whined.

"They locked the back door behind us," Harlan cursed. "We've landed in Doomstar and we can't get out."

"What?" Napoleon meowed. "What is it? Where am I? Harlan, help me!"

Harlan couldn't even reply. There was nothing he could say or do. He felt like drinking twenty-five glasses of Gulpease. His love was going insane and he couldn't help her. They were trapped in Doomstar and he couldn't make their escape. He hated himself.

His moment of terror was like a spark. As soon as it had started, it was over. Nothing had caught flame. Harlan had smothered it himself. He had to stay strong, even for those he had already repeatedly failed. He was their only hope in the face of whatever was out there. He grabbed the feline and pushed Roscoe behind him. He turned toward the stage door as it started to open.

"We're not doing it!" Mess wailed.

"I know," said a grim Harlan.

Bright light flooded the doorway. A form was framed in it, infused with glowing illumination. The figure stepped in, followed by five more. "Welcome," said Stan. Jerry, Louis, Bob, George, and Julius stood behind him, smiling. "Welcome to Doomstar. Now, what were we talking about again?"


"Let me explain," said Stan affably. "Guys, get yourselves out of here." The five walked past the cowering LOSTers and started carrying and dragging their own corpses toward the door. Stan smiled at the trio as the others went about their work. "Nice to have you back," he socialized.

"You, too" Harlan replied, missing none of the sardonic irony.

"Ah, yes," Stan laughed. "The FOW is at it again." He pronounced it "foe."

"The Federation of Worlds?" Roscoe corroborated.

Stan nodded. "There's a war on. Every once in a while, they kill us all," he said mildly. He continued when the others were too stunned to speak. "Oh, sure. They've done it five, six, maybe seven times now. We figure whatever FOW planet is attacking us, it has to be at least six months away, since that's the shortest time between secret superweapons so far."

"You don't know who's invading you?" Harlan asked incredulously.

"Not invading," Stan corrected. "Attacking. We've never seen the aliens. We've only seen their SS weapons." He shrugged. "We're fairly certain it can't be the entire FOW, of course, and that whoever it is, they want the planet intact."

That made sense. If they hadn't, Harlan had little doubt that the might of the Federation would have decimated the world by now. There would have been nothing for the *Shooting Star* to land on. As the five other FMs finished dragging their doubles out and started taking Zero and Spot from the chair, Harlan put together a psychological profile of the Doomstarrers. He did not like what he saw, heard, or thought.

"What's the bops agh?" Napoleon meowed vacantly.

"The Bureau of Public Safety and General Health," Stan said immediately. Any question from a revolutionary hero deserved an immediate answer without question.

"What's the hit coat?" The feline was chirping the questions with an empty, mild expression. Harlan could tell she was running on automatic, almost in savor.

"The Hitcote . . . Well, he's the Hitcote, isn't he? The Hitcote is the Hitcote." Realizing that wasn't enough for a virtual demigod, Stan reconsidered. "Maybe the SIRBOF Regs will know."

"What's the sirboff regs?" Napoleon mewed.

"The Singular Insular Ruling Body of Friends," said Stan. "Regulators. They have to register you in."

"No more ECG?" Napoleon giggled. "No more U.W.?" She kneeled luxuriously and scratched her side along Harlan's leg.

"Stop that," he said, putting his hands under her arms. "Stand up."

"I'm hungry," she mewed, rolling her head on Harlan's shoulder. "You're nice and warm."

"Stop that!" he commanded. The feline finally snapped out of it.

"Sorry," she apologized. "Harlan, something's happening."

"I know."

"No, something else. Something . . ."

"Control yourself," he said tersely. "So," he said agreeably to Stan. "You got rid of the Earth Central Government? The United World?"

"ENSUB?" Roscoe added.

"Oh, sure," Stan assured them. "We streamlined everything. The SIRBOF is much better than those things."

The first Reg was named Woody. The second Reg was Joe. They sat in an open, airy shack in the tropical paradise which was Doomstar's lowest level. "It is an honor and a privilege for us to register you," said Reg number one. "The *Hartman-Barker* told us of your coming."

"Just a formality," said Reg number two. "The *Hitcote* prophesied your return, but we have our regulations."

Both men started poking tensor squares on small slates they held in one hand.

"Full names?"

"Napoleon."

"Full name."

"Napoleon."

"Is that your full name?"

"You know it is!"

"Planet of origin?"

"Mandarin."

"Earth name?"

"Mandarin."

"That's the Earthen explorer name?"

"That's the only name I know!"

"Planetality?"

"Feline."

"Are you now or were you ever a citizen of Earth?"

"No." Napoleon had a self-satisfied look on her face.

"Are you now or were you ever a citizen of Doomstar?"

"No."

"Never?"

"Never. I was a resident." Harlan realized she was playing with the Regs.

"Are you now or were you ever a resident of Earth?"

"Yes." Like a cat played with her prey.

"For how long?"

"Sixteen years." That surprised the space bullet.

"Reason for departure?"

"You know."

"I can't fill this in. You must." The Reg didn't even look up.

And so it went, through "Is that Harlan Trigor?" "Is that Trigor with an 'e'?" and the infamous "Do you have any alien food, drink, product, or weapon to declare?"

"The space bullet suit."

"The what?"

"My space bullet suit."

"What?"

"My Destinian self-contained armament suit."

"Oh, Weinstein-Hubbell," Woody swore. Napoleon laughed when she realized that they were using Larry's creator as a swear word now. "No criteria."

It was Harlan's turn to say, "What?"

"No criteria. We have no criteria for a space bullet suit," said Woody.

"We'll have to create one," said Joe. "The SBS? The SS? The DS?"

"DS?" Woody asked.

"Destinian Suit. The DSBS?"

"The DSCAS?"

"The Spab? The Spallet? The Deslet?"

"The ARM-IT!" Woody exclaimed. And that was it. By then all the non-Doomstarrers knew that the SIRBOF was at least twice as long, twice as complex, and twice as bad as the ECG.

But finally their questions were over. There was time for one from Napoleon. "What's the hit coat?" Her voice had slowly degenerated to a catlike squeal which grated on Harlan's mind.

"The Hitcote?" Woody answered. "Why, he's our leader."

"You are our deities," Joe agreed. "And he is our leader."

"But what does hit coat mean?" the feline wondered.

The Regs were stymied until Joe hit upon a retranslation of her question. "Oh, of course! You will see him. You must see him! He has to see you. Let us take you to our leader." So it was that the three leery travelers were following Woody, Joe, and Stan along the wide beige paths of the Double El (Lower Level/Double L).

"Oh, sure," Stan said once again. "Everyone wants to come down here. The waiting list is prodigious." They passed a lovely grove with an elegant building housing tall, vaguely familiar statues. "Ah, this is one of our Clat Temples." They peered at the sculptures to recognize the girl in the fur coat, the handsome blond man, and the guy in the bumpy purple suit. Clat—CLone-cAT. Naturally, deities had to have a religion.

"But that doesn't look anything like me!" Napoleon

complained, pouting. The statue had no cat ears, cat paws, whiskers, and only the hint of a tail. Stan just smiled vacantly and agreed.

Harlan took the time to consider the situation carefully. Could the planet dropping the SS weapons on Doomstar be Nest? Obviously, the planet didn't have the facilities to bomb the place back. All they had were great clone factories. Clo-Facs, no doubt. So when the population was eradicated, they were automatically reproduced, complete with memories. Memories of their degradation by TMs, memories of the Noah's Ark Operation, memories of their bloody revolution, and memory after memory of death after death after death. What would that do to a person? Harlan himself remembered what he had seen on the VU screen. The TMs had deadened the FMs and SMs with drugs to keep these cloned human beings pliant. Now the Doomstarrers were obviously doing it to themselves—to forget, to control the incredible shame and self-loathing they had to feel. Harlan couldn't help but feel sorry for the cheerfully insane people of this anguished planet.

Sympathy was something Harlan couldn't be practical about. The FOW war was something he could. If it was the Mantases who were trying to wipe Doomstar clean, the key question was why. His thoughts were interrupted when he bumped into Napoleon. She had stopped in her tracks and was spitting at the ground.

Harlan looked over her clenched teeth, blazing eyes, and claw-ready paws to the two foozles who had frozen in place ten paces from them, at the crosswalk. The little things hadn't changed. They were still somewhere between two and three feet tall on their hind legs, dressed in shiny blue skirts and/or tunics, and were, basically, adorable-looking puppy dogs.

Not only had their appearance not altered, but their manners were the same as well. Instead of barking or howling or countering Napoleon's aggression in any way, they simply stopped, looked the hissing feline over, and then one said, "What's your problem?"

Harlan put himself between the canines and Napoleon. At this moment he had taken on a new, invisible peacemaker suit. "Pardon us," he quipped. "She's regressing."

The foozles were unimpressed. "Oh?"

"Certainly," Harlan replied, a grin growing on his otherwise mirthless face. "Cats and dogs have distrusted each other for centuries."

"I'm not a dog," said the second foozle.

The first interrupted. "That's uninteresting," he said flatly. The creatures had never been ones for either diplomacy or dishonesty. "Will she attack us?"

"Not yet," Harlan said.

They didn't like the sound of that, so the pair backed away, looks of concerned distaste on their faces. "What was that all about?" Roscoe whispered to Trigor as the space bullet did his best to soothe the feline. Harlan scratched the cat's neck with brisk strokes. He looked away from her intense eyes.

"What are they doing here?" he snapped at the Regs and Stan.

"What?" Woody said defensively. "The foozles?"

"Yes," Harlan said pedantically. "The foozles. Weren't they exiled along with the Mantases?"

"They just returned," said Joe. "Mantases are our enemy, but there's nothing wrong with foozles."

"They're descended from puppies," Stan said. So that theory was generally accepted now, Harlan thought, that all aliens were originally Earthen creatures which had mutated, gained intelligence, and returned from the stars. Even on Doomstar, Earth was commonly acknowledged as the center of the universe.

Even so, Harlan was hard-pressed to remain silent. His

sister, Hana, had told him what the foozles did to her on Destiny, how they were teamed with the Mantases.

"Even though they followed the Mantases' orders," Hana had told him, "they still seemed to be in control. They were always speaking their feelings so honestly, they almost seemed to be making sarcastic jokes. They would never fail to question a command they didn't like or agree with, and at times their attitude bordered on open insubordination."

Harlan had been proud of her. Even after her terrible ordeal on Jackpot, she was able to relate details of her captivity without emotional collapse. She was, indeed, a daughter of Destiny.

"Please." Woody sought to calm the deity's sudden anger. "Do not concern yourself. The Hitcote awaits." The group moved on amid the Double El luxury. The perception of sky was cunning. It was actually the floor of the next highest level but designed and implemented in such a way that it gave the impression of being a natural Earth-like atmosphere.

Illumination, too, seemed to be natural. It came from everywhere, but Harlan's enhanced senses could pick out light sources along both horizons and under their feet. The world had an inner glow. That, as well as everything else that had occurred since they touched down, made the soldier think—hard. The strategy channels in his mind clicked like dominoes until he devised a theory that fit the evidence. Harlan took a final moment to enjoy his role as peacemaker. It had been fun. But now it was time to return to his more natural guise of one of the universe's great warmongers.

"What's this?" he wondered as the Regs and Stan stopped the entourage before a bunkerlike construct with a single door.

"The Hitcote," said Woody. Other than the five, there was no one else in sight. Although the population could be recreated automatically, it was obvious that Double El, at least, was vastly underpopulated.

"What are you doing?" Harlan pressed as the Regs started stabbing their tensor slates.

"It's the Hitcote," Stan said in surprise. "No one can see the Hitcote except the chosen ones. To enter, the new EASE must be properly entered."

"Ease," Napoleon mewed.

"Entry and Secret Exit code," Stan revealed. The feline nodded and they all waited as the Regs struggled with the complex series of signals which would make their leader available to their returned demigods. Napoleon spent the time trying to rub against Harlan's leg, and he spent the time trying to stop her.

It was different this time. The feline was not treating Harlan's limbs like a scratching post or a tree. The look in her eyes as she gazed up at him was unmistakable. He was looking at a wild animal.

"Stop that," he demanded quietly, pulling her up. She immediately embraced him. "Stop that," he said. She kissed him passionately. So passionately, in fact, that Stan's smile widened and Roscoe felt like looking away. "Stop that," he said a third time when he finally managed to extricate himself.

She was panting, her chest heaving. "Estrus," she gasped.

"What?"

"Cheshire, Harlan, I'm in—"

"Don't say it." He didn't need this on top of everything else. In cats, the estrus cycle could last as long as forty-five days. Unless they found and destroyed Nest soon, Napoleon would go nuts with desire. But their immediate concern was how to keep her off him. Whenever he'd stop her from going to all fours, she'd hug and kiss him. She couldn't seem to decide how to respond to her heat—as a cat or a humanoid.

Doomstar took care of the problem, but with solutions like this, they didn't need disasters. A mob of people appeared in the distance, coming toward them. "Worshipers?" Roscoe said hopefully when he saw Stan's aghast expression.

The clone said nothing, just stared in fear at the oncoming crowd. Harlan moved Napoleon out of his way as they held each other. "They're all women," he noted. Napoleon looked over her shoulder and through smoldering eyes saw the throng of human females marching purposefully toward them. She also saw the things in their hands.

The Regs didn't look up until the weight of the women's marching feet started to shake the ground. Woody gaped and Joe blanched. They returned to their task with a renewed vigor born of panic. "Who are they?" Harlan demanded of Stan point-blank.

"The SM Bees," he gulped, still staring at them.

S, Roscoe pondered. Sex. M, Machine. B? He gazed at the faces just coming into view. Angry, purposeful faces. Blank, emotionless faces. Hysterical, bloodthirsty faces. "Battalions!" he gasped.

The trio stood in the wide open spaces without a lick of cover or protection as the Sex Machine Battalion bore down on them. Dozens of crazed female clones driven mad by the decades of degradation heaped on them by the TMs.

"But we're your deities!" Roscoe exclaimed. "I'm . . . we're not True Men! We didn't do anything to them!"

"It makes no difference," Harlan guessed when Stan remained silent. "Hundreds of years of abuse in their collective mind. There has to be a release. They have to have some kind of revenge."

"They're going to kill us!" Pound realized.

"Tear us limb from limb," Stan said softly, emptily. "Mutilate us."

"What's that in their hands?" Napoleon asked, Coven-isms dampered by the situation. They were angled implements with a thick rectangular barrel and flat handle.

"Their FM Bees," Stan said darkly. "Hurry!" he demanded stridently of the Regs. But they were going as fast as they could. The Hitcote door was not opening.

"What in the . . ." Roscoe started before he physically started. They could all see the SM Bees clearly. They were no more than a hundred feet away. At the very crown of the mob, leading her sisters to the man who had kept her in theatrical captivity for twenty years, was the resurrected Phyllis—otherwise known as Spot.

# TWENTY

Napoleon marched to meet them. She made a magnificent female figure, her back straight, her eyes blazing, her fur shining in the Double El light, her tail lashing. "Stop!" she demanded. Even the SM Bees could not deny her. "Back off."

To Roscoe's astonishment, the halted mass showed signs of confusion. Some actually stepped back. But that was before Phyllis looked around and rallied her sisters. "Sisters of Mercy," she called, giving new meaning to the epithet SM, "we must be strong and united! Do not be deterred by the alien Earth Mother." She returned her gaze to the men, looking directly at Roscoe. "If you prick us, do we not bleed? If you poison us, do we not die? And if you wrong us . . . shall we not revenge?"

The crowd went wild with support. Spot smiled at Roscoe. She was using Shakespeare's words as her own. His magic was hers to the unknowing mob. But Napoleon knew some Shakespeare too.

"Away!" she yelled. "And mock the time with fairest show. False face must hide what the false heart must know." The mob was confused. This feline was speaking exactly like their leader, seemingly accusing Phyllis of duplicity.

"What though care killed a cat," Spot said directly to the feline threateningly, quoting from *Much Ado About Nothing*. "Thou hast mettle enough in thee to kill care." Phyllis had chosen to warn Napoleon, which gave the cat the upper hand. She continued to sway the crowd rather than converse with the ex-actress.

"Who can be wise, amazed, temperate and furious, loyal and neutral in a moment? No man!" she cried, speaking from *Macbeth*. "Stand not upon the order of your going, but go at once!" Napoleon's strength could not be denied, but she only knew two Shakespeare plays. Phyllis knew all of them.

"It will have blood, they say! Blood will have blood!" *Macbeth*.

"I am in blood," Napoleon immediately replied from *Macbeth*. "Stepped in so far, that I should wade no more!"

Spot was furious. The feline had changed the line slightly to fit her own meaning. This was Shakespeare! It was not done! "Blow, winds, and crack your cheeks!" she raged from *King Lear*. "Rage! Blow! You cataracts and hurricanes, spout till you have drenched our steeples, drowned the cocks! You sulfurous and thought-executing fires, vaunt-couriers to oak-cleaving thunderbolts, singe my white head! And thou, all-shaking thunder, strike flat the thick rotundity of the world! *Crack* nature's molds, all germens spill at once *that make ingrateful man!*"

But she wasn't through. She wouldn't let Napoleon get the upper hand again. "Oh, a kiss. Long as my exile, sweet as my revenge!" *Coriolanus*. "And now I'll do it.

And so he goes to heaven. And so I am revenged."
*Hamlet*. "Then, kill. Kill, kill, kill, kill! Kill!" *King Lear*.

The mob roared its pent-up anger and surged forward.
Stan took one last hopeless look at the frenetic Regs, then
jumped in front of the feline. "No!" Spot shot him with
her FM Bee.

The projectile sank into Stan's stomach, pushing him
back into Napoleon. Harlan had clearly seen the small
missile's trail, and it wasn't because of his vaunted eyesight either. The bullet had traveled like a knife and sank
into the man's skin, then completely disappeared.

Stan turned his pain-twisted face to the feline. "Get
back," he managed to gasp. Napoleon hopped away and
Stan's middle exploded between his fingers.

"Burster!" Roscoe realized with disgust. "They're
Fake Man Bursters!"

Napoleon danced back to protect her mate. Roscoe
jumped behind Harlan as well. The Regs flattened themselves against the bunker door, their fingers still flying
across the tensors. Trigor didn't dare distract them with
any questions.

Stan jumped as he died, trying to block Phyllis. He
collapsed, almost in two pieces in front of her. A red
puddle started to grow at her feet, forcing her to walk
around the horrid corpse. It delayed her just long enough.

She smiled at the other LOSTers, then turned her head
and opened her mouth to command the Sisters of Mercy.
She froze in midmotion, her arm up, gaping off to the
right. They all saw Zero running from the other side of
the bunker. "Spot, no!"

Napoleon saw the SM mouth her lover's name. But she
lowered the gun at his middle all the same. He slowed,
then stopped, his hands out. All the SM Bees' heads were
turned toward him. "Please, Spot, don't," Zero
admonished.

"The last line," she mumbled. "You . . . we . . ."

"Don't do this," he requested carefully.

"Run," she whispered to him. "Get away."

"You don't have to do this."

"Yes," she nodded. "I do. You don't know ... you weren't ... you didn't ..." The remembered pain was finally torn away for one split second. Zero took the advantage.

"Yes, you're right!" he proclaimed loudly. "I wasn't there! I didn't do anything to you! None of us did! It was the TMs! The TMs did it, not the FMs!"

The Regs fell over backward. The bunker door had swung open.

"That's right!" Spot screamed, turning and pointing at Roscoe. "And *he's* a TM!"

Harlan threw Pound over the Regs. The director fell on his stomach and slid all the way down the hall. Harlan picked up Napoleon and threw her. She vaulted through the air, over the Regs, and landed on all fours. "Come on!" he yelled at Zero. He didn't wait for him, so when he turned back in the bunker entrance, he saw the Regs and Zero lined up, blocking the door from the outside. "Get in!"

Woody shook his head. "We are not chosen," said Joe. Their hands were stabbing their slates still.

Harlan tried to grab them, but the SM Bees' fingers and weapons were faster. Trigor saw the burster bullets hitting them in the torsos and the long female fingers wrapping around their arms, necks, and hair. They looked like white worms digging in and out of the men's flesh. "Close the door!" they screamed.

It slammed shut as their bodies started to explode. Napoleon had leaped between Harlan's legs to do it. The obstruction automatically relocked. They could hear the FM Bees blasting outside. "Thank Trigor," Roscoe gasped.

"No," he said. "Thank Napoleon." He walked to the

end of the short plain hall. There was a hole in the floor there just big enough for their bodies. There was a pole off center in the hole. "We must slide down using the walls and the pole to keep from going too fast," he reasoned.

But Roscoe wasn't able to forget what had just happened so easily. "They wanted to rip me apart," he marveled. "I never did anything to Spot. I don't even know those other women!"

"They're giving vent to something they probably never experienced themselves," Harlan said, peering down the tube. "It was their previous selves who had been debased by the TMs centuries ago. Somehow it's been building up inside every new clone for that long." Roscoe gulped. No wonder everybody on Doomstar was nuts. "Well, we might as well get this over with," Trigor sighed. "Napoleon. Napoleon? Napoleon!"

The feline was staring into empty air as if hypnotized. Roscoe touched her back. She howled, flung herself into the air, and ran crazily around the room. Harlan expertly tackled her as she passed a third time and wrestled her to the floor. "Snap out of it!"

Rationality came back to the feline as she lay spread-eagled under the soldier. "I was thinking about my spitter," she marveled. "And all of a sudden there it was in front of me. Scared the living Cheshire out of me, that I can tell you."

"I didn't see any spitter," Roscoe complained.

"It's her imagination," Harlan told him. "A cat's vivid imagination, no doubt." He looked back down to see estrus in her eyes again. He got up very quickly. Napoleon stretched out sensually on the floor.

"Do we have to see this hit coat?" she purred enticingly.

"Yes."

"Oh, pooh." Napoleon rolled over onto her stomach as

Harlan marched to the hole in the floor. He was just about to step in when the feline was there, snarling into the pit.

"Oh, come on, Nap," he grumbled in exasperation. But she was too far gone to respond. She was spitting and scratching at the hole as if ... as if she had cornered a juicy hunk of frightened vermin.

"I'll go," Roscoe offered, but Harlan held him back, a finger to his lips. He circled the pit, then leaned over and whispered into Napoleon's ear. She grabbed a quick kiss, then slid back. She crawled over to Roscoe and motioned for him to kneel down.

"Tell me a story," she asked. "I have to stay sane."

Pound looked nervously over at Trigor, who was silently lowering himself into the hole with his arms and legs spread wide against the tube's sides. He told her the first tale that came into his head. "Lord knew she was right when she left that heartless brute with her heart at his feet," he began from *Her Lustful Passions*. "Hot tears of shame stung her dark, sultry eyes. . . ."

The foozles were taken completely by surprise. They had been waiting at the bottom of the passage with their Pawprint Piercers, ready to kill the LOSTers as they slid in. Instead, Harlan stuck in the bottom of the tube, waiting for his own moment to strike. As soon as the foozles' attention was diverted by a groan coming from the table behind them, Trigor slid out.

The canines had a chance, but hardly one worth mentioning. Suffice to say that within seconds the foozles were in the corner of the severe white room, their weapons were in Napoleon's paws, and Roscoe and Harlan were on either side of the table, looking down into the deeply canaled face of the Hitcote.

He was an old, old man in a plain, foot-length robe. He was clean shaven and his fingernails were short, but his hair was white. There was a small box under the tabletop from him and a bigger box on the floor under him.

"Who are you?" Roscoe asked the heavy-lidded, watery blue eyes.

His voice was very small, distant, weak, and slow. It took him exactly fifty-six seconds to say, "Hartman-Barker," hitting every vowel and consonant with breathy agony.

"Another TM!" Pound marveled at Harlan.

"H-I-T-C-O-T-E," Trigor spelled. "Human in the Center of the Earth." He looked up at Roscoe meaningfully. "Their leader."

"The last True Man," the director realized. "What's wrong with him?"

"He's ancient, that's what," said a foozle. Napoleon snarled, sending the little creature back against the wall.

It took the Hitcote twenty-seven seconds to get out, "Governor."

"He's a governor?" Roscoe wondered.

"Machine," the Hitcote said in nineteen seconds.

"It's the thing under the table," Harlan related, kneeling. "He's attached to it."

"Oh, this is torment," said the foozle. "It slows down his metabolism. He's got more diseases than you can count on all eight paws and toes." They ought to know. The trio had discovered that the religious Doomstarrers had the aliens guard the Hitcote, since no FM or SM was worthy. As if the foozles were. "As if puppy dogs are," Roscoe had snorted.

"They're not puppy dogs," Harlan revealed. "They're not descended from Earthen canines at all." And now, since the foozles seemed willing to speed up the Hitcote's interrogation, Trigor turned back to them. "Your planet is in the Federation, isn't it?"

The foozles said nothing. "You're the ones who have been dropping the SS weapons, and when that didn't work, you came down here to find out what went wrong, didn't you?" The foozles remained silent. "Everything had Earthen-based names," Harlan explained somberly to Roscoe, "Mantases, felines, Coven, Jackpot, even Destiny—except for 'foozles.' Every alien creature acted in a similar manner to their original Earthen antecedent—except the foozles."

"They showed no fear toward Napoleon as a cat at all," Pound remembered.

"No." He watched the doglike creatures evenly. "You made a deal with the Mantases to infiltrate Earth. The boogers seemed to be using you, but you had been using them all along. Hadn't you?" Not a foozle lip so much as quivered.

"Why?" Roscoe inquired. "What on Earth could you possibly be afraid of?" The foozles stared ahead as if they hadn't heard.

"You may not be genetically afraid of felines," Harlan said, "but you've got plenty to fear from Napoleon, in any case. Nap? Make them talk."

She only had to lean forward to get one of the creatures conversing. "What wasn't there on Earth to be afraid of?" he said angrily. "This planet is incredibly, astonishingly dangerous. They're incredibly stupid, yet manage to survive almost everything. They're incredibly suicidal, yet hold on to their short, miserable lives with clawing, homicidal desperation.

"Do you know about this Doomstar of theirs? Do you know how the ecological system is set up? It seems to work perfectly, on a superficial level, but the Double El is bathed in enough radiation on a daily basis to kill residents twenty years earlier than someone on the HL."

"Highest Level," said the other foozle dryly.

"Earthen corruption has totally permeated too many solar systems," the first foozle asserted. "But I don't want to proselytize. I'm not telling you anything new. Earthen

lore is filled with such cautionary tales. And you yourselves are no strangers to Earthen cruelty. What do you
care what we do to this planet, these people?"

They made a good point. Roscoe looked at Harlan with
concern.

"Normally," Trigor said placidly, "nothing. But there
are other concerns."

"What?" asked a foozle and Roscoe at the same time.

"Boogers," growled Napoleon with a wicked grin.

"What about them?" the foozle replied too quickly.

Harlan joined Napoleon, his manner efficient and
assured. "A test," he announced. "You answer everything, or I let the feline get to you."

"I don't know if I can control myself for long," Napoleon told him tersely. Neither Trigor nor Pound knew
whether she was acting or not.

"You're not from Earth."

"No."

"Your planet is in the Federation of Worlds."

"Yes."

"Why destroy Doomstar?"

"We were assigned to investigate Earth. To keep the
Federation informed. We reported on the danger and
were reassigned to destroy the planet. When the Fake
Men and Sex Machines did it for us, we reported the new
danger. The clone population was so abused, so tortured,
and so confused, the Federation didn't see our assignment as a slaughter. Rather, we were putting Doomstar
out of their misery."

"How are you going to do it?" The foozles balked.
Napoleon nearly punctured the one nearest her in a
spasmodic thrust. Her intensity managed to surprise even
Harlan. She was indeed coming unstuck.

"That," the foozle said, pointing to the box under the
Hitcote's table.

"Pee kay gee," the deteriorating human said in a world's record of ten seconds.

The foozles answered Harlan's look this time. "Planet Killing Gadget," they translated. "PKG." Roscoe especially looked at them in disbelief. "When on Doomstar . . ." one shrugged.

"Having failed to wipe out the population," Harlan amended his previous theory, "you came to plant a bomb in the center of the world."

"Yes."

"You're not protecting the Mantases?"

"No." That rendered Harlan speechless.

"What are we waiting for?" Roscoe inquired. "Go on."

"The foozles don't lie," Trigor informed him, guessing on the basis of what he had seen, what Hana had told him, and what he knew. "For some reason they can't or won't." He didn't bother getting corroboration from the creatures themselves. If it wasn't true, they'd only lie anyway.

"Harlan," Napoleon whined, "they're not in league with the boogers. What are we going to do now?"

It only took him a second to adjust. Although he disliked planets that decided to destroy other planets just on principle, he could see the Federation's cold-blooded practicality at work. It seemed as if he would have to be just as cold-bloodedly practical. "But you did have a deal with the Mantases once?" he double-checked. The foozles nodded. "Well, then," Harlan said with a wide smile. "How would you like a new deal?"


"It was the only thing that made sense," Harlan elucidated as they made their way into space within the escstar. "If the Coven spell worked, Nest couldn't be a fixed planet. It had to be a world the Mantases invaded and used for their occasional birthings."

"A different planet for each birthing," Roscoe marveled.

"Mandarin was one," Napoleon growled with certainty.

"And now Earth," Harlan said, equally certain.

Roscoe surveyed the space between Doomstar and its satellites. "But there are no Mantas ships here."

"Star Nosed Moles dig into a planet's surface," said the foozle. "They make the underground tunnels the boogers need to lay and hatch their eggs."

"Even the Doomstarrers could see changes in the moon," Harlan continued. "But who would notice anything on a planet that was already falling apart?"

Therein lay Trigor's deal with the foozles. Basically it went, how would you like it if Doomstar knew of your duplicity, or how would you like to maybe destroy two planets with one PKG? Who knew what would happen to Doomstar's delicate syzygy if one of their satellites was blown up?

They had left the bunker by the secret exit, which deposited them far away from the SM Bees. So they never got to see the crazed women waiting with strange patience while Spot cried miserably over the second corpse of her beloved Zero.

They didn't get to see Mess or Muse either. By the time the team returned to the *Shooting Star*, the two compubots were useless. No matter how much Roscoe or Napoleon called their names, there was no reply. They were so deep in savor that the only system still on inside the LOST ship was the thing.

Ultimately, they all went into space: Harlan, Napoleon, Roscoe, and the two foozles. When the space bullet and feline transferred to the foozle ship, Roscoe stayed in the esc-star, in light orbit, to serve as a combination lookout and witness. No one had to say that the meek director would be a liability in battle.

Instead, Harlan and Napoleon bent double and squeezed into the two-ball-connected-by-a-tube-shaped spaceship to start their hasty, desperate assault on the newly discovered Nest. The tension just managed to keep the cat cognizant of her human intelligence. Half the time she wanted to run screaming from the craft. The other half she wanted to chew on the canines' heads.

Gerister, in the meantime, had her own concerns. "Is she dead?"

"There is a seventy-five percent certainty of it," Broston replied.

"Was it seen?" the steel-blue insectoid inquired.

"There is no complete assurance," said the black-colored male Mantas in reply. "If our kind did not destroy her, then the females or canine creatures might have."

"Then she may yet be alive."

Broston did not question her concern. It was their duty to question. They were but two of the many assigned to guard Nest from all possible danger. "If so, she is unarmed, unprepared, and immediately recognizable. There is a ninety-two percent certainty that she could do nothing."

"There is an eight percent chance that she could," Gerister reminded the male. They did not even mention the man. With the weapons they had on board, he was not a threat. He was not even a bother. In fact, as of just a few short days before, he had practically become an ally.

"There is always a percentage of negative probability," Broston agreed. "Nothing is certain. That is why we are here. Let us make certain our precautions are complete."

"Very well," the female Mantas declared. "The psychological imaging of the feline is saturated throughout our counsciousness. We are prepared for her immediate destruction if she is even glimpsed. A psychic alarm will begin, triggering the killing command. At a possible loss of half the present population, she will be hunted and dispatched."

"And their ships? The LOST ship?"

"The same procedure. All Mantas craft not directly concerned with the Resurrection Rule will begin immediate destruction programs as soon as the craft is sighted."

"So," said Broston proudly, "she can't get in. She can't do anything."

"That is what they said on Earth," Gerister reminded him gravely. " 'They can't get out. They can't do anything.' "

"Honor the day," Broston responded gravely. "Honor the race."

"Honor The Rule," they both said, touching antennae.

The Mantas ship comm-link suddenly came alive with the voice of a foozle. "Star Nosed Mole, this is Efwon. Permission to come aboard."

The Mantases' mandibles shuddered as Gerister made contact with the foozle ship. "Efwon, you are not welcome here at this time."

"Who is this?" was the alien's irritable reply. "Groxmore, is that you?"

The insectoid marveled at the foozle's attempt to name a single Mantas out of thousands. "This is Gerister."

"Gerister, don't be stupid." The foozle was its usual abrupt self. "We know what's going on with you; just like you to know what's going on with us. Do you think we'd come all the way out here just to get in the way? We've got information on the feline and her companion. Open up; we're coming in."

"We cannot allow you on board," Broston took over. "What is your information?"

"Oh, no," said Efwon. "Nothing for nothing. My . . .

companion is wounded. We're not talking until we're on board."

Gerister looked at her own companion meaningfully. "The foozles do not lie. We risk the resurrection by not knowing what they have to say."

"Come alongside," Broston told the foozle. "We will link." As the two ships aligned just over the Earth's cracked, rotting surface, the Mantases opened their minds to their race, preparing to feed them all the information their allies were about to give them. On the far side of the Earth, away from prying Doomstar eyes, the lone Star Nosed Mole's airlock seal opened.

The snaking blue bolt ripped the door completely off its hinges, snapped it in two, and hurled it into the far wall. For a split second, the ARM-IT just stood there, hovering outside the opening, but then it shot inside, its arms tearing from its granite sides.

The space bullet was a Mantas-seeking missile. Inside the suit Harlan felt like smashing walls, but he knew they needed the Star Nosed Mole. What they didn't need was the insectoids inside it. He reveled in their slaughter, ashamed of himself for it. But the shame hardly diminished the pleasure as his once ineffectual bolts and blasts decimated heads and exploded Mantas bodies.

He made a circuit of the ship's halls and rooms, like a vastly superior mouse in a maze, his weapons like spider's legs crawling into every crevice to sting all there to death. Gerister's and Broston's brains only communicated the anguish and sharp pain of sudden death as the green, red, and blue bolts came from everywhere to tear, slice, and punch holes in them.

Harlan Trigor stood in the air, letting newly found power wash over him as the Destiny weapons killed, then cleaned the unscathed ship of the insect creatures. He was the neutron space bullet—killer of creatures, not things. His armaments danced across, around, and through the ship until he was the only living thing in it.

"That's the problem with boogers," said Efwon as he stood in his ship's doorway. "No imagination."

"You're on your own," said the other foozle with the bandage around his upper arm. Since the foozles didn't lie, it was necessary for Napoleon to actually wound one to get the Mantases to lower their guard. "Everything in the planet must know something's wrong. I don't envy you."

"I don't even like you," said Efwon. "Get this cat out of here!"

Harlan returned to scoop up the spitting feline in his slate-colored arms. This close to Earth the Coven spell had taken almost complete control. Napoleon was howling and clawing the air in anger and fear. She tried to scratch the space bullet and scramble from his arms. He held on while linking his suit's controls with the Star Nosed Mole's.

The airlock closed and the foozles were gone. It was just Harlan, Napoleon, and the PKG.

Trigor dragged the cat to the secure-seats and strapped her in, keeping one big space bullet hand on her chest. "Nap, please," he begged. "Concentrate. Hold on for just a little while longer!" To his despair, she just started caterwauling. Blinding his eyes to the sight, he set the Star Nosed Mole on a course straight toward the Earth's surface.

He could see it in his suit's "eye"—a cracking chocolate cover on a gooey caramel surface over a chunky, grinding interior. And inside . . . inside he could only imagine the caverns made by the special equipment of the Mantas ships. He knew all there was to know about these craft now. He knew how blasts came from the star noses, cutting a hole for the ship to burrow into. He knew how they dug tunnels along which they could adhere their birthing larvae.

There was none of that on this security ship, but the mole's construction was clear enough. Its records revealed all. How the larvae solidified and took shape. How the new blue, black, and gray unisexed, winged Mantases took form inside. How, just at the moment of their awareness, the rockets blasted the self-contained "eggs" into space. How the eggs would arrive on a planet like horrible hail.

The Star Nosed Mole screamed through the negligible Earth atmosphere. Napoleon's cries became whimpers and then mews as the pressure pushed her deep into the insect-shaped seat. Harlan ground his teeth together and locked the space bullet feet to the floor as the Mantas ship dove like an arrowhead to the ground.

The star nose blasted automatically. The ship sank into the soft planet surface. The rockets and O'Neil Drive kicked in. The craft twisted and sank through the molten goo which was once Earth.

Harlan kept the mole away from the others, but nothing else was sacred. He could practically hear the outraged screams of the protecting Mantases as well as the developing ones as he guided the ship across the tunnels, ripping through stone walls, scrambling larvae.

The ship sank and sank and sank. Only seconds had passed since the foozle ship had first pulled up alongside. Harlan couldn't give the surprised enemy any time to plan or regroup. For all their vaunted shared intelligence, the Mantases had not expected this. They couldn't even begin to understand this. They may have licked Earthen and Destinian technology, but they knew nothing of foozilian.

The PKG was set. The foozles had explained enough so the space bullet could understand its functions as well. Within seconds of arriving at the center of the planet, the weapon would detonate, taking Earth, the Mantases, the Star Nosed Moles, the new race, Harlan, and Napoleon with it.

Roscoe watched the ship disappear into the ground, tears in his eyes. He was but a single man, floating in space, crying for the friends he only recently obtained and lost.

The other Mantas ships dared not strike out at the invading mole. The Rule wouldn't let them threaten any other eggs. Those ships able to get a clear shot at the intruder were impotent. The same shields that protected them from the space bullet protected them from each other. The invaded Star Nosed Mole arrived at its destination without major incident. All engines kicked off as the pirated vessel settled into the center of the hollowing world.

Harlan felt like laughing. The foozles hadn't had to make any deal with them after all. The resurrection would have destroyed Earth as readily as the Planet Killing Gadget. When the moles' rockets shot the eggs off, the world would have become a crumbling pincushion. The gravity of the moon and Doomstar would have torn it apart. But there was no love lost between the two alien races. The foozles probably included the Mantases in its list of Earthen evils anyway.

Instead, Trigor sighed and unscrewed the top of his suit. The Mantases needed the same atmosphere humans did, so there was no danger of suffocating in the ship. He could spend his last moments with his love as the Mantases helplessly awaited their unknowing Armageddon.

How many times had they been certain of impending death? How many times had they told each other of their love? What good would it do to repeat those same things now, he wondered as he peeled the exoskeleton off and pulled himself from the suit.

This time there could be no doubt. They were in the center of a self-destructing planet with a planet-killing device, surrounded by millions of their most dreaded enemies. There was not only no way out, there were several no way outs.

Trigor dropped lightly to the ship floor. He turned to the secure-seat he had strapped Napoleon to in order to take one last look at his beloved. The feline was no longer there.

It was just as well, he thought as he surveyed the Star Nosed Mole's interior with his human eyes. The Coven spell had made mush of her brain. It would not be like gazing at his lady love. It would have been like watching a mate or a wife in an insane asylum from the other side of one-way glass. It would have been someone he no longer knew.

Better he should remember her as she was when he loved her. Better she should wander the bowels of the ship on all fours, retarded, unknowing of the cataclysmic end to come. Better they should both die like this. It was fitting somehow . . . poetic . . . a tragedy worthy of the Bard himself.

"Nothing in his life became him like the leaving of it," Harlan Trigor said softly to himself, sitting on the floor before the square PKG. "He died as one that had been studied in his death, to throw away the dearest thing he owned as 'twere a careless trifle."

But then the man turned his eyes toward the ceiling. He did not care to die with another person's words on his lips. He had to hurry before the device could detonate. "Your quest is completed, my beloved," he whispered. "We are mated in this, if nothing else. I honor your ancestors and my own in this act of sacrifice. Eternity will be ours."

Harlan stared at the Planet Killing Gadget. "From the

womb I am born. It is what I must be. We're divers for glory, and the sky is our sea."

Behind him, the empty, hollow space bullet suit raised its arm; one forefinger pointed at the back of Harlan's head.

# TWENTY-ONE

It all came as a total surprise to Trigor, which was the biggest surprise of all. He did not hear the space bullet suit's arm rise, he did not hear its forefinger pointing and he didn't hear Napoleon's mad scramble. Instead, he felt the firm, furry body knocking him down and to the side, and saw the green bolts burrowing into the PKG box.

To say that Harlan was flabbergasted was to put it mildly. His head spun almost three-quarters around, taking in the feline's face, the pointing suit, and the collapsing foozle supersecret weapon. He was humiliated, but his chagrin didn't stop him from hurling the cat off him and rolling away.

The two reunited in the corner of the mole's bridge. There was just enough time to talk as the empty space bullet suit, with its head flung back like a parka hood, moved its arm awkwardly toward them.

"Nap . . . what . . . ?" It was impressive he could get that much out considering the way he felt.

"It's alive!" she screeched, hurling herself aside this time. Harlan threw himself in the opposite direction as a blue lightning bolt licked the wall where they had just been. He rolled to one knee beside the devastated Planet Killing Gadget. His peripheral vision took in its charred wall plating and its ruined interior, while he stared up at his nine-foot-tall suit, the exterior of himself, which pointed a deadly, accusing finger directly between his eyes.

His leg muscles expanded, sending him in a backward somersault over the destroyed and defused bomb as the yellow-orange blast made killing sleet on the bridge floor. Trigor's back slammed on the Mantas console, his breath coming in tortured gasps. This was his worst nightmare come to horrid life. For a split second, he thought the PKG had detonated, he had died, and the life-force had found him worthy of only this hell.

But then he instinctively knew that this was not a death dream. His suit had become alive without him in it. The awful truth had to be that the Mantas-stolen Destinian technology had progressed this far. That the unified minds of the insectoids were powerful enough to control the immensely complex inner workings of the ARM-IT. That *had* to be the truth! It explained the suit's slow, seemingly painful movements. It explained that the thing was moving at all!

So now he had an explanation, but he had no escape. The Mantas bridge was wide, but not wide enough. It was tall, but not tall enough. It was long, but not long enough. As soon as the Mantas minds completely controlled the device, Harlan would be riddled with rays the way the Mantases had been before him.

Harlan couldn't stop staring at the suit. It had become the living dead, a terrifying zombie turning on its master. Well then, so be it. If Trigor himself had brought his means of destruction aboard the ship, then let it kill him. He had had enough.

The headless granite monster pointed accusingly at the soldier. Green bolts poured out of its finger.

Harlan didn't think he had blinked. A moment later he realized he had not. It had been the golden, fiery form of the feline which had obstructed his view. Napoleon had come between him and his ultimate fate. She had come to protect her adored with the last defense she had left—the Lil Stone.

The green bolts sank right into the smooth blue gem as if drawn into it by a magnetic force. At that moment their entire adventure linked together like a dragon that had been chasing, then finally bit on to its own tail. The circle was complete, the cycle ended. Napoleon had carried the stone throughout their quest, her hand only going to it at this moment of extreme panic.

She answered his unspoken question through tight lips as the space bullet bolts sank into the blue rock. "If it works, you don't have to understand it."

"Nap!" he gasped. "You're . . . !" He didn't want to say "sane."

"The spell was broken almost as soon as we landed," she informed him in a rush.

"It was completed," he realized. "There was no need for it to continue!" He could see her arm muscles bunching under the pressure of the space bullet bolts. He lunged forward to help her.

"No!" she cried. "This is more magic. Who knows what makes it work?" Harlan was going to counter her statement, but his mouth closed when his brain remembered all the unexplainable things they had already experienced. It was just possible the Lil Stone only worked in her paws.

The green bolts terminated. For a few scant seconds, the Star Nosed Mole bridge was quiet. There was only

Trigor on his rear behind a crouching Napoleon, who was facing a silent, headless nine-foot-tall pointing hulk of slate-colored space debris.

"The PKG?" the feline started.

"Definitely destroyed," Trigor reported, looking at the wreckage sadly.

"Back to square one," Napoleon growled. "And here I thought we'd be saved because this SS weapon would destroy things and not people instead of the other way round." According to the Doomstarrers, the previous attacks had killed all the people and not touched the things.

It was these words that made Trigor realize what the motionless suit was capable of when the insectoids finally figured it all out. If it couldn't destroy them, then it could destroy the ship. And the Lil Stone would be useless against millions of tons of molten rock.

Harlan leaped up and dove over Napoleon's bent body. He ran in space, driving his feet toward the space bullet's open neck. He fell in the suit as if dropping through a manhole, tearing at the exoskeleton covering.

"Harlan!" she shrieked. "Get back here! I can't protect you in there!"

"You can stop the bolts," he grunted, harnessing himself inside. "But you can't stop it! Maybe the stone is a magnet for the blasts as well, but what will happen if the Mantases get this thing flying?" On cue, the suit began to shiver, then quake, then start jumping in the air. A lightning bolt lashed out, only to disappear into the deep blue face of the gem.

Another bolt went up, and then another, and another, then a quarter dozen, then a half dozen, then a full dozen more. Suddenly the shoulders of the beast were filled with lightning bolts, all heading for the ceiling, but all bent in midflight as if sucked into the blue Finally Finished rock.

Trigor linked with the suit. He felt the satisfying surge of oneness and power he always felt, but behind it was the mutineering control of the insectoids, all eagerly trying to eject, imprison, or eradicate him. He struggled to control the suit, which fought like a newly freed slave.

The bolts were followed by blasts that were so close they seemed tied to the lightning's tails. Napoleon had to grab the Lil Stone in both paws to keep from being thrown back by the force of the attack.

"Get the ship to the surface!" Harlan yelled. "We've got to get the suit out of range! We've got to . . . . escape!"

"What about the birthing?" Napoleon yelled back over the shrieking sounds of the suit's assault.

"What about it?" Harlan boomed. "What can we do?"

"Fry them!"

"Try!"

Napoleon whirled toward the Mantas controls while still holding the Lil Stone before the space bullet suit. Her free paw wandered across the tensors and sensors, which lit as the heat of her limb passed overhead.

"I can't figure it!" she yelled at Harlan.

"I don't know," he answered. "I may be able to fly it. But they might be fooling me. I might guide us right into their clutches!"

"Go ahead," Napoleon suggested loudly, still studying the controls. "We've got little left to lose."

In response, the ship lurched backward from its central resting place. Napoleon fell back on the board, her legs off the floor. She forced them down again and the claws that had been torn from her long ago tried to tighten. All the while she held the gem up in a firm grip.

The Star Nosed Mole began to spin backward toward the Earth's crumbling surface. Harlan grunted and ground his teeth together as he tried to wrest total control of his suit back from the thousands of insectoid brains.

He could feel them all inside his head in their original form: tiny bugs crawling across his mind. He tried to crush them under invisible feet.

"Ugh," he said as his muscles locked into the mole's defenses. Destinian weapons blazed on the outside of the surfacing craft, rending tunnel walls and ripping open half-formed Mantases. The ship tore through the delicate strata, killing tens of almost-born insectoids. Harlan heard them and their guardians screaming in pain, horror, and rage.

"It's no trap!" he announced. "They wouldn't allow me to kill their new race!"

"Good," Napoleon supported, holding the gem up like a cross to ward off the granite vampire. Into this rock the Mantases poured the might of the Destinian ARM-IT. They unleashed its power in answer to the mole's attack.

The feline was hurled off the deck and plastered against the wall over the console by the force of the united armament. All the space bullet's weaponry seared through the air and drilled into the Lil Stone as Napoleon desperately tried to keep her grip. She dared not let go in case its mystical power came from her.

"Turn it off!" she howled from behind the sputtering roar.

"I'm trying!" The weapons winked out, depositing the feline on all threes atop the control board. The mole's rockets blasted on, sending the ship lurching sideways through more tunnels. The cat leaped from the console and Harlan turned off the devices she had accidentally turned on as the space bullet suit swung upside down.

It bounced like a pogo stick all over the room, seemingly trying to shake Harlan out. He slowly stopped the jumps and righted the suit as the Mantas ship returned to its surface course. "We can't turn the larried thing around until we reach the atmosphere," Trigor cursed. "*Then* we'll have to get those rockets working."

Napoleon got up tentatively. "You back in control?"

"I think so. I'm pretty sure." The feline kept the gem up in any case. "We'll be reaching the surface in just a few seconds. Get yourself strapped into the secure-seat." It wasn't easy with one paw, but Napoleon got herself seated and had just linked the first strap into its safety restrainer when the suit shot up to the ceiling.

The space bullet slammed so hard on the bridge top that the clang reverberated through the halls. The shoulders of the suit left a dent in the surface. It looked as if Harlan's head had been rammed through to the next level's floor.

Napoleon couldn't even bring herself to call his name as the suit floated purposefully downward. The shock of seeing his lolling head and closed eyes was too much for her vocal cords. The suit had knocked its master out.

Napoleon clawed at the secure-seat as the space bullet suit surged in her direction. She held the stone up, but there were no death rays coming. She howled when she realized it meant to crush her, not fry her.

She never did get the Cheshire seatbelt undone. Instead, she wriggled out from under it just before the space debris sought to embrace her. The suit flattened the chair instead, ripping open its sides from the pressure and bending its steel supports. Napoleon tumbled and rolled away on the ground.

The space bullet tried to step on her as she went, the linked slate feet denting the deck as it hopped after her spinning form. Cheshire, Cheshire, Cheshire! If only the stone fired in addition to defended!

Napoleon rolled out into the hall and found her legs under her. She ran toward the rear of the ship, hoping to find a cubbyhole the suit couldn't crush or jam into. As she turned the corner, she saw the space bullet float out of the bridge area.

"Harlan!" she yelled, hoping to wake him up. She

screamed his name loud enough to wake the dead. "*Harlan!*"

The Mantases searched for her through the suit. It looked for her through millions of insectoid eyes. It went through the empty, winding, narrow halls of the Star Nosed Mole, carrying the unconscious soldier inside them. They silently tracked her, mentally calling her name.

At first they followed her voice, but when that died out, they simply followed the trail of her inner warmth. As they went they learned more about the suit. They used its powers against her, following an invisible trail that was as strong as her scent. They followed until her intangible spirit seemed so strong it practically surrounded them.

That was when the Star Nosed Mole broke the Earth's surface and Napoleon fell on them from above.

The Mantas ship seemed to gasp and gulp air as the screeching feline dropped from her hiding place over a doorway. She landed on the space bullet's shoulders as the mole settled on the shifting Earthen ground. It sailed like a boat as Napoleon tore at the exoskeleton covering Harlan's head.

The space bullet suit roared its displeasure. The suit surged up. Blasts erupted all around her as she held the Lil Stone high above her head. The gem touched the ceiling as the rays surged into it. The feline swung it across the ceiling as if drawing a line. The bolts followed, disappearing into the rock but cutting a hole open at the same time.

Napoleon scrambled into the jagged tear in the surface as the suit plowed through. The feline climbed right out of the Mantas ship into the light. She gasped for breath as the molten surface of the Earth seemed to burn the atmosphere around her. The heat didn't kill her immediately, but it would eventually. And there was just enough air to allow her to crawl, gasping.

She hugged the ship's outer surface to keep from slipping into the orange lava sea all around her, turning her head to see the suit wedged in the narrow opening. She felt her fur singeing against the hot metal as she wiggled around to hold the Lil Stone forward.

All the space bullet weaponry went to the stone. The suit was momentarily trapped. Napoleon pulled herself forward, grabbing at Harlan's smoking hair. Still holding the stone, she pushed her arms down into the open neck of the ARM-IT. Her paws snaked under her beloved's arms. Using all her strength, she dragged him from the traitorous uniform.

She fell back, his warm, welcome weight atop her. She held him to her, her eyes closed, her lips twisted in a satisfied smile. "We tried, my love," she whispered to him. "Who knows?" she wondered as the ship began to sink through the lava. "Maybe the power of the stone will kill them all. Only we'll never know. . . ."

She wrapped her arms and legs around him, the Lil gem still tightly clenched in one paw. As she lay back to die, her tail encircled his waist. The suit poured forth its destructive force, but it only sank into the blue rock, nailing the lovers, dying, burning, and unconscious, to the Star Nosed Mole's surface.

Soon there was silence. There was still the heat and the pain, but at least her mind was clear. Maybe this was death, with the last sensations in life still holding on. It could be a lot worse. At least the form of Trigor was still in her arms.

But no such luck. This was not death. Her eyes snapped open at the sound of the voice. The voice she knew. The voice she knew almost as well as her own.

"Wake up, will you, Nap? We don't have all day."

No, this *had* to be death. How else could you explain the presence of the voice that belonged to someone she had left millions of light-years away? "Larry?"

"You were expecting maybe Bishop-Fortune?" The words were bantering, but the tone was serious. "Get that dead weight off you and sit up. We're going to try a pickup run."

"Larry?" She looked over Harlan's back to where the voice emanated from. It came from the space bullet suit. Maybe it was haunted.

'Of course Larry," it said. "Look up."

She reacted accordingly. The Earthen sky was filled with ships. Doomstar square ships and something else. There was one other craft that wasn't one of the plain VU Port (tm) encrusted rectangles. It was a cone shape above a tube covered with extra circles, spears, and squares. It was the Earth Ship *Black Hole*.

"Harlan." She shook him. "Harlan, wake up." She prayed that the blow didn't cause permanent damage. She couldn't bring herself to feel the area where he had struck the ceiling. Happily, his eyelids fluttered. He looked at her and smiled weakly.

"Ow," he said.

"Are you all right?"

"Headache," he grimaced.

"Look." He smiled weakly again. "You'll feel better," she suggested.

He looked and he did, after a double take. The *Black Hole* swooped down and hovered directly alongside the sinking Star Nosed Mole. An airlock door opened and two men jumped out, carrying air canisters and face masks. They helped the feline and soldier get them on and led them back to the entry bay.

As the door slid shut behind them and the ship took off again, the Doomstar craft soared toward the planet, their weapons blasting. Harlan and Napoleon saw none of it. They were beyond caring at this point. The miracle of their rescue was no more amazing than their previous escapes, only there had been so many. After surviving a baker's dozen of certain deaths, the soldier and the feline had to keep from getting cocky.

Instead, they meekly followed their immediate rescuers through the vaguely familiar halls of the rescue ship. Napoleon helped the wounded Harlan along, ignoring her own burns and charred fur. All that was finally forgotten when they reached the bridge.

The pilots stood with their backs toward Harlan and Napoleon so they could survey the devastation taking place in the ship's screens. The Doomstar ships were making quick work of the Mantas hatching, blasting the Star Nosed Moles and the tunnels beyond. Their bolts detonated the Mantas ships, which burned most of the larvae, then the following bolts danced through the tunnels, destroying whatever was left.

"Glass houses . . ." said one of the pilots softly in the same voice that had come over the space bullet suit's comm-link.

"They were so well protected against Earthen and Destinian weaponry," Harlan painfully surmised, "they had no defense against the most basic of Doomstar weapons." Napoleon nodded and smiled in agreement. She had been so intent on getting her revenge, it never occurred to her to elicit the help of the Doomstarrers. After seeing the Mantas might, she had subconsciously thought they would've been no help.

Such a thing never occurred to either of the pilots. They stood among technology Harlan recognized as Destinian, but couldn't identify. But both he and Napoleon could easily identify the pilots. They would know the back of their heads anywhere.

Larry and Hana Trigor turned to face his best friend and her brother. Napoleon and Harlan almost lost their smiles, but just managed to keep them on. The relief overwhelmed their surprise.

Both Larry and Hana were at least thirty years older.

## TWENTY-TWO

The magic was happening.

There had been so much magic so far. The magic of Earth, the magic of Destiny, the magic of Finally Finished, the magic of Shakespeare, the magic of Doomstar, and ultimately, back to the magic of Coven where Harlan Trigor wanted to have his single wish fulfilled.

Roscoe Pound walked among the resplendent planet features, appreciating them all the more for what he had experienced. "For it so falls out," he murmured, quoting from *Much Ado About Nothing*, "that what we have we prize not to the worth. Whiles we enjoy it, but being lacked and lost, why, then, we rack the value, then we find the virtue that possession would not show us whiles it was ours."

He had lost so much. . . . He remembered the faces of his actors. He remembered his beautiful ship. He even remembered the Earth he had left. As cruel, as unfair, as bigoted as it was, it had still been his home. And it had

had its beauty. But the Mantases, FLIT, and the humans' own stupidity and cruelty had robbed it all from him. Still, in its place, the eccentricities of time and space had given him something greater. Something more valuable and precious.

"This is the very ecstasy of love." *Hamlet*. "As sweet and musical as bright Apollo's lute, strung with his hair, and when love speaks, the voice of all the gods makes heaven drowsy with the harmony." *Love's Labour's Lost*. "For aught that I could ever read, could ever hear by tale or history, the course of true love never did run smooth." *A Midsummer Night's Dream*.

For all the violence of their adventure, did love burst in its many splendors as the heroic, surviving group attempted to understand their rescue and escape. The love first washed over the TM director when the friends and brothers were reunited. It had only been four years, Harlan and Napoleon time, but forty years Larry and Hana time. In the interim, the pair had led the planet Destiny to ever greater heights of justice and self-sufficiency.

Even so, the pair immediately took heed when the strange compubot message arrived, begging them to traverse time and space on a certain course at a certain speed to aid in the final destruction of the Mantases. Hana had become a Destinian warrior-priestess in the intervening years and was as ready and eager as Larry to help her brother. Roscoe looked at the Destinian pair now, sitting some ways away, facing each other, their foreheads together.

There was a certain sadness about the pair. He had heard Harlan mention it. Something about the pain suffered on Jackpot, something about the warrior-priestess' vow of chastity. "Therefore love moderately, long love doth so . . . too swift arrives as tardy as too slow," Roscoe quoted from *Romeo and Juliet*. Sometimes he wasn't too sure what Shakespeare was talking about, but, whatever it was, he was certain the Bard was right.

They had all sought an answer to their reunion on the *Shooting Star*, where a different and strange love bloomed. For, as much as Pound had called Muse and the others had called Mess, only one voice answered. A voice both male and female. A voice that rose through the fog of savor, a voice that had called across the cosmos to reach Destiny, a voice that called itself—MUSS. The Multi-Unit Symbiotic System.

Roscoe headed back to his repaired ship now. No longer was it a star-shaped craft, home of the Light Orbit Space Theater. Two of its five points had been destroyed. It now looked like an abstract view of a rising or setting sun. It was now rounded on one side with three triangles on the other. Roscoe thought about it. "Juliet is the sun," Romeo had said. But Henry IV had said something else again: "I will imitate the sun, who doth permit the clouds to smother up his beauty from the world. Then, when he please again to be himself, he may be more wondered at by breaking through the foul and ugly mists."

So be it, then! The *Shooting Star* no more. Now, instead, another grand union. Roscoe mentally dubbed his new ship the *Juliet Henry*.

He supposed he should see the happy couple once more before he left. They might appreciate the company. After all, the Coverners were rarely about. Not since the Back Side effect of Harlan's wish had made the mountain disappear and the town return. Love again, the love Sparx the Elder had for the witch who had brought the mountain down in the first place. He had run to the newly returned town as soon as it had appeared in place of the mount, his face aglow with wonder and hope.

The happiness of his expression when he returned to collect his things left no more room for doubt. Love was the greatest magic, the most powerful spell.

Roscoe stopped outside the small house. He looked in the window to the bedroom. No, he couldn't interrupt that excruciatingly beautiful scene. Harlan sat on the edge of the bed beside the feline, who lay propped up against the headboard. Across their laps was the result of Harlan's wish.

Four offspring, two male, two female, ranging from the totally feline to the almost totally human. Almost, since each child had a long, luxurious, fur-covered tail. And each had an equal-sized piece of the Lil Stone—one as a pendant, one as a bracelet, one as a belt buckle, and one as a necklace.

The magic had let the alien biologies mate. Somehow, some way, this quartet was the result. "The web of our life is of a mingled yarn, good and ill together," Roscoe thought. "There's place and means for every man alive. Whate'er the course, the end is the renown. All's well that ends well."

He continued on toward the *Juliet Henry*, remembering how he had felt in that esc-star high above the Mantas-infected Earth. More than his twenty years on the planet, more than the twenty years in space, the fugitives had taught him how to care. It was as if those years had been his gestation and he had been newly born with the feline-human children. It was he who had been resurrected on Earth as the insectoids had been destroyed.

Roscoe Pound strode onto the ship's bridge, appreciating the renewed fixtures. This was now his craft. It was no longer a stage for fantasy; it was the place of his reality. No longer would he direct scenes from offstage. He would be a participant in the real battles, the fights that made a difference. Or so he hoped. After all, he was not a soldier. He was an artist. But . . .

The faces came into his mind one at a time: his own, sixty years after Harlan and Napoleon's, though only ten years their elder. Larry, twenty years older than he, though he had lived a life at least eighty years ago. Time and space, space and time . . .

"Muss?"

"Yes?" she/he said musically.

"Prepare for takeoff."

"Destination?"

"Back home." There was a war on. The Earth had not been destroyed. Only the Mantases. Doomstar still existed, as did the Federation of Worlds. As did the foozles. And woven throughout the fabric of the planet's history and the conflict were the lives of the four: Larry, Napoleon, Harlan, and Hana. Now five, Roscodopolis-Pouneri. He too would have his place.

"For all the universe's a stage," the man said. "And all the people merely players. They have their exits and their entrances, but . . . !" He smiled as s/he instigated ALP. "One man, in his time stream, can play many parts."

The *Juliet Henry* headed back toward Earth as Roscoe Pound trumpeted the war cry.

"Doomstar Forever!"